Praise for Jenny Colgan

'I love this book! It's funny, page-turning and addictive... just like Malory Towers for grown-ups'
Sophie Kinsella

'I have been waiting twenty-five years for someone to write a bloody brilliant boarding school book, stuffed full of unforgettable characters, thrilling adventures and angst and here it is.'
Lisa Jewell

'A wonderful first novel that had me in tears and fits of laughter. Definitely an A*!'
Chris Manby

'If you were a fan of Malory Towers or St Clare's books in your – ahem – youth, you'll love this modern boarding school based tale... Top of the class! ****'
Closer

'This brilliant boarding school book, with its eccentric cast of characters and witty one-liners, should prove an unmissable dose of nostalgia. Whether you've recently left school, have rose-tinted memories of it or are a teacher looking for some escapism from classroom dreariness, this book will certainly score A*'
Glamour

'Good old-fashioned fun and escapism ... A fabulously fresh and fun read ****'
Heat

'This is Malory Towers ... for grown-ups'
Company

'If you're looking for delightful childhood reminiscing or perhaps are the person who fantasised about being in a boarding school as a youngster, then this is the book for you!'
BookPleasures.com

Jenny
COLGAN
Class

sphere

SPHERE

First published in Great Britain as a paperback original
in 2008 by Sphere
This reissue published by Sphere in 2016

Copyright © Jane Beaton, 2008

'The Choosing' by Liz Lochhead from *Dreaming Frankenstein and
Collected Poems* is reproduced by permission of Polygon, an imprint
of Birlinn Ltd. www.birlinn.co.uk
'Christmas' © Sir John Betjeman by kind permission of
the Estate of John Betjeman
'The Crystal Set' © Kathleen Jamie 1995
'Journey of the Magi' by T. S. Eliot reproduced by kind permission
of Faber Ltd / The T. S. Eliot Estate

A CIP catalogue record for this book
is available from the British Library.

ISBN 978-0-7515-5329-1

Typeset in Palatino by M Rules
Printed and bound in Great Britain by
Clays Ltd, St Ives plc

Papers used by Sphere are from well-managed forests
and other responsible sources.

MIX
Paper from
responsible sources
FSC
www.fsc.org   FSC® C104740

Sphere
An imprint of
Little, Brown Book Group
Carmelite House
50 Victoria Embankment
London EC4Y 0DZ

An Hachette UK Company
www.hachette.co.uk

www.littlebrown.co.uk

For my mother

Acknowledgements

Thanks to Jo Dickinson, Emma Stonex and all at Little, Brown; The British Poetry Library; W. Hickham; Kathleen Jamie; and Gunn Media Inc.

Characters

Staff

Headteacher: Dr Veronica Deveral
Administrator: Miss Evelyn Prenderghast
Deputy Headteacher: Miss June Starling

Cook: Mrs Joan Rhys
Caretaker: Mr Harold Carruthers

Physics: Mr John Bart
Music: Mrs Theodora Offili
French: Mademoiselle Claire Crozier
English: Miss Margaret Adair
Maths: Miss Ella Beresford
PE: Miss Janie James
Drama: Miss Fleur Parsley

Governors

Dame Lydia Johnson
Majabeen Gupta
Digory Gill

Pupils

Middle School Year One

Sylvie Brown
Imogen Fairlie
Simone Pribetich
Andrea McCann
Felicity Prosser
Zazie Saurisse
Alice Trebizon-Woods
Astrid Ulverton
Ursula Wendell

Hello, hello. I know, a pre-introduction, that is WEIRD. Sorry. But I wanted to write a quick note to explain what this book is all about.

A few years ago, I wanted to read a boarding school book, having loved them when I was younger. But I couldn't find one for grown-ups. So I wrote a couple.

We then decided, we being me and my publishers, to release them under a different name. I can't remember why now. It SEEMED like a good idea at the time.

Anyway, regardless, *Class* and *Rules* came out and they had lovely reviews. But as it turned out, absolutely nobody bought them at all, having never heard of Jane Beaton, which was perfectly understandable, but also made me very sad as I loved writing them and was very proud of them.

As the years have gone on, though people keep finding their way to them, little-by-little, finally last year somebody wrote the publishers a letter saying, 'do please let me know what happened to Jane Beaton, as I kept checking the obituaries in case she died' at which point we thought, okay, ENOUGH IS ENOUGH. So we are now bringing them out again as Jenny Colgan novels this time, and hopefully I'll get to finish the series (there are going to be six of course), and everything will all work out nicely this time.

They are a couple of years old, but I haven't changed anything except one thing: when I wrote them originally I had in my mind for Simone, the scholarship girl, a pretty unusual surname I'd heard on a little-known lawyer back in a 90s trial and stored away.

For obvious reasons since then, we've decided to change the name 'Simone Kardashian' :). She will now be Simone Pribetich in honour of one of my dearest friends, Anouch, who is also Armenian.

Everything else remains exactly the same, and I so hope you enjoy reading these books as much as I loved writing them. Do let me know, on @jennycolgan or track me down on Facebook, of course. As Jenny, probably, not Jane :).

With love,

Jenny xxx

Chapter One

Purple skirt *no*. Grey suit *yes* but it was in a crumpled ball from an unfortunate attack of dry cleaner phobia. Black, definitely *not*. Ditto that Gaviscon-pink frilly coat jacket thing she'd panic bought for a wedding and couldn't throw away because it had cost too much, but every time she came across it in her wardrobe it made her shiver and question the kind of person she was.

Job interviews. Torture from the pits of hell. Especially job interviews four hundred miles away which require clothing which will both look fantastic and stand up to seven hours in Stan's Fiat Panda, with its light coating of crisps. Oh, and that would do the job both for chilly Scotland and the warm English riviera. God, it sucked not being able to take time off sometimes.

Maggie Adair looked at herself critically in the mirror and decided to drive to Cornwall in her pyjamas.

Fliss was having a lie in – among the last, she thought, of her entire life.

I can't believe they're making me do this, she thought. I can't believe they're sending me away. And if they think they're fooling me with their jolly hockey-sticks utter bloody bollocks they can think again. Of course Hattie loves it, she

1

bloody loves anything that requires the brain of a flea, a tennis racket, a boys' school on the hill and eyelash curlers.

Well I'm not going to bloody love it. I'll sit it out till they realise how shit it is and they'll let me go to Guildford Academy like everyone else, not some nobs' bloody hole two hundred miles away. Why should I care about being sent so far from London just as everyone else is getting to go to Wembley concerts and on the tube on their own? I'm nearly fourteen, for God's sake. I'm a teenager. And now I'm going to be buried alive in bloody Cornwall. Nobody ever thinks about me.

I'll show them. I'll be home after a month.

Breakfast the next morning was even worse. Fliss pushed her All-Bran round her plate. No way was she eating this muck. She'd pass it on to Ranald (the beagle) but she didn't think he would eat it either. She patted his wet nose, and felt comforted.

'And I don't know for sure,' Hattie was saying, 'but I think they're going to make me prefect! One of the youngest ever!'

'That's wonderful, sweetie,' their mother was saying. 'And you can keep an eye out for Fliss.'

Fliss rolled her eyes. 'Great. Let everyone know the big swotty prefect is my sister. NO thank you.'

Hattie bit her lip. Even though she was eighteen months older, Fliss could still hurt her. And she wasn't *that* big.

'Behave yourself,' said their father. 'I don't want to hear you speaking like that.'

'Fine,' said Fliss, slipping down from the table. 'You don't have to hear me speaking *at all*. That's why you're sending me away, remember?' And she made sure the conservatory doors banged properly behind her as she mounted the stairs.

'Is she really only thirteen?' said her mother. 'Do we really have to put up with this for another six years?'

'Hmm?' said her father, buried under the *FT*. Selective hearing, he reckoned. That's all you needed. Though he couldn't help contrasting his sweet placid elder daughter with this little firecracker. Boarding school was going to be just what she needed, sort her out.

Dr Veronica Deveral couldn't believe they were still interviewing for staff three weeks before the beginning of term. It showed a lack of professionalism she just couldn't bear. She glanced in the mirror, then reached out a finger to smooth the deep furrow between her eyes. Normally she was without a hint of vanity, but the start of the new school year brought anxieties all of its own, even after thirty years, and Mrs Ferrers waiting for the very last minute to jump ship to Godolphin was one of them.

So now she was short of an English teacher; and with eighty new girls soon turning up – some scared, some weepy, some excited, some defiant, and all of them needing a good confident hand. She put on her reading glasses and turned back to the pile of CVs. She missed the days when she didn't need CVs, with their gussied up management language, and fancy euphemisms about child-centred learning, instead of simple common sense. A nicely typed letter without spelling mistakes and a quick once-over to see if they were the right stuff – that used to be all she needed.

Still, she mused, gazing out of the high window of her office, over the smooth lawns – quiet and empty, at least for a few more weeks – and up to the rocky promontory above the sea, which started just beyond the bounds of the school. It wasn't all bad. These ghastly 'inclusiveness' courses the board had suggested she attend – no one would ever instruct

Veronica to do anything – had been quite interesting in terms of expanding the range of people the girls could work with.

They had such hermetic upbringings, so many of them. Country house, London house, nannies and the best schools. Oh, there was divorce and absent parenting, and all the rest, but they still existed in a world in which everyone had help; no one had to worry about money or even getting a job. Now, wasn't there an application somewhere from a woman teaching in a Glasgow housing estate? Perhaps she should have another glass of mint tea and look at it again.

'La dee dah.'

'Shut it,' Simone said.

'La dee dah.'

'Mum! He's doing it again!'

'Joel!'

'I'm not doing *anyfink*.'

Simone tried to ignore him and concentrate on an early spell of packing, which was hard when he wouldn't get out of her tiny bedroom. And, even more irritating, she could kind of see his point. Even she'd winced at the straw boater, and the winter gloves on the uniform list, though at first she'd been so excited. Such a change from the ugly burgundy sweatshirt and optional (i.e., everyone wore them if you didn't want to get called a 'slut') grey trousers and black shoes at St Cats.

She tried to ignore her annoying younger brother, and bask once again in the memory of the day they'd got the letter. Not the months and months of long study that had gone on before it. Not the remarks from her classmates, which had got even more unpleasant the more she'd stayed behind and begged the teachers for extra work and more coaching – most of the third years were of the firm conviction

4

that she'd had sex with every single teacher in the school, male and female, in return for the highest predicted GCSE grades the school had ever seen, not that there'd been much to beat.

She'd tried her best to keep her head high, even when she was being tripped in the corridor; when she couldn't open any door without glances and whispers in her direction; when she'd spent every break-time and lunchtime hiding in a corner of the library (normally forbidden, but she'd got special permission).

No, she was going back to the day the letter came. In a heavy, thick, white envelope. '*Dear Mr & Mrs Pribetich . . . we are pleased to inform you that your daughter Simone . . . full scholarship . . . enclosed, clothing suppliers . . .*'

Her father hadn't said very much, he'd had to go out of the room for a minute. Half delighted – he'd never dreamed when he'd arrived in Britain that one day his daughter would be attending a private school – he was also annoyed that, even though it was a great opportunity for Simone, he wasn't paying for it himself. And he worried too for his sensitive daughter. She'd nearly worked herself ill for the entrance exams. Would she be able to keep up?

Simone's mum however had no such reservations. She flung her arms around Simone, screaming in excitement.

'She just wants to tell everyone,' said Joel. But Simone hadn't cared. She'd been too busy taking it all in. No more St Cats. No more burgundy sweatshirts. No more Joel! No more being paraded in front of Mamma's friends ('no, not pretty, no. But *so* clever! You wouldn't believe how clever!'). Her life started now.

It had to be around here somewhere. Just as she was ferreting with one hand for the last of the Maltesers in the bottom

5

of her bag, Maggie crested the hill in the car. And there it was.

The school most resembled a castle, perched by the sea. It had four towers – four houses, Maggie firmly told herself, trying to remember. Named after English royal houses, that was right. Wessex; Plantagenet; York and Tudor. No Stuart, she noted ruefully. Maggie mentally contrasted the imposing buildings with the wet, grey single-storey seventies build she'd left behind her up in Scotland.

Uh oh, she thought. What was it Stan had said? 'The second you get in there you'll get a chip on your shoulder the size of Govan. All those spoilt mimsies running about. You'll hate it.'

Mind you, it wasn't like Stan was exactly keen for her to broaden her horizons. He'd been in the same distribution job since he left school. Spreading his wings wasn't really in his vocabulary. But maybe it would be different for her. Let's face it, there had to be more out there than teaching in the same school she grew up in and having Sunday lunch round her mum's? She had to at least see.

Veronica Deveral rubbed her eyes. Only her third candidate, and she felt weary already.

'So,' she asked the wide-eyed young woman sitting in front of her. 'How would you cope with a difficult child . . . say, for example, one who doesn't think she should be here?'

The woman, who was wearing pale blue eyeliner that matched both her suit and her tights, and didn't blink as often as she should, leaned forward to show enthusiasm.

'Well,' she said, in refined tones that didn't quite ring true – junior acting classes thought Veronica – 'I'd try and establish a paradigm matrix of acceptable integral behaviours, and follow that up with universal quality monitoring and touch/face time. I think non-goal orientated seeking should be minimised wherever appropriate.'

There was a silence.

'Well, er, thank you very much for coming in Miss . . .'

'Oh, I just like the kids to call me Candice. Promotes teacher–pupil sensitivity awareness,' said Candice sincerely.

Veronica smiled without using her lips and decided against pouring them both another cup of tea.

Getting changed in a Fiat Panda isn't as much fun as it looks. Maggie tried to imagine doing this in the car park of Holy Cross without getting a penknife in the bahookie, and couldn't manage it. But here, hidden out of sight on the grey gravel drive, it was at least possible, if lacking in the elegance stakes.

She put her make-up on using the car mirror. Pink cheeks, windswept from having the windows open for the last hundred miles, air-con not quite having reached Stan's mighty machine. Her dark, thickly waving hair – which, when properly brushed out by a hairdresser was really rather lovely but the rest of the time required lion taming – was a bit frizzed, but she might be able to get away with it by pulling it into a tight bun. In fact, frizzy hair in tight buns was exactly what she'd expect a boarding-school teacher to wear, so she might be right at home. She smoothed down her skirt, took a deep breath and left the car. Straight ahead of her, the sun glistened off the choppy sea. She could probably swim here in the mornings, lose the half stone caused by huddling in the staffroom ever since she'd left college two years before, mainlining caramel wafers in an attempt to forget the horror that was year 3.

Maggie stepped out onto the gravel drive. Up close, the building was even more impressive; an elaborate Victorian

7

confection, built in 1880 as an adjunct to the much older boy's school at the other end of the cove, the imposing building giving off an air of seriousness and calm.

She wondered what it would be like full of pupils. Or perhaps they were serious and calm too. At the very least they were unlikely to have ASBOs. Already she'd been impressed by the amount of graffiti on the old walls of the school: none. Nothing about who was going to get screwed, about who was going to get knifed . . . nothing at all.

No. She wasn't going to think about what it would be like to work here. This was just an experiment, just to see what else was out there before she went back to her mum and dad's, and Stan, in Govan. Where she belonged. She thought of Stan from weeks earlier, when she'd talked about applying.

'"Teacher required for single sex boarding school",' she read out. '"Beautiful location. On-site living provided. English, with some sports".'

Stan sniffed.

'Well, that's you out then. What sports are you going to teach? Running to the newsagents to get an Aero?'

'I'm trained in PT, thank you!' said Maggie sniffily.

'It'll be funny posh sports anyway, like polo, and lacrosse.' He snorted to himself.

'What?'

'Just picturing you playing polo.'

Maggie breathed heavily through her nose.

'Why?'

'You're frightened of horses, for one. And you'd probably crush one if you keep on eating bacon sandwiches like that.'

'Shut up!' said Maggie. 'Do you think being Scottish counts as being an ethnic minority? It says they're trying to encourage entries from everywhere. Apply in writing in the first instance to Miss Prenderghast . . .'

'A girls' school with free accommodation?' said Stan. 'Where do I sign up?' He thought she was only doing this to annoy him, even when the interview invitation arrived.

'Dear Ms Adair,' he'd read out in an absurdly over-exaggerated accent. 'Please do us the most gracious honour of joining us for tea and crumpet with myself, the queen and . . .'

'Give that back,' she'd said, swiping the letter, which had come on heavy cream vellum paper, with a little sketch of the Downey school printed on it in raised blue ink. It simply requested her presence for a meeting with the headmistress, but reading it had made her heart pound a bit. It did feel a bit like being summonsed.

'I don't know why you're wasting your time,' Stan had said, as she'd worried over whether or not to take the purple skirt. 'A bunch of bloody poncey southern snobs, they're never going to look at you anyway.'

'I know,' said Maggie, crossly folding up her good bra.

'And even if they did, you're not going to move to Cornwall, are you?'

'I'm sure I'm not. It's good interview experience, that's all.'

'There you go then. Stop messing about.'

But as they lay in bed in the evening, Stan snoring happily away, pizza crumbs still round his mouth, Maggie lay there imagining. Imagining a world of beautiful halls; of brand new computers for the kids that didn't get broken immediately. Books that didn't have to be shared. Bright, healthy, eager faces, eager to learn; to have their minds opened.

It wasn't that she didn't like her kids. She just found them so wearing. She just wanted a change, that was all. So why, when she mentioned it, did everyone look at her like she'd just gone crazy?

*

The main entrance to the school was two large wooden doors with huge circular wrought-iron door knockers, set under a carved stone lintel on which faded cut letters read *multa ex hoc ludo accipies; multa quidem fac ut reddas*. Maggie hoped she wouldn't be asked to translate them as one of the interview questions. The whole entrance-way, from the sweep of the gravel drive to the grand view out to sea, seemed designed to impress, and did so. In fact it hardly even smelled of school – that heady scent of formaldehyde, trainers, uneaten vegetables and cheap deodorant Maggie had got to know so well. Maybe it was because of the long holiday, or maybe girls just didn't smell so bad, but at Holy Cross it oozed from the walls.

The doors entered on to a long black and white tiled corridor, lined with portraits and photographs – of distinguished teachers and former pupils, Maggie supposed. Suddenly she felt herself getting very nervous. She thought back to her interview with James Gregor at Holy Cross. 'Good at animal taming are you?' he'd said. 'Good. Our staff turnover is 20 per cent a year, so you will forgive me if I don't take the trouble to get to know you too well just yet.'

And she'd been in. And he'd been right. No wonder Stan was bored with her looking at other options. After all, college had been great fun. Late nights out with the girls, skipping lectures, going to see all the new bands at King Tut's and any other sweaty dive where students got in free. Even her teaching experience had been all right – a little farm school in Sutherland where the kids didn't turn up in autumn (harvest) or winter (snowed in), and had looked at her completely bemused when she'd asked the first year to write an essay about their pets.

'What's a pet, miss?'

'My dad's got three snakes. Are they pets, miss? But he just keeps them for the rats.'

Then she'd come back to Glasgow, all geared up and ready for her new career, only to find that, with recruitment in teachers at an all-time high, the only job she could find was at her old school, Holy Cross. Her old school where the boys had pulled her hair, and the girls had pulled the boys' hair and it was rough as guts, right up till that moment in fifth year when big lanky Stanley Mackintosh had loped over in his huge white baseball boots and shyly asked her if she wanted to go and see some band some mate of his was in.

The band sucked; or they might have been brilliant, Maggie wasn't paying attention and no one heard of them ever again. No, she was too busy snogging a tall, lanky, big-eared bloke called Stan up at the back near the toilet and full of excited happiness.

Of course, that was six years ago. Now, Stan was working down the newspaper distributors – he'd started as a paper boy and never really gone away, although it did mean he was surprisingly well informed for someone who played as much Championship Manager as he did – and she was back at Holy Cross. They never even went to gigs any more, since she left college and didn't get cheap entry to things, and she was always knackered when she got home anyway, and there was always marking.

Back in Govan. And it didn't matter that she was still young, just out of college – to the students, she was 'miss', she was ancient, and she was to be taken advantage of by any means necessary. She'd ditched the trendy jeans and tops she'd worn to lectures, and replaced them with plain skirts and tops that gave the children as little chance to pick on her as possible – she saw her dull tweedy wardrobe as

11

armour. They still watched out to see if she wore a new lipstick or different earrings, whereupon they would try and turn it into a conversation as prolonged and insulting as possible.

Once she'd dreamed of filling young hearts and minds with wonderful books and poetry; inspiring them, like Robin Williams, to think beyond their small communities and into the big world. Now she just dreamed of crowd control, and keeping them quiet for ten bloody minutes without someone whacking somebody else or answering their hidden mobiles. They'd caught a kid in fourth year with a knife again the other day. It was only a matter of time before one got brandished in class. She just hoped to God it wasn't her class. She needed to learn another way.

The elegant tiled corridor leading off the grand entrance hall at Downey House towards the administrative offices was so quiet Maggie found she was holding her breath. She looked at the portrait right in front of her: a stern looking woman, who'd been headmistress during the Second World War. Her hair looked like it was made of wrought iron. She wondered how she'd looked after the girls then, girls who were worried about brothers and fathers; about German boats coming ashore, even down here. She shivered and nearly jumped when a little voice piped, 'Miss Adair?'

A tiny woman, no taller than Maggie's shoulder, had suddenly materialised in front of her. She had grey hair, was wearing a bright fuchsia turtleneck with her glasses on a chain round her neck and, though obviously old, had eyes as bright as a little bird's.

'Mrs Beltan,' she said, indicating the portrait. 'Wonderful woman. Just wonderful.'

'She looks it,' said Maggie. 'Hello.'

'I'm Miss Prenderghast. School proctor. Follow me.'

Maggie wasn't sure what a proctor was but it sounded important. She followed carefully, as Miss Prenderghast's tiny heels clicked importantly on the spotless floor.

Veronica glanced up from the CV she was reading. Art, music, English . . . all useful. But, more importantly, Maggie Adair was from an inner-city comprehensive school. One with economic problems, social problems, academic problems – you name it. So many of the girls here were spoiled, only interested in getting into colleges with good social scenes and parties, en route to a good marriage and a house in the country . . . sometimes she wondered how much had changed in fifty years. A little exposure to the more difficult side of life might be just what they needed – provided they could understand the accent . . . she put on her warmest smile as Evelyn Prenderghast knocked on the door.

Oh, but the young people were so *scruffy* nowadays. That dreadful suit looked as if it had been used for lining a dog's basket. And would it be too much to ask an interviewee to drag a comb through her hair? Veronica was disappointed, and it showed.

Maggie felt the headmistress's gaze on her the second she entered the room. It was like a laser. She felt as if it was taking in everything about her and it made her feel about ten years old. You wouldn't be able to tell a lie to Dr Deveral, she'd see through you instantly. Why hadn't she bought a new suit for the interview? Why? Was her mascara on straight? Why did she waste time mooning at all those portraits? She knew she should have gone to the loos and fixed herself up.

'Hello,' she said, as confidently as she could manage, and suddenly decided to pretend to herself that this *was* her school, that she already worked here, that this was her life. She gazed around at the headmistress's office, which was panelled in dark wood, with more portraits on the wall – including one of the queen – and a variety of different and beautiful objects, that looked as if they had been collected from around the world, set on different surfaces, carefully placed to catch the eye and look beautiful. Just imagine. Maggie looked at a lovely sculpture of the hunting goddess Diana with her dogs, and her face broke into a grin.

Veronica was quite taken aback by how much the girl's face changed when she smiled – it was a lovely, open smile that made her look nearly the same age as some of her students. Quite an improvement. But that suit . . .

Veronica was frustrated. This girl was very nice and everything – even the Glaswegian accent wasn't too strong, which was a relief. She hadn't been looking forward to an entire interview of asking the girl to repeat herself. But so far it had all been chat about college and so on – nothing useful at all. Nothing particularly worthwhile, just lots of the usual interview platitudes about bringing out children's strengths and independence of thought and whatever the latest buzzwords were out there. She sighed, then decided to ask one question she'd always wondered about.

'Miss Adair, tell me something . . . this school you work at. It has dreadfully poor exam results, doesn't it?'

'Yes,' said Maggie, hoping she wasn't being personally blamed for all of them. She could tell this interview wasn't going well – not at all, in fact – and was resigning herself to the long trip back, along with a fair bit of humble pie dished up by Stan in the Bear & Bees later.

Dr Deveral hadn't seemed in the least bit interested in her new language initiatives or her dissertation. Probably a bit

14

much to hope for, that someone from a lovely school like this would be interested in someone like her from a rough school. Suddenly the thought made her indignant – just because her kids weren't posh didn't mean they weren't all right, most of them. In fact, the ones that did do well were doing it against incredible odds, much harder than the pony-riding spoon-feeding they probably did here. She suddenly felt herself flush hot with indignation.

'Yes, it does have poor results. But they're improving all the—'

Veronica cut her off with a wave of the hand. 'What I wonder is, why do you make these children stay on at school? They don't want to go, they're not going to get any qualifications . . . I mean, really, what's the point?'

If anything was likely to make Maggie really furious it was this. Stan said it all the time. It just showed he had absolutely no idea, and neither did this stupid woman, who'd only ever sat in her posh study, drinking tea and wondering how many swimming pools to build next year. Bugger this stupid job. Stan had been right, it was a waste of her time. Some people would just never understand.

'I'll tell you the point,' said Maggie, her accent subconsciously getting stronger. 'School is all some of these children have got. School is the only order in their lives. They hate getting expelled, believe it or not. Their homes are chaotic and their families are chaotic, and any steadiness and guidance we can give them, any order and praise, and timekeeping and support, anything the school can give them at all, even just a hot meal once a day, that's what's worth it. So I suppose they don't get *quite* as many pupils into Oxford and Cambridge as you do, Dr Deveral. But I don't think they're automatically less valuable just because their parents can't pay.'

15

Maggie felt very hot suddenly, realising she'd been quite rude, and that an outburst hadn't exactly been called for, especially not one that sounded as if it was calling for a socialist revolution. 'So . . . erhm. I guess I'm probably best back there,' she finished weakly, in a quiet voice.

Veronica sat back and, for the first time that day, let a genuine smile cross her lips.

'Oh, I wouldn't be so sure about that,' she said.

Simone held her arms out like a traffic warden's, feeling acutely self-conscious.

'We'll have to send away for these,' the three-hundred-year-old woman in the uniform shop had said, as all her fellow crones had nodded in agreement. 'Downey House! That's rather famous, isn't it?'

'Yes it is,' said her mother, self-importantly. Her mum was all dressed up, just to come to a uniform shop. She looked totally stupid, like she was on her way to a wedding or something. Why did her mother have to be so embarrassing all the time? 'And our Simone's going there!'

Well, obviously she was going there, seeing as she was in getting measured up for the uniform. Simone let out a sigh.

'Now she's quite big around the chest for her age,' said the woman loudly.

'Yes, she's going to be just like me,' said her mum, who was shaped like a barrel. 'Look – big titties.'

There was another mother in there – much more subtly dressed – with a girl around Simone's age, who was getting measured for a different school. As soon as they heard 'big titties', however, they glanced at each other. Simone wished the floor would open and swallow her up.

As the saleslady put the tape measure around her hips, Simone risked a glance out of the window. At exactly the wrong time: Estelle Grant, the nastiest girl in year seven, was walking past with two of her cronies.

Immediately a look of glee spread over Estelle's face, as she pummelled her friends to look. Simone's mum and the lady were completely oblivious to her discomfort, standing up on a stool in full view of the high street.

'Can I get down?' she said desperately, as Estelle started posing with her chest out, as if struggling to contain her massive bosoms. It wasn't Simone's fault that she was so well developed. Now the other girls had puffed out their cheeks and were staggering around like elephants. Simone felt tears prick the back of her eyes. She wasn't going to cry, she *wasn't*. She was never going back to that school. Nobody would ever make her feel like Estelle Grant did, ever again.

'Now, your school requires a boater, so let's check for hat size,' the lady was saying, plonking a straw bonnet on her head. This was too much for the girls outside; they collapsed in half-fake hysterics.

Simone closed her eyes and dug her nails into her hands, as her mother twittered to the sales lady about how fast her daughter was growing up – and out! And she got her periods at ten, can you imagine?! The saleslady shook her head in amazement through a mouthful of pins, till Estelle and her cronies finally tired of the sport and, in an orgy of rude hand signals, went on their way.

Never again. Never again.

Chapter Two

Maggie Adair was making the long trip a second time, but now she was a little more organised, and didn't mind at all. She kept glancing at the heavy card envelope on the seat beside her, as if it were about to disappear if she didn't keep it under constant attention.

When it had arrived, just two days after she'd returned from Cornwall ('Did you make friends with any sheep while you were there?' Stan had said, and that was all he'd asked her about it), she'd got a huge shock. Then she'd assumed that anything arriving this quickly could only be a rejection, which was belied by the size of the envelope. Sure enough:

'. . . we would be pleased to offer you the post of junior English mistress . . .'

And that was all she read before dropping it on the floor. 'Oh,' she said.

'What is it?' said Stan, lumbering down the stairs with his polo shirt buttoned up wrong and sleep still in his eyes.

'Uhm . . . uh . . .' she looked up at him, realising she was about to drop a bombshell. 'I got that job.'

'What job?' said Stan. He wasn't quite himself before two

cups of builders' tea in the morning. Then, as he reached the kettle, he stopped suddenly and turned round. 'The posh job?'

Maggie nodded. Her hands were shaking, she just couldn't believe it. Dr Deveral had given nothing away at all and she'd driven the whole evening back convinced she'd wasted her time – the woman next in line for the interview looked like Gwyneth Paltrow in a netball shirt, for goodness' sake.

Stan stared at her. She wondered how long it had been since she'd really looked at him – really taken in the person she'd been with since the last night of school. He'd put on weight, of course, they both had, and they'd never again be as skinny as they were then, at seventeen. But his spiky hair still stuck up in all directions, and he still looked a mess whether in his work clothes, his pyjamas or his kilt. Even now she could feel toast crumbs compelling themselves towards him from all corners of the kitchen. Her daft Stan.

'But you can't take it,' he said, doggedly, staring at her.

Maggie stared back at him and realised that, up until that moment, she hadn't been quite sure what she was going to do.

'But I want to,' she said, slowly.

Simone watched as her mother piled the car high with silver foil packets.

'Mum, you know, they feed us there.'

'Yes, but what kind of food, huh? Bread and jam! Cup o' tea!'

'I like bread and jam.'

'Too much,' said Joel. 'You look like a jam roly-poly.'

'Shut up! Mum, tell Joel to shut up.'

Her mum raised her heavily painted eyebrows, sighed, and continued packing the car. It was a five-hour drive, but her mother had enough stashed away for a full scale siege. There were cottage cheese doughnuts, meatball soup, pickled cabbage in jars . . . It looked like a toss-up for her mother: was she going to starve to death at school, or were they all going to succumb on the drive?

'Jam roly-poly! Jam roly-poly!'

Simone concentrated very hard on her Marie Curie biography. Perhaps she'd had a small very annoying brother whose constant torments had strengthened her resolve to become a great heroine of science.

Dad was already sitting in the driver's seat. He'd been ready to leave since seven a.m., even though they didn't have to be at the school until teatime. He was wearing a suit and tie, even though he normally went to work in overalls. The tie had teddy bears all over it. She and Joel had bought it for him for Father's Day years ago. It didn't look very good, but she wasn't going to say anything. He was in a right mood. He should be happy for her, she thought. It wasn't like he would miss seeing her – most days he was out the house to work before they'd got up for breakfast, then he got back after eight o'clock, ate his dinner and fell asleep on the sofa.

Simone glanced at her suitcase. She wished it wasn't so tatty. It had been her grandfather's, and her dad had brought it over from the old country. It had been made to look like leather but here and there where the fabric was torn you could tell it wasn't really, there was cardboard poking through. Bogdan Pribetich was stencilled on the top of it, and it smelled musty – like it had been put in the attic with someone leaving some old socks in it.

Still, inside were her new clothes – she couldn't think of

them without being pleased. She knew the 'Michaelmas term' list by heart:

Navy blazer with school crest
Bedford check winter-weight skirt
Navy V-necked jumper with school crest
4 x white short-sleeved blouse
2 x T–shirt with school design for Drama lessons
2 x white polo shirt with school crest
Navy games skirt
Navy felt hat with school crest
Navy cycle shorts
Navy sweatshirt with school crest
Navy tracksuit trousers with school crest
Royal blue hockey socks
Navy swimming costume with gold stripe
Navy swimming cap

She'd tried everything on, but only once, so she didn't get it crushed. Her mother had invited lots of her aunties round (they weren't all her real aunties, but she'd called them aunty for so long sometimes she couldn't even remember who she was actually related to) and they'd made her do a fashion show for them in the living room, as they ummed and ahhed and talked about the quality of the cloth and the weight of the material and Simone had done the occasional slightly clumsy turn, as her mother warned people eating the *mamaliga* not to get their fingers on any-thing and Joel played up like a maniac, running around being a very noisy Dalek, desperately trying to regain some of the attention.

Now, ironed a second time, it was all tightly packed up in the suitcase, with underwear, tights and socks squeezed in the gaps in between. Simone had wanted to ask whether or not she'd be getting a new bra; just one wasn't really enough, but her mother hadn't mentioned it and it hadn't come up, so she kept quiet. Her father had looked at her, navy blue from top to toe and smiled, a little sadly.

'You look quite the little English lady,' he'd said. Simone supposed it was meant to be a nice thing to say, but she wasn't 100 per cent sure.

'What's the matter with everyone?' Maggie had said to her sister as she was preparing to leave. 'It's just a job.'

'I don't know,' said Anna. 'I suppose I just always thought you'd be teaching Cody and Dylan, you know? That they'd always grow up with their auntie in the school.'

But Cody, the eldest, was only three, Maggie thought, even if, with his shaved head and Celtic football club shirt, he looked like her year 2 troublemakers already. But that meant in nine years' time everyone thought she'd still be exactly where she was. She didn't want that to happen. She wasn't going for ever. She was going to get some experience, somewhere excellent, then come back to Glasgow and apply it where it was needed, that was all.

Anna had passed over a glass of warm white wine; it was after hours in the salon, and she was putting navy blue streaks in Maggie's hair. She'd been experimenting on Maggie for so long Maggie hardly noticed any more – in fact it had helped at school, made her a bit more trendy having a hairdresser for a sister who used her as a free guinea pig, despite the occasional results that made her actually resemble a real guinea pig.

'I'd better be able to wash this out before I go,' she warned. Anna ignored her.

'And the thing is, Maggie, kids round here, they need

22

good teachers. They need people like you who are dedicated, who care about things. What do you want to go wasting your time with a posh bunch of nobs who already have everything and are only going to leave school and sit around on their arses waiting for a rich man for the next fifty years?'

Maggie looked at her glass. 'Well I want to . . .' she said. Then she tried again. 'If I stay here . . .' That didn't sound right either. 'The thing is, Anna, I just want to get out a bit. If I keep on here . . . it's not that it's bad or anything . . .'

'But it's good enough for all of us,' said Anna.

'That's not what I mean. But I think I'll just get jaded and a bit bitter . . . I won't be a good teacher. I won't be good for the kids, I'll just turn into one of those rancid old harridans, like Fatty Puff. Mrs McGinty. Just shouting all the time. I think it'll be good for me to work in a different place for a while, just get some more experience. Then come home.'

'And Stan agrees with that, does he?' Anna slapped on some colour with what felt like malice. Maggie wondered if it was time for a chop. What did southern teachers look like?

Veronica smoothed down her soft grey cashmere cardigan. She supposed pearls weren't exactly fashionable any more, but then what was fashionable was just so horrific she could hardly bear to think about it – in fact, if she could stop the upper sixths coming back from holiday with tattoos she'd be delighted. Didn't their parents even mind? Half of them were so busy working or having affairs they probably didn't notice. All those little butterflies and fairies on their shoulders or down their backs. Surely they'd live to regret them. Veronica tried to imagine having a tattoo when she was at school, but she couldn't. It wouldn't even have

23

crossed her mind; she might as well have been told not to fly upside down. She'd forbidden them time and time again, but it didn't seem to make any difference; they got to the Glastonbury Festival and every sensible thought flew right out of their heads.

So, her pearls might not be fashionable, but they had been her mother's best. She remembered so vividly her mother getting ready for a night out. She'd wear stiff petticoats under her skirt – satin was a favourite. She liked ice cream colours: pistachio, pale pink. And she wore 'Joy' by Yves St Laurent. You didn't get that much these days either; for years Veronica hadn't been able to smell it without being taken straight back to her childhood. She'd crouch down by the dressing table (her mother wouldn't let her on the bed in case she creased the counterpane) and watch in awe as her mother deftly applied powder, lipstick, and a block mascara. She'd thought she was the most beautiful woman in the world.

All of that was before, of course. In fact, those were the only happy memories she had of her mother, painted and pretty, heading out with her father, with his hair scraped down with oil.

Later on, it had been snatched meetings in Lyons Corner Houses, her mother having told some lie to her father to get out of the house, as Veronica's belly got bigger and bigger. On one of these wet and rainy occasions, as they sat over scones and tea with damp coats and dripping umbrellas, both trying to avoid looking at the empty third finger of Veronica's left hand, her mother had handed her the small box, wrapped in cloth.

'Just,' she muttered, 'something to pass on. If it's a girl I mean. Your father won't notice.'

That night, back at the convent – the grim home for

unmarried mothers she'd been despatched to – sitting stoically as she always did after the nine p.m. curfew, whilst other girls sobbed their hearts out on the cold, greasy-blanketed cot beds that lined the walls, or talked defiantly about how their men would come for them, she had let the pearls run over her hands like water, feeling their perfect smoothness and cool beauty.

Veronica shook her head briskly to clear her brain, and focused on what she'd say to the new parents this afternoon. In fact, the pearls would help there. They normally did. They said, this is what our school is about: class, family, traditional values. That was what the school was about. The pearls were from somewhere else altogether.

It had not been a girl.

Fliss was in her favourite spot, underneath the cherry tree in a far corner of the old orchard. No one could see you there from the house, unless they stood on the roof. She had the new Jacqueline Wilson, Ranald, and a bag of cherries she'd filched from the kitchen, but it wasn't doing the trick. All she could think of was that they were sending her away. OK, so she hadn't exactly covered herself in glory at Queen's middle; she winced as she thought back to her report cards. 'Felicity has plenty of ability but tends towards laziness'. 'If she focused, she'd do as well as her big sister'. 'Felicity's conduct does occasionally give cause for concern'. And so on and so on, blah blah blah. She didn't care. School was stupid, and now they were sending her somewhere even stupider. Great. She obviously didn't come up to her parents' high standards, so they were just chucking her out like rubbish. She cuddled Ranald.

'It's easy for you,' she whispered into his panting neck. 'You don't have to go to bloody school. I wish I were a dog.'

Ranald whimpered his agreement, as the grass ruffled gently in the breeze.

And she wondered what would be the best way out of there. Not expelled – too much trouble. Just a way of showing them that the local school, with her real actual friends and not some of Hattie's horrid swotty cast-offs, would be best. At the local school in Guildford they were allowed to go into London when they were fifteen, *and* they didn't have to wear uniform. So completely the opposite of Downey bloody House then.

'Hurry up!' she could hear her mother shouting. 'We have to go or we'll get stuck on that bloody A303 again, and I'm quite old enough as it is.'

Finally ensconced in the car, Fliss flicked through *Cosmo Girl* and sighed loudly for the nine hundredth time.

'I *told* you,' said her dad. 'We're nearly there.'

'I don't give a . . . crap . . .' said Fliss, wondering how strong a word she could get away with when they were on the motorway with nowhere to stop, and she was leaving for ever anyway, '. . . how far it is to go. You can just keep driving as far as I'm concerned. Why couldn't we bring Ranald anyway?'

'Because I didn't want the window open the entire way,' said her mother, looking crossly out of the window. Hattie had her head well and truly down and was supposedly reading one of her swanky upper-fourth books but Fliss could tell she hadn't turned over a page in nearly twenty minutes. She'd considered instituting back-of-the-car territory wars, but that really did make the parents stop so it probably wasn't worth it. It didn't look like they'd had any last-minute changes of heart.

'So last night,' she said airily, staring at the pylons flicking past, 'you didn't, say, have some kind of psychic dream that said how awful it was to lose a child when they were very very young?'

Her parents both ignored her, only glancing at each other. After the sulks and the door slamming had had no effect, she was doing what the *Sugar* magazine problem page suggested and presenting logical sides to her problem.

'You know, studies show that marriages are at very great risk from empty nest syndrome when the children leave home. Of course, for *most* families this doesn't happen for years yet. Think what a higher risk you must have trying to do it so early.'

Fliss's mother turned round awkwardly in the front seat of the Freelander.

'Darling,' she said. She'd had her roots done, Fliss thought. She used to be really proud that her mother looked after herself – she was more in shape than Hattie was, that was obvious. But now she wasn't sure; her mother spent half the blooming day at the hair salon or getting her nails done, and Fliss wondered if she didn't have to bother with all that crap, maybe she'd have more time for not having to send her away to school. She thought of her friend Millie's mum, who had long grey hair. Millie always said it was a huge embarrassment and that her mum made her feel absolutely brassic whenever she turned up anywhere because she looked a million years old, but Fliss liked going round there. Millie's mum was always cooking something for dinner and taking lovely bread out of the Aga or playing with the dog in their big messy kitchen. Fliss sometimes thought this was how mummies were meant to be. Mind you, when Millie came round to her house she liked to go upstairs and secretly try on some of Fliss's mum's make-up.

Fliss's mum didn't cook much. She heated stuff up for them, with a big sigh, as if it were a terrible chore to take the wrapping off a Waitrose packet. She let them have a lot of ketchup with their veg, though. She was always dashing out and complaining about being tired, though she still found plenty of time to go out in the evenings or have dinner with their dad or do a million things that seemed a bit more important than making soup or something.

It wasn't that she wasn't fun, though. Sometimes they'd all go to London and hit Selfridges and Harvey Nicks and their mum would buy them cool clothes and say, 'Oh, this is too naughty' when she got her credit card out and then take them for smoothies – Hattie and Fliss would rather have gone to McDonald's, but if they mentioned it their mother would say, 'Got to watch those hips girls!' so they didn't mention it any more.

They'd also do their best not to fall out on those trips. Falling out meant fewer goodies. So they'd go to Oxford Street, and Hattie would get posh face cream for her spots, and Fliss would get lip gloss, and they'd try on loads of things in Top Shop which was miles better than the one in Guildford and when they got home their dad would cover his eyes and go 'Oh my God, how have my girls been trying to bankrupt me today' but he didn't mean it really, he was actually quite pleased. Then they'd do a fashion show with all their new kit unless they'd got anything too short, when their dad would call them a Geldof girl and make them hide it away.

Fliss sniffed hard. There wouldn't be much more of that. She bet there wouldn't be a Top Shop in the whole of Cornwall, not even a tiny concession one. She thought back over her hideous school uniform, all heavy navy blue which didn't really work with her blonde hair, and the stupid hats and elasticated gym knickers. She hated it! She hated it. She hated it.

She let out another long sigh. So did her mother.

'It's only Cornwall,' Maggie had said, for what felt like the millionth time. 'It's not the moon! There's not even a time difference! It's only for ten weeks at a time, they get loads of holidays.'

The only person who'd been completely sanguine about the whole thing had been her headmaster, funnily enough. 'Jumping from the sinking ship?' he'd said on the phone, as she nervously steeled herself to say she was leaving not long before the start of term. 'Don't blame you. Don't worry about notice, there's enough wee lasses kicking around at the moment who'll jump at your job.'

'Right then.' Maggie had felt quite insulted. OK, she hadn't exactly thought that everyone would be standing on their chairs like in *Dead Poets Society*, but it would have been nice to think that her headmaster would remember her name.

On the home front, though, she thought as she travelled through Birmingham and down towards the west, the Fiat Panda making its displeasure known with suspicious little grunty noises, it hadn't been like that at all. Although no one would say it out loud, it seemed to be the general consensus that she'd gone all snobby on Govan and thought she was too good for them all, especially Stan.

'You know I'm not leaving you,' she'd whispered, late at night, after another evening of Stan studiously ignoring her whilst eating a fish finger sandwich in front of *A Question of Sport*.

'So, just moving out of the house to the other end of the country. I'm so glad that's not leaving me,' Stan had said.

'It's only for a few weeks at a time! You can fly down to Exeter for weekends!'

'Well, I'll have to, won't I? You're taking the car.'

'I need the car.'

'You need, you want, your job, your things,' said Stan, turning over. 'Yes, Maggie. I know it's all about you.'

They hadn't even made love since she'd got the job offer. Maggie was worried. Why wasn't she more upset?

Chapter Three

Veronica stood up at the lectern and surveyed the hundreds of girls and their parents, crowding out the long hall. Part of the original cathedral structure, the long hall retained its original features – two rows of stern looking carved stone angels, punctuating the tall arched windows that lined both sides. They seemed to be gazing down on the girls, kindly, but with a look in their eyes that suggested they'd not be amused by any mischief. That's what Simone had thought anyway. Her own mouth had been permanently open since their old car had drawn up on the sweeping gravel drive. She'd seen the pictures – *pored* over the pictures, of course – but nothing had really prepared her for the scale of the great grey towers, silhouetted against the blue sea and sky. She simply couldn't believe this was her new home; her place. Even Joel had been temporarily stunned into silence.

'Zoiks,' he'd said finally. 'It looks like Hogwarts.'

It didn't really. It looked like a castle from long ago, set against the wind and the waves. Simone, whose tastes in reading were running quite quickly in advance of her age, was lost in a Daphne du Maurier dream, looking at the oriel windows set in the towers, and the ivy clambering up the north side.

She came back to earth with a bump as her dad, who'd

been quiet the whole journey, followed the temporary signs pointing towards the 'parents' car park'. Simone's heart started to pound even harder. This was it! She was here! She looked at the other cars entering the car park. There wasn't a single other ancient, creaky old beige Mercedes Benz there, and there certainly wasn't one with a gold-encrusted tissue box holder in the back seat. The car park was full of 4x4s, new shiny Audis and BMWs, huge creamy Volvos and even a couple of Bentleys, which she only recognised when Joel went, 'Fffooo! Bentleys! They cost, like a million squillion pounds!!! And the insides are made out of gold and diamonds and stuff.' And when their mother told him to be quiet, in an uncharacteristically nervous sounding voice, he was for once.

The car rolled to a stop.

'Let's get on with it then,' growled her father.

Oh God, what the hell was that? Fliss squinted at the big ugly car blocking their way to the entrance.

'Great,' she said. 'I see they run a minicab service.'

'Felicity,' said her father, in his 'trying to tell her off' tone of voice, which never worked. Hattie had already jumped out of the car, spying several thousand of her very closest friends and screaming at them at the top of her voice. Fliss rolled her eyes. She'd met Hattie's friends before, when they came up to visit, and she thought they were all pants. As slowly as she dared she drew her hockey stick out of the boot, and turned round to see a dumpy girl emerging from the hideous brown car.

The girl was plump, with rather sallow skin and hair tightly pulled back in a ponytail. She was already wearing her full school uniform; didn't she know you got to wear your home clothes on your first day?

She looked over at Fliss with a brave, friendly smile on her face. Oh great, new girls time. Better luck next time, podge, thought Fliss viciously. She didn't want friends here. She had her friends. In Guildford. Where she was going back to, just as soon as she'd figured this place out. As she turned round to pick up her suitcase, a large woman, obviously the girl's mother, and dressed in what looked like evening wear – a lot of black and sequins – clambered out of the front of the car.

'Simone! Simone!' she screeched at the top of her voice. The entire car park turned round. 'We've got a present for you!'

Simone, as the plump girl must be called, gave an embarrassed looking half smile and turned round as her mother handed over a small package and then looked directly at Fliss's mum.

'It's an extra bra,' she announced proudly, out of the blue, just like that, as if it was the kind of thing you would just say in normal conversation to everyone in the world. 'They grow up so fast, no?'

'Yes they do,' said Fliss's mum, with the smile she got on her face whenever she wanted to get moving somewhere down the street and they got stopped by someone who wanted them to sign up for charity.

'I am Mrs Pribetich, Simone's mother. This is Simone's first day.'

No kidding, thought Fliss, looking at Simone's skirt, which hung way down below her knees. Fliss was already planning on rolling hers up as far as she could get away with. And then a bit further.

'Caroline Prosser. Hello.'

Her mother gave a rather limp handshake. Mrs Pribetich raised her eyebrows looking at Fliss and Hattie.

'I think maybe our girls will be friends, yes?'

Not in a million years, thought Fliss, digging her hockey stick into the gravel.

Not in a million years, thought Simone, catching the look of disgust on Fliss's face. And on her mother's, come to that.

'Welcome,' Veronica said. It was nice to have the whole school quiet; that wouldn't happen again for another year. 'We're very pleased to welcome you here to Downey House; for our returning girls, and our new ones.'

She addressed the little ones – she knew they were thirteen, not exactly babies, but they looked so young, with their scrubbed faces and long hair. Not like the older girls, who were affecting to slouch against the back of the hall, as if assembly was just too unutterably dull for words. The school – a middle and upper school – started at year three when the girls were going on fourteen, and ran up to an upper sixth. There were just over three hundred and fifty students.

Of course they were just as nervous, she knew – they had their new haircuts; their new experiences of whatever the summer had brought them, ready to be shared and picked over with the other girls. Would they still be friends? Would someone have a boyfriend when they didn't? Would they pass their exams? The jutting lips, cutting-edge outfits, careful hairstyles and overuse of make-up (the rules about that didn't kick in till the next morning) betrayed just as many nerves as the little plump sallow-skinned girl just in front of the lectern, whose right knee was jiggling so hard she wanted to put her hand on it.

Maggie spied the little girl jiggling too. Her heart went out to her. She didn't mind sitting up at the front of the room with

34

all the other teachers – she was used to that. She was just a little unnerved by the level of scrutiny going on. At Holy Cross you got a quick once-over whilst the pupils worked out the best nicknames they could for you, so if you had a big nose, or big breasts, or anything else about you whatsoever, so much the better. Then they went back to either ignoring you or working out persecution tactics.

Here, it felt oddly like being judged by a group of your peers. You didn't need to glance too long at the girls here to realise just how big the poverty gap in Britain was. Very few of these girls were overweight – there were a few plump with puppy fat, but it was a healthy, pink-cheeked big-bummed horse riding look, thought Maggie; not the gloopy rolls that accumulated on so many of the girls at her old school through endless processed meat and pastry and no fruit and veg. And regardless of the cover of the school's prospectus – which looked like those old Benetton ads – there was a lot of homogeneity; blonde hair, pale skin. One or two staggeringly beautiful black girls who looked like (and probably were) African princesses of some kind; some Middle Eastern girls too, but nothing like the ragtag mix of Polish, Hindi and patois she'd been used to.

Her mind jumped to the surprisingly comfortable suite of rooms in the East Tower that Miss Prenderghast had shown her to. There was a pretty sitting room with a lovely view out to sea (currently rather grey and imposing), a floral sofa and a round dining table. She also had a small bedroom at the back with a single bed covered by a toile counterpane. Maybe when Stan came down they could book a bed and breakfast somewhere. Nobody had asked about her marital status, but there'd been a few glances at her empty ring finger, which was quite funny. She was also to share a small office, though with whom she didn't yet know, where she was expected to meet the girls and take seminars for the older ones preparing for university.

Bringing herself back to the assembly, she glanced round at her fellow teachers; she'd only had ten minutes to try and meet as many of them as possible. The deputy head, and head of English – in effect her immediate boss – was a pinched woman, far too thin for her age, called Miss Starling. Not Ms. The Miss was unmistakeable. She'd obviously been at Downey House for about nine thousand years and wasn't intending to look on Maggie as anything else but an interloper till she'd been there three generations, probably. From first glance (or rather, the first time Miss Starling had said, 'Now, I know that modern com-pre-HEN-sive teaching doesn't emphasise discipline, but here, Ms Adair, we like SIlence in the classroom', over-emphasising odd syllables and making, not for the last time, Maggie figured, reference to her more humble beginnings), Maggie had guessed that Miss Starling might be a teacher the pupils respected, but not one they liked or enjoyed. Which felt like such a shame; if you couldn't have a bit of fun and interest in English, you were unlikely to get it anywhere in the curriculum.

Then there was Mam'selle Crozier, the French mistress. Maggie had liked her immediately. Tall and slender – *mais bien sûr* – she looked like she too might be quite stern but in fact had immediately let out an infectious giggle and said in a low voice how '*superrr*' it was to have someone around her own age, and that they must go out for a drink, which cheered Maggie immensely; she'd had images of lots of long dark evenings in her room on her own, correcting papers and worrying about whether Stan had eaten any vegetables.

'Do not worry,' the French teacher had said. 'Some of them are leetle sheets, but that is simply teaching, *non*? And the rest are superrr.'

Maggie was sitting in the front row on the stage, waiting to be introduced to the school. She felt a shot of adrenalin run through her and a distinct shiver of nerves.

Veronica hoped she'd done the right thing employing Margaret Adair. She looked so nervous sitting there, and quite out of place in the same old suit – she'd really need to have a word. She knew students had debts and so on these days, but this was quite ridiculous, there was no excuse for not grooming yourself. She hoped the girls would understand her and not start laughing the moment she opened her mouth (this hadn't occurred to Maggie) – the accent really was very Glaswegian. However. Nothing ventured, nothing gained.

'I'd like to introduce our new English teacher, replacing Mrs Ferrers,' she said. 'Ms Adair has come to us all the way from Glasgow. She's worked in different types of schools that have given her a real view of life at the sharp edge, which I think is going to make her a huge asset here at Downey, so please give her your warmest welcome, girls.'

'Sink,' said a voice next to Fliss. They were sitting cross legged on the floor. Fliss didn't think she could keep it up for much longer – what was it, some kind of prison camp torture? Nobody else seemed to mind, but her calves were killing her.

'What?' she whispered. She was sitting next to a beautiful black-haired girl, with dark blue eyes and a slightly supercilious expression.

'She's a sink teacher, isn't she? Obvious. "Life at the sharp edge". They must be getting desperate.'

Fliss glanced sideways with some admiration, not only for the girl's obvious prettiness. She was obviously annoyed to be here too.

'Do you know lots about the school?' she whispered, as Maggie stood up on stage, thanked everyone nicely and said how much she was looking forward to . . . blah blah blah. She sounded like that politician who made her dad swear whenever he came on the radio. Oh God, if the teachers were going to be crap too, that was all she needed. She looked about Hattie's age.

'Enough to know I don't want to be here,' said the girl. 'Hello. I'm Alice.'

'Fliss. I don't want to be here either.'

'Excuse me,' came a voice. 'Are you two chatting?'

It was Miss Starling. She was their head of year so they'd met her already. Fliss felt a thrill of fear.

'No, miss,' said Alice contritely, looking innocent.

'A teacher is talking,' said Miss Starling. 'Not a peep out of you two please. On your first day too!'

Maggie felt her face burn up. She was furious. How dare another teacher impose discipline when she was talking? She'd immediately been shown up as an amateur in front of the whole school. She shot a quick glance at Miss Starling, a glance not missed by Veronica. Interesting, thought Veronica. Quite the little spark of temper in there. But she was quite right; June Starling had absolutely no business telling off girls in front of other teachers; it was sheer showing off. Perhaps it was time for the school song, the rousing 'Downey Hall', named after the original building. She nodded to Mrs Offili, the hearty, beefy and universally adored head of music, who banged down on the piano with a rousing hand.

We are the girls
The Girls of Downey Hall
We stand up proud

And we hold our heads up tall
We serve the Queen
Our country, God and home
We dare to dream
Of wider plains to roam
We are the girls
The Girls of Downey Hall.

Simone, having learnt the song off by heart before she arrived, had jumped up with pride when she heard the piano start up. Quickly, she'd realised she was first up, and that her enthusiasm was being met with sniggers from some of the surrounding girls. She felt her face flame pink, before the teachers all stood up too and there was a general shuffling of chairs being pushed back and feet clomping up on the dusty wooden floor.

To Simone, used to a *laissez-faire* comprehensive environment, everything so far had passed in a whirr of queues and laundry bags and a blur of girls running all around. Quite a lot of the girls, it seemed, already knew each other from their 'prep' schools. Simone didn't know what a prep school was, exactly. And they were all so ... they were so small, and petite, and pretty. Or, the ones who weren't small were tall and willowy, like reeds, with long limbs lightly tanned by the sun. One or two were even wearing sandals showing painted toenails.

Miss Starling, the head of Plantagenet House, to which she'd been assigned, had terrified her – simply glancing up briskly, saying, 'You're the scholarship girl, are you? Well done. Well, we hope to see a lot of work out of you. Not just for yourself, but to inspire the other girls. In fact, I don't expect to have to pay you much attention at all. You know what will happen if you don't pull the finger out, don't you?

There's a lot of girls from backgrounds like yours that would kill for the opportunity. Don't mess it up.'

'No, miss,' Simone had said, her head pointed directly towards the floor.

'No, Miss Starling,' Miss Starling had said.

'No, Miss Starling.'

They were called in to meet the headmistress too before her parents left. Simone just wanted them to go. She could see they didn't belong, and they felt it too. The other mothers were all chic and sleek looking; they had short blonde hair and wore gently draping things in soft colours, or smartly tailored suits, or even slim-cut trousers. Nobody was wearing a large black dress with sequins at the neck, nobody, even if Simone's mum had announced that she thought everyone would dress like the Princess Diana so she was going to too.

Simone was in awe of the headmistress's office immediately. It was so beautiful. The far wall was a heavy old-fashioned print wallpaper, but nearly obscured by paintings which, although different in styles – some abstract, some figures, a large oil painting of a horse that Simone adored immediately – all seemed to blend together well. The other wall was filled with floor-length windows that looked straight out over the cliffs and out to sea. Many had been the badly behaved girl who'd sat there, staring and wishing herself on a boat, far, far away!

Veronica looked up from her desk. She was aware – more than any of the other teachers or students knew, or ever would – of the difficulties of coming from one world into the next. Many of the scholarship girls they got were what she thought of as the 'genteel poor': middle-class girls whose parents had fallen on hard times, but still knew the value of an excellent education. Some of them went through the school quite happily with no one even knowing; the school gave a grant for uniforms, and families scraped together for the rest, so it was only the lack of Easter suntans and talk of new cars at seventeen that would give the game away, and then only to a close observer.

From her first glance at Mrs Pribetich's hair, however, she realised that this was something else – a genuine girl from a difficult background. Her heart softened as soon as she looked at Simone, whose body was pasty from too much time in with her books, and fat from too many sweets and biscuits, no doubt given as well-intentioned treats. She needed lots of fresh air, exercise, good food and encouragement of the right sort; she sensed the problem might be prising Simone away from her books, rather than the other way around.

'Welcome,' she said. Over the years Veronica's voice had become incredibly genteel. Simone might have felt more at home if she'd known how it started out. 'Welcome to Downey House.'

'Thank you,' said Simone. Her mother nudged her. 'I mean, thank you for the opportunity to attend your, ehm, august seat of learning, and I hope that I'll be a credit to you and this institution for many years to come.'

Veronica stifled a smile. Actually she could do with more girls coming in with that attitude, even if they were forced to learn a rote speech.

'Well, good. Thank you. That's nice to hear.'

'We're just so proud of her,' said the mother. 'You know, she's such a good girl, and so obedient and never stops studying . . .'

Veronica ignored her, but in a positive way.

'Simone,' she said. 'We're very pleased to welcome you here. Many girls aim for a scholarship to Downey, and very, very few succeed. It's a great achievement.'

Simone went bright pink and stared at her lap.

'But, now you're here, I want you to take advantage of everything we can offer you. Downey House isn't just about books and exams, although those are part of it. It's about becoming a confident, rounded young woman. It's about being able to take on the world. So I don't want you to chain yourself to the library. I want you to get out there; to enjoy the fresh air; to make good friendships with the other girls; to participate in as many sports and societies as you can and to throw yourself into everything with as much enthusiasm as you've thrown yourself into getting in here.'

Simone nodded mutely. The idea of her becoming a confident young woman like the ones she'd seen standing around the assembly hall, so terrifyingly beautiful and self-assured – well, she'd never be like that in a million years, about as long as it would take her to . . . get on a pony. But she knew she always had to agree with what the teacher said.

'You'll get a lot out of Downey House – as long as you give a lot back.'

Simone looked up through her glasses. What an unprepossessing child, thought Veronica. Just one big bundle of nerves. She really did hope the school would knock some of it out of her, and not drive her more into herself.

'Yes, miss,' said Simone.

Simone's mother had finally been persuaded to get back into the car, howling and wailing, just as the very last of the parents were setting off. Simone watched her, her insides clenching with embarrassment. Not one of the other mothers had clung to their daughters, weeping huge tears, and certainly none of the other fathers had had to pull off the mothers and practically fold them into the car.

From above, though, through one of the dormitory windows, the girls were watching.

Each spacious dorm took four girls and had its own bathroom, comfortable single beds that the girls brought their own duvet covers for, and a cupboard, desk and bedside cabinet for each one. Fliss Prosser looked down from her assigned room into the car park below (sea views were reserved for older students).

'Look at this,' she scoffed to Alice, who was in the same dorm. 'God, if my mother did that I'd be so embarrassed.'

'So's she,' pointed out Alice. 'But still – eww.'

They both looked over to the still empty bed in their room. The third was taken by a quiet student called Imogen, who'd unpacked her belongings immaculately and immediately sat down at her desk with her back to the room and started to swot up on their maths course. But the fourth was ominously empty.

'Oh God,' said Alice. 'That means . . . she's ours! The hippopotamus!'

'Ssh!' said Fliss. It wasn't nice, really it wasn't. But Alice was so pretty and funny and lively, it was impossible not to want to be her friend.

'What if she makes big snuffling heffalump noises at night? And cries all the time? And leaves hairs all down the sink? It'd be *terrible*.'

Fliss couldn't help herself. She snuffled up her nose and did a pretty good imitation of grunting.

'Snorty . . . I'll just sleep here . . . SNORT.'

'Got any turnips I can eat?' said Alice. 'That's what we have back in my country.'

'Yes,' said Fliss. 'My mum had some decorating her hat!'

The girls collapsed into fits of giggles that suddenly went silent. There, framed in the doorway, pale and scared looking, was Simone.

Fliss's first instinct was to apologise. Simone looked like a

43

wounded animal; like Ranald with a thorn in his paw, and her instinct was for kindness, and to look after the weaker person. But she felt Alice's eyes upon her, sizing her up to see what she would do. And Fliss remembered how cross she was to be there, and how she certainly wasn't going to worry about anyone else.

'Oh, hi,' she said, in a disdainful tone of voice. 'I suppose that's your bed then.'

Maggie sat on her bed with her hands clasped. It was odd; she felt like she didn't know what to do. She tried ringing Stan again, and this time she got him. She had the weird feeling that he wasn't picking up his mobile before. It was odd, that sense that she felt he was there, but deliberately not answering the phone. It wasn't like him; normally he was thrilled to hear from her in the day.

'Hiya,' he said, in a neutral tone.

'Hi sweetie,' she said, trying to sound as normal as possible. 'How are you? How are you doing?'

'I'm not in hospital,' said Stan irritably. 'I'm just having my life as normal, remember? It's you who's disappeared.'

'I haven't disappeared,' said Maggie, rolling her eyes. She didn't want an argument, just a friendly voice when she was hundreds of miles away, in a tower of a castle filled with four hundred people she didn't know.

'Hmm,' said Stan. He was eating.

'Are you having chips?' she asked him. Dinner had been perfectly serviceable, but undeniably plain, lamb chops, green beans and mash. Some chips from the Golden Fry down the road suddenly felt like a fabulous idea.

'Uh huh,' said Stan.

'Are they good?'

'Why, are youse somewhere too poncey for chips now?'

44

'I am actually,' said Maggie. 'There must be some at the seaside. But I think the school is a chip-free zone. That's what you pay for.'

'People paying to be deprived of chips,' scoffed Stan. 'Sounds a pretty stupid set-up to me.'

Maggie found herself agreeing with him – anything to hear his voice soften.

'So, how is it then?' he asked grudgingly. 'Do you live in a castle now?'

'It is a bit like a castle actually,' Maggie admitted. 'It's very formal, much more than I thought. All the girls have to stand up when the head passes, that kind of thing.'

'Bloody hell. Do they still get caned and stuff?'

'No, not here. Apparently the boys' school over the hill still does, but only for real transgressions. And even that's only because the parents like it, apparently – they never do it really, they just put it in the prospectus.'

'Sick,' whistled Stan.

Maggie wanted to tell him about all the new teachers she'd met, and the grand hall, and her neat little suite of rooms, and how excited and trepidatious she was about the next morning and taking her first class. But she knew deep down that he wouldn't – couldn't – share her enthusiasm and that it wasn't really fair to try and make him.

'So, how was your day?' she asked, timidly.

Stan paused. 'It was the same as every day,' he said, as if surprised she'd asked. 'Same old jerks, same old distribution problems. Oh, no, hang on, I came home to an empty house with no dinner. That was a bit different.'

Maggie didn't take the bait. She was so tired anyway, it had been such a long day. 'I'll be back soon,' she said soothingly. 'And you must come down. We'll find chips, I promise.'

Stan made a non-committal grunt, then there was a silence.

'Well, I'd better get to bed,' Maggie said. 'Big day tomorrow and everything.'

'Yeah,' said Stan. 'Well, you have a big day tomorrow. Mine is pretty small, I expect.'

'Hmm,' said Maggie, feeling tired of his whingy tone, and then guilty for being annoyed. 'Well, goodnight then . . .'

Stan either didn't hear the appeal in her voice – for him to say something nice, to say he loved her or he missed her; anything at all. He either didn't hear it, or he ignored it.

Veronica couldn't believe it had taken her all day to get round to opening the post. Yes, she was terribly busy, but even so . . . Miss Prenderghast would have taken care of much of it this morning, but would still have left out the pieces she felt Veronica should see – invoices to initial; letters from concerned parents or applicants; and government circulars trying to interfere with things, which she generally binned immediately.

This was different, however. It was from the charities commission – many private schools were registered charities and, as such, didn't pay tax – talking about an assessment.

Veronica's school was exempt from Ofsted inspections, belonging as it did to the private sector. However, there were 'voluntary' assessments that could be carried out which worked in roughly the same way. They were becoming less and less voluntary as parents became more and more savvy about standards and league tables, and Veronica knew, deep down, that she wasn't going to be able to refuse – she'd put them off in the past, and if she put them off again, it would start to ring warning bells.

Sitting up in bed, she smoothed her neat grey hair behind her ears. If she hadn't ruthlessly trained it out of herself, she would have sworn. The last thing she needed was people picking over the school, nosing their beaks into her affairs. This was a wonderful school and she ran it very well. And beyond that was nobody's business.

Chapter Four

Maggie woke up blinking at the unfamiliar sunlight glancing off the rough white painted ceiling of her small bedroom. At first she had no idea where she was. Then she remembered, and a sharp bolt of excitement ran through her. She, Maggie Adair, was assistant head of English at one of the smartest girls' schools in the country! She was going to take fine young minds and fill them with words, and creativity and learning and . . .

A loud bell roared and Maggie jumped out of her skin. It sounded like a fire alarm, but didn't last. She looked at her phone. Seven o'clock! Did the bells really start ringing at seven o'clock in the morning? Every morning? This she was not going to like.

Still, she was up now. She went to the window and opened it wide, inhaling the lovely, ozoney air off the sea. Why had she never lived by the sea before? Why had she always looked out on housing estates and not the little white hulls of trawlers bobbing off in the distance? Because she couldn't afford it, she supposed. Well, she was coming up in the world now. As she gazed out in a reverie, she heard a frantic cursing next to her in what sounded like French. She leaned over and looked to her left. Sure enough, there was Mademoiselle Crozier and, tumbling from her fingers, a lit cigarette.

'Hello,' she said. Mademoiselle Crozier was wearing a black satin robe that looked incredibly luxurious for a teacher. Maggie instantly swore to finally get rid of her old towelling dressing gown that Stan had repeatedly pointed out made her look like the Gruffalo.

'*Merde*,' said Mam'selle. 'Oh, it's you. I 'ave dropped my cigarette.'

'Won't they think it's one of the girls?'

'*Mais oui*, and then there will be a grand inquisition, *non*?' She stared gloomily at the grass below. 'Perhaps it will all catch on fire and the evidence will be gone.'

'We could sneak down and pick it up,' offered Maggie. 'I won't tell anyone.'

'Sank you,' said Mam'selle. 'It is strictly *non* here, *non*?'

'*Oui*,' said Maggie smiling. 'Shall we go for breakfast?'

Mademoiselle rolled her eyes. 'You have not tried the coffee. No breakfast for me. But please, call me Claire.'

Maggie felt pleased. She thought she was going to like Mam'selle. Then she thought about her first class, and her chest tightened uncomfortably. It was one of the first forms, or what she thought of as year three – there were four forms, one from each house, so hopefully they'd be as nervous as she was and not inclined to try and trip her up. She *hoped*.

She had her lesson plan set out, based on what had worked well with her smarter pupils at Holy Cross, and had chosen for her first years a book she'd found the most terrifying thing she'd ever read when she was a teenager, *Brother in the Land*, about a young male survivor of a nuclear holocaust in England. She found it worked perfectly by being so scary that, if you got it as your first book, you also assumed that the teacher was very scary and might well bring down Armageddon on your head at any time. Almost as effective as displaying lots of strong discipline, and vastly easier. Obviously there was the odd complaint from parents when their thirteen-year-olds started wetting their beds again, but surely they were made of sterner stuff at boarding school.

Pulling on a jumper over her pyjama bottoms, she decided it was too beautiful a morning to waste; and that there wasn't much point in not living on a housing estate any more if she didn't get out and enjoy it.

The main hall, with its plaster angels, was eerily quiet – the girls were all in their towers, she assumed, brushing teeth and getting ready for the day. She padded across the hall in her Birkenstocks – ugly, but incredibly useful – and out into the dewy morning.

Goodness, but it was beautiful. The crests of the distant waves were whipped white, the morning with its last streaks of pink in the air. A fresh pure salty wind was blowing that felt as though she was getting her brain washed.

First, Maggie rounded the East Tower and peered at the grass. Sure enough, there was a handful of butts, some with lipstick around them. Surely Claire didn't wear lipstick to bed? Well, maybe the French did that kind of thing – Maggie had never had a friend from another country before. She took a bag out of her pocket and started lifting them up.

'Ah,' came a voice. Maggie looked up. It was Miss Starling, immaculate in a purple tweed suit. Maggie smiled nervously, conscious of her old University of Strathclyde sweatshirt and pulled-back hair.

'Good morning,' she said. She had to get it into her head that this woman was a colleague, not her teacher. Her boss, yes, but not her housemistress.

'Miss Adair. Good morning!'

She stared at Maggie with the cigarette butts in her hand. 'I don't know if it was made clear at the interview, and I

50

know things are different in . . . our more *deprived* parts of the country, but we don't tolerate smoking at this school. At all. It's against the law and it's a bad example for the girls. When you're in town, I suppose, if you must, but it's *completely* forbidden on school property . . .'

'I don't . . .' stuttered Maggie, looking at the butts in her hand. Miss Starling raised an eyebrow. Maggie considered dropping Claire in it, but realised she couldn't. 'Uh, all right.'

'Well, let us say no more about it. Off for an early morning walk?'

Maggie nodded, not knowing the right answer.

'Very good. Helps the constitution. Good day!'

Maggie watched her stalk off, feeling a little weak and trembly. This was ridiculous. She couldn't be frightened of her boss. She thought of her old head of English, Mr Frower, invariably known as Percy, even though the children weren't old enough to remember how he'd got his nickname. He'd nipped out for fags in the middle of lessons and was regularly to be found sticking on videos of shows only roughly connected with the topic and wandering off for a sit down. The time two of his children fluked their way to 'B's, they practically had to have a party for him. Oh yes, things had changed.

Maggie struck out for the clifftops, feeling, despite her telling off, that the world belonged to her. The only soul she could see was a gardener, down in the far end of the grounds. There was a whole team of gardeners. 'I have a whole team of gardeners,' Maggie thought to herself with a grin, and almost broke into a skip as she headed towards the garden gate.

'Look at that,' said Alice scornfully, looking out of their dormitory window as the small figure of Maggie could be seen, wandering over the grounds. 'What on earth is she wearing? What does she think she looks like? Are those *pyjamas*?'

Fliss had never seen a teacher in pyjamas before. She couldn't resist taking a peek.

'God,' Alice said. 'Look at the arse she's displaying to the world! That is rude, man.'

Fliss looked at herself in the mirror. Then she looked at Alice, who was combing out her long dark hair and looked beautiful and extremely confident. She needed a bit of that. She'd love to be so sure of herself. So she nodded and joined in.

'Isn't it true they all eat deep fried Mars Bars in Scotland?' she said.

'I don't know,' said Alice. 'It's impossible to understand a *word* they say. I think they all have heart attacks, though. Which should get us out of double English.'

Quietly, as if trying to make herself as small and unnoticeable as possible, Simone shuffled past into the bathroom. She was wearing huge pink pyjamas covered in little pictures of dogs. She'd noticed that the other girls wore slinky Calvin Klein bottoms and tiny little vest tops to bed, which showed off their little Keira Knightley tummies and high round breasts. How did they know what to wear to bed? Was there some sort of a memo sent round? Her mum had bought her these pyjamas because they'd both thought they were cute, and they were cheap in Primark, and nice cosy flannel, because Mrs Rishkian down at the laundrette had heard that these boarding schools weren't heated and she'd need to be nice and warm.

Alice regarded her steadily in the mirror.

'Nice pyjamas,' she said in a neutral tone.

'Thanks,' said Simone, colouring and looking for her toothbrush.

'Primark?' Alice asked.

'Yes!' said Simone, amazed that this gorgeous girl seemed to be making reasonable conversation with her.

Alice looked at Fliss. 'I'd never have guessed.'

Fliss felt bad. 'I'm going to go and get dressed,' she said. 'Your pyjamas are cute, Simone.'

Alice rolled her eyes.

The blowing blustery clifftops brought some of Maggie's confidence back. She felt exhilarated by the whipping waves and the clouds racing over the sky, as the sun steadily warmed her back.

'*I wandered lonely as a cloud!*' she shouted into the head of the wind. '*That floats on high o'er vales and hills . . .*'

Getting into it now she started to declaim louder and louder, enjoying the sensation of roaring into the wind and being so very far away from everything she found familiar.

'*. . . And then my chest with pleasure fills,*' she concluded, throwing out an arm to a hovering audience of gulls and cormorants, and imagining her new class applauding and being inspired and moved by poetry. '*And dances with the daffodils!*'

'Oh, very good,' came a voice, and, from almost directly beneath her feet, a man emerged from the undergrowth, clapping.

'Shit!' shouted Maggie and jumped back, almost losing her footing.

'Sorry, sorry!' said the man, putting up his hands to make it clear he wasn't a threat. As well he might, thought Maggie, hiding in the undergrowth next to a girls' school. She fumbled in her pyjama pockets for her mobile phone. Maybe she'd have to call the police. She hadn't brought it. Shit. Shit. She felt her face flush.

'It's OK' he said. 'I was on the path, see? It goes just below here. I was walking my dog.'

As if to prove this to her he whistled and a lovely mongrel bounded up, hopping joyously.

'Oh what a nice dog,' said Maggie, unable to help herself. She was fairly sure that paedophile perverts didn't have nice dogs. 'What is it?'

'A bitter,' said the man. 'Bit o' this, bit o' that, you know?'

She smiled, despite herself. 'I was just . . .'

'Yes, what *were* you doing? I can see you're questioning my motives, but I'm afraid you are *much* more suspicious. Out shouting loudly in your underwear?'

Oh God. Maggie felt her face get even redder. 'I was just practising some poetry. And these are perfectly decent pyjamas, thank you.'

'Well, you obviously haven't seen the hole in the back. And a bit of Wordsworth. Very nice. Although I think you'll find it's "my *heart* with pleasure fills".'

'I'm the new English teacher at Downey House.'

'*Are* you?' His face split into a wide, slightly manic grin. 'Well, very nice to meet you, New English Teacher at Downey House. I'm your opposite number.'

He stuck out his hand. Maggie stuck hers out to meet it before realising it was covered in cigarette ash from picking up Claire's butts. She quickly pulled it back and scratched the dog's neck instead. The man didn't seem to mind.

'What do you mean?'

'I'm David McDonald. Head of English at Downey Boys.'

Maggie still didn't know what he was talking about.

'The boys' school? Over the headland? Downers? That's what the boys call it. Or Downey's Syndrome, if they're in the mood to be really horrid, which as we know all boys are. You'd think they'd use a bit of imagination . . .'

Maggie wasn't entirely sure how to get him to stop talking.

'Oh,' she said, just pitching herself in in the middle. 'Wow. Hello then!'

'We'll be seeing a bit of each other then,' said David. Maggie realised to her horror that she was meeting a new professional colleague (and possible ally – though his grin was a bit loopy she liked his dog) whilst still in her damn pyjamas. She was going to bin these things asap. 'Inter-school debates, that kind of thing. Are you interested in drama?'

'Uh, yes, definitely.'

'I think I could tell by your excellent presentation. Well, good. We should talk about that sometime.'

'Uh huh,' said Maggie, embarrassed now by her wild hair bushing around her face and her nicotine-stained fingers.

'Well, I'd best get going. The brutes will be going feral. And as for the boys . . .'

'OK then,' said Maggie, smiling. 'OK. Bye.'

'Come on, Stephen Daedalus!' It took a minute for Maggie to realise he was shouting on his dog. 'See you around!'

'Uh, yeah OK!'

But her voice was swept away on the wind as she watched him descend back along the cliff path.

Back at the school, things were much, much busier, even though Maggie hadn't been away twenty minutes. She realised immediately one of her worst fears – who on earth had she thought she was, dashing out onto the moors without a second thought? Catherine from *Wuthering Heights*? Yes, probably. Impetuous behaviour; always a fault in her, she knew, particularly unsuited to being a teacher.

The front courtyard was teeming with girls looking for

their classes. Oh no, Maggie thought crossly. She was going to have to go through the whole courtyard, full of girls, in her pyjamas. Which possibly had a hole in the back – she wasn't 100 per cent sure she believed the rather mischievous looking Mr McDonald. On her very first morning. This kind of thing, she knew, could ruin a teacher's rep for ever. At her old school a new recruit, Mr Samson, had turned up on his first day with a stain on his tie. He'd spent the rest of his career as Bird-shit Samson, and never knew why. She had such a short time to make a good impression – she was already going to seem so strange and foreign to most of them, at least if it worked the other way as to how strange and foreign they felt to her.

Stupidly, she found herself hiding behind her parked car. What was she going to do? What? Wait until they all went into lessons? But then she'd be late! That wasn't much better, Miss Starling would doubtless have a thing or two to say about it. Who was she less afraid of, the girls or Miss Starling? She wasn't sure.

Veronica replaced her teacup thoughtfully as she considered drawing down the blinds. Was that her new teacher hiding out in the car park? *Surely* not. Obviously she'd gone out on a limb with the appointment, but it was rare that her judgement was quite as poor as that. Oh, that would be all she needed, a new headache to add to the other things they were going to have to go through this year. She returned her gaze to the pile of paperwork on her desk. Examiners were suggesting commencing over a three-week period during which they would sit in on classes, talk to selected pupils (selected by whom, Veronica wondered drily), look at the school accounts and generally poke their big noses into everything. Including, Veronica worried, herself.

Goodness me, what *was* that ridiculous Scottish girl doing? The whole point of this school was to teach young ladies calm and order, not how to run about in their smalls, something half the sixth form needed almost no practice in anyway. She would definitely have to have a word.

'Pssst,' came a voice. On the verge of panic, Maggie cut her eyes to the side. There, sidling through the car park and squeezing through the very small spaces between the cars with an elegant swing of her hips, was Claire.

'What are you doing? *Qu'est-ce que vous faites?*' she demanded, obviously so used to teaching in two languages she didn't really let it go at any other time. As she got close Maggie could smell the cigarettes on her breath.

'I can get out but I can't get back in,' whispered Maggie frantically. 'I've never taught at a school where there were people *all the time* before.'

'That ees no problem,' said Claire. 'Follow me.'

And she sidled off (Maggie found it difficult to get through some of the smaller spaces between the parked cars) all the way round the building, via the hedges, to a small door round the back of their turret that Maggie hadn't even noticed.

'Fire exit,' explained Claire. 'It should not be open from the outside, huh, it will encourage the girls to misbehave. But for one morning only . . .'

'I think,' said Maggie, 'you behave worse than any of the girls here.'

Claire smiled. 'You cannot get a reasonable loaf of bread from here to Le Touquet,' she said. 'One must do sometheeng for fun, *non*?'

Maggie made it upstairs, showered, changed and into assembly with mere moments to spare. She was ready.

Chapter Five

Fliss looked at the card as she stood by the old-fashioned wooden pigeon holes, trying to ignore all the older girls shouting and gossiping to one another. Alice had disappeared and she felt entirely on her own. Half of it made her want to sneer and rip it up. Half of it made her want to cry.

Our darling Felicity, the card said. *We know this is the first day of a great adventure for you. You may not think we are doing the right thing, but we think you will thrive and grow up into the wonderful young woman we know you can be.*

Fliss's throat had got a lump in it just then. She was glad no one else was around to see.

So do what you can to make us proud and we know you'll be happy too.

All of a sudden she felt a whirl in her stomach as someone picked her up and spun her round.

'All right baby sis?'

It was Hattie. She was wearing her prefect's badge proudly on her blazer and her navy jumper tied loosely over her shoulders in a way Fliss couldn't help finding extremely irritating.

'Hey,' said Hattie, grabbing the card out of Fliss's hands. 'Is that from home?'

'Give it back!' said Fliss. 'It's private mail! It's MINE!'

'Don't be silly,' said Hattie, who'd never had the faintest

problem with bursting into Fliss's room at odd times of day, or flicking through her diary (which Fliss kept out in the stables now). 'What could they possibly be writing to you that they wouldn't want me to see?' She scanned the note quickly. 'Oh yeah. They sent one just like this to me.' She sniffed.

'Did they?' Fliss felt immediately crestfallen. She'd thought she'd detected Daddy's hand in the card; that he had wanted to send her some reassurance, try and suggest that he hadn't really wanted her to go at all, that they loved her too much.

'Yeah, yeah. It's just meant to make you work hard. Mind you, did the job for me.'

'What do you mean?' said Fliss, red-faced and upset.

'Oh yeah, I didn't want to come here either. Thought you'd get to stay behind having all the fun. But I did what they said, and it's been the making of me,' said Hattie. 'I might even make captain of netball this year. So. Listen to them. They know what's best for you.' She gave a patronising smile. 'And so do I. Even if you don't think so at the moment.' She bustled off importantly.

Fliss's fists clenched by her sides and she felt fury burn up inside her. So everyone knew what was best, did they? Well, they'd see about that! She wasn't going to turn into a useless pi busybody suckbutt like Hattie, no way.

'Hello Fliss,' said Alice, wandering up, looking pristine in an oddly impertinent way – her uniform was a little too tidy; her shirt a little too white. It looked as though she was challenging you to say something about it. 'Want to pretend we got lost and be late for class?'

Fliss realised one of her fists was clenched, and slowly let it unfurl.

'Sure,' she said.

*

59

Simone looked round the empty classroom. Where was everyone? Was she in the right place? Her skirt button was rubbing. She shouldn't have had that extra slice of bacon this morning. But the breakfast had been brilliant; fried bread and sausage and yoghurt and fresh fruit. No coffee, like she got at home, except for sixth formers, but she'd had tea with four sugars and there was no one to tut like her mum did. Plus she'd heard the girls say they only got a top-up feed on the first morning so she should make the most of it.

The refectory was a high-ceilinged panelled room, with high-set windows, long wooden tables and benches that sat eight or ten; the room's bad acoustics meant that whilst the clanging of knives and forks was always loud, it was some-times difficult to hear even your neighbour. Hence everyone shouted.

From where she'd been sitting on the end of the row by herself, Simone couldn't believe all the other girls seemed to have coupled up already. How was that possible? It wasn't that she wasn't used to eating by herself; God, at St Cats it had happened all the time. But how had all these girls man-aged to fit in so quickly? Even their haircuts were similar. Was there some memo that went round that said you had to have long silky straight-cut hair without a fringe, as well as the PE kit and a boater? Had she missed it? She'd stroked her fuzzy plaits nervously. Simone didn't realise that a lot of these girls came from the same small number of 'feeder' schools that educated them to take the exam. Half of them had already met at pony club; or their mothers were friends, having been to the same school twenty years before.

Sitting at the end of the row she'd watched them enviously as she stuffed two sausages inside a sandwich and covered it liberally in ketchup.

'Oh, this food is great,' one girl was saying.

'Heavenly.' But, oddly, neither of them was actually eating. Carefully, one of the girls had fished a piece of kiwi fruit out of the fruit salad and popped it in her mouth.

'I'm stuffed,' she said. 'Huge supper last night.'

'Ya, me too,' said another.

'And my tuck is just to die for,' said a third. 'My mother sent me an entire bloody fruit cake. I think I ate the whole thing.'

Simone had stuffed down the rest of her sandwich and sidled away as quickly as she could, to puzzled glances from the others. As soon as she was nearly out of earshot, naughty Alice had said, 'I just can't make up my mind – transfer from Roedean or, perhaps . . . *scholarship*?' And the whole table had dissolved in laughter.

Now Simone sat alone in the English classroom, trying to figure it all out.

Assembly and roll call over – a lengthy and tedious allocation of classrooms, timetables, groupings and house leaders – Maggie was at last ready to teach her first lesson. All her classes were Plantagenets, and she had a pastoral role towards Middle School 1. So, thought Maggie, running it through her head. Pregnancy, skag, fighting and usually the first time they got thrown out of the house and temporarily rendered homeless. Oh, no, hang on. It wouldn't be like that here. With any luck it would only be periods and missing tennis racquets.

She looked through it all nervously in the staffroom. Some modern poetry, nothing too frightening, plus the novel. She was looking forward to *Wuthering Heights* and *Tess* for the older ones; she'd never been able to teach those before, as the boy halves of her classes, even the small senior ones, groaned and rolled their eyes laboriously whenever they

61

came out, whereas the girls could just float away on a cloud of doomed romance. Although, she wondered, maybe all the girls here would have read those books already? They were going to be way ahead of what she was used to. What if this was the equivalent for them of Noddy stories?

Well, it was on the curriculum, so that was what they would have. The A-level students, who came in in the afternoon, were doing Chaucer. She cursed. She hated Chaucer, always had done. So hard to interpret and not that funny when you finally managed it. Still, Miss Starling had just told her, before dashing out to get over to Tudor, that the A-level students were quiet, studious girls in this house, expected to do extremely well and good self-starters. They way she'd said it left Maggie in no doubt that the reason they were such paragons of virtue was because of Miss Starling's immaculate regime, that she had no wish of changing.

Well, we'll see, thought Maggie, smoothing down her checked jacket in the ladies and checking she didn't have any grass in her hair, just as the bell tolled again loud and clear. Maggie took a deep breath and headed out to her classroom.

'Hello,' she said cheerily to the lone girl, a chubby lass who seemed to be eating. 'I'm Miss Adair. The new English teacher.'

'Hello, miss,' mumbled Simone, embarrassed that she'd been caught out. Her mother had sent her some *mamaliga* cakes in the post – she must have posted them before they'd even left yesterday. The grease had stained through the wrapper, but they tasted of home; so good she didn't care. Even the smell made her think of them all sitting on the big brown settee, watching *X Factor* and bugging their dad to let them phone in again. She even missed Joel kicking her in the ankle when he thought she was taking up more than her fair share of the cushions. She had a lump in her throat. What was she doing here?

'Are you eating?' asked Maggie, thinking as she always did, how much saying this made her sound like a teacher.

'Yes miss,' said Simone, turning a deep shade of purple. In trouble! On her first day.

'Well, are you allowed to eat with your other teachers?'

'No, miss.'

'So why do you think I'm going to be any different? Give me that please.'

Snivelling, Simone handed up the parcel of home. Maggie debated throwing it in the bin – it looked like soggy bread and smelled very peculiar – but she could sense with this girl she probably wasn't going to have to be too tough.

'You can pick it up after school,' she said. Simone nodded numbly.

Great, thought Maggie. Been here ten seconds and have already reduced my first pupil to a dumbstruck sodden mess.

'What's your name?' she asked kindly.

'Simone.'

'Do you need a tissue, Simone?'

Simone nodded quietly, whilst Maggie retrieved one from the packet no sensible teacher did without in her handbag. She was about to ask if the girl was all right, when suddenly, with a noisy chatter, the main river of schoolgirls burst into the room.

Chatting, yelling, giggling, they were making a lot of noise, Maggie knew, to cover up their essential nerves at this, the start of a new school, with new girls and new ways of doing things. Although the way this lot threw themselves about, it was as if they'd known one another for years. She was used to first years being a little more cowed than this, if only because the ones at Holy Cross weren't sure whether they were going to get mugged at break time for their mobile phones.

Maggie gave them a couple of minutes to choose their seats and settle down. The desks were the old-fashioned kind she hadn't seen in years – wooden, with proper lids and inkwells, scored and scratched with years of discussion about who loved whom and which pop group was the best, etched by compasses.

Then she wrote her name up on the board and turned round to face them all.

'Hello,' she said. 'I'm Miss Adair. For those of you who are new here, I'm also new here, and very happy to be. Here. Now, who can tell where my accent is from?'

Maggie had expected to be able to start some friendly banter, but no one said a word. She looked around the class until a few people tentatively raised their hands. She picked a dark-haired girl at random.

'Scotland?' said the girl, as if slightly puzzled that she'd asked such a stupid question.

'That's right,' said Maggie. 'Have you been there?'

'Well, my family own an estate there,' said the girl, looking bored.

'OK, well done,' said Maggie trying not to show that she was flustered. 'Who else has been to Scotland?'

Pretty much the entire class raised their hands. Maggie wondered if she'd have got the same response if she'd said the Caribbean, or America, or France. Probably. Thirteen years old and they'd done it all. She noticed her little muncher hadn't raised her hand yet. She'd have to keep an eye on her.

'Well,' she said. 'I thought, just for us to get acquainted, we could start with a Scottish poem, from the land of my birth. A great poet, called Liz Lochhead. Then we can discuss it, see what you think, and open up the floor.'

The girls opened their jotters obediently, with only one low groan from the back. Maggie's heart sank a little. Maybe she'd just ignore this one. She knew she needed to flaunt her authority at an early stage, but maybe not just yet.

'It's called "The Choosing",' she said. And she read the beautiful verse, of two girls growing up, one to go on to study and do well for herself, one forbidden by her father to continue her schooling, the first spending all her time in the library, running in to her pregnant friend upstairs on the bus, 'her arms around the full-shaped vase that is her body'. Maggie remembered so well the first time she'd heard it; how clearly she had identified herself with the two girls on the estates. That she would be the one in the library, with the prizes there for the taking. Was it having the same effect? She cast half an eye in their direction. Perhaps this was wrong. There wasn't a choice for these girls. Of course they would succeed. Effortlessly. Failure wasn't an option when you could pay thousands of pounds a year to buy your girls the best education possible.

But they listened politely enough, and she tried to elongate her vowels and not roll her r's too much to give them a fair shot.

'So . . .' she said, leaning back, trying to look cool and collected and utterly unfazed by the new world she found herself in. 'Any thoughts?'

There was a long moment when nobody moved a muscle in the class and Maggie had that thought she sometimes got that she should have done primary teaching after all and they could have just pulled out some colouring-in books at this point.

Fliss sat at the back, and glanced at Alice, whose eyes were dancing, full of mischief. Alice nodded. 'Go on,' she whispered. Fliss rolled her eyes. Alice giggled.

'You two,' came Maggie's voice firmly. 'Do you have something to say?'

'Well, the thing is,' drawled Fliss, quite amazed at where on earth she'd found the courage. 'I'm afraid I didn't really understand what you were saying.'

Maggie felt the class stiffen.

'Was it English?' Fliss went on, scarcely believing her own daring.

Maggie stared at her. 'Well you'll find out,' she said. She rifled through her file, scarcely able to believe she was doing it, and pulled out another poem.

'Why don't you read this to the class, if your diction is so much better.'

She stared at Fliss who stared back. She couldn't mean it, could she? She couldn't possibly be expecting her to read something out loud?

Maggie was doing her best inside to look steely. That was the only way, she kept telling herself. Be tough, and you only had to do it once. And never, ever let them get to you.

She held up the paper. 'Out at the front please. What's your name?'

'Felicity Prosser,' Fliss mumbled, her cheeks going scarlet. Maggie was surprised to see her blushing. Obviously not quite as shameless as she liked to pretend. Still, she wasn't going to back down now.

'Out you get then.'

For a short period nobody moved a muscle. Then, gradually and as sulkily as she could manage, Fliss pushed herself out to the front of the class.

'What's this?' she asked.

'Some foreign poetry,' said Maggie. 'Read it to the class, please.'

The class stared at Fliss, looking awed and amazed. She felt her face burn but didn't feel she had any choice.

Gradually, haltingly she began:

'Go fetch to me a pint o' wine,
An' fill it in a silver tassie,'

Felicity kept her head down and muttered into the paper.

'That's a cup,' said Maggie. 'Speak louder, please.'

'That I may drink, before I go,
A service to my bonnie lassie.'

'That means girl,' said Maggie.

'I know,' said Fliss.

'OK. Sorry, it's just you said you didn't understand foreign.'

'I'm sorry, miss.'

'Keep reading, please.'

As Fliss stumblingly reached the second verse, even she could see it was quite exciting, and the class was looking interested as she intoned,

'The trumpets sound, the banners fly,
The glittering spears are rankèd ready;
The shouts o' war are heard afar,
The battle closes deep and bloody;'

And when she reached the end, Maggie checked and saw the class were listening intently. Good. It had worked.

'That's Robert Burns,' said Maggie. 'One of the greatest

poets that ever lived. Do you think you're still going to have trouble understanding Scots? I have lots more poems here that we can move on to if you don't.'

'I'm sure I'll be fine, miss,' said Fliss, still feeling sick with the humiliation.

'All right. Sit down please.'

Maggie turned back to her class.

'Right. Now where were we? On Liz Lochhead. Does anyone have any trouble with translation?'

Everyone else fervently shook their heads.

'All right. Comments, please. The sheets are on your desks.'

There was a long, long wait whilst it seemed as though no one was going to speak. Until, finally, a small girl tentatively raised her hand.

'Yes. You,' said Maggie, in a much friendlier voice, pointing her out. 'Can you say your names too, when you answer? Makes my job easier.'

'I'm Isabel,' said the girl, and Maggie jotted it down on her seating chart.

'What did you think, Isabel?'

'Well, she kind of feels sorry for the other girl, but a bit jealous too, doesn't she?'

After that the class relaxed and went much better. Except for one girl, sitting at the back. I will never forgive her, thought Fliss. Never.

'Simone?' asked Maggie. 'Who do you empathise with in the poem?'

Simone had loved the poem. That was her. All those other girls at school could just go out and get pregnant and she was going to go and do something else. She had to articulate it. She had to get it out. Flushing horribly in front of everyone she stuttered.

68

'The poet,' she said. 'I mean, she was going to the library and getting on with her life and . . .'

'Not the vase?' came a voice from behind her. The whole class sniggered. Simone was by far the heaviest one there. Immediately her face turned bright pink and she stared down at her desk.

'Who said that?' said Maggie, annoyed. Fliss was delighted. It wasn't just going to be her who hated this teacher.

As always happens in schoolrooms, the girls imperceptibly moved away from the culprit, leaving her encircled. Maggie glanced at her chart.

'Alice Trebizon-Woods?'

Alice was a pretty blank-faced girl with long dark hair and an innocent looking expression Maggie didn't trust for an instant.

'Yes, miss.'

'Did you interject?'

'Did I what, miss?'

Maggie waited a couple of seconds.

'Did you want to say something to Simone?'

'I was just adding to the debate, miss. About whether she felt like the other woman. I thought we were opening up the floor.'

There wasn't much Maggie could say to that.

'Well, keep things out of the realm of the personal, please.'

Alice opened her eyes wide and blinked them.

'I wasn't, miss.'

'Continue, Simone,' said Maggie, but Simone couldn't, and stared hard at her desk. Maggie stared hard at Alice and made a mental note to mark her card. The other girls too, all new, stared at the bold girls in the back desk, impressed.

*

'Hi, Stan.'

There was a long pause.

'Yeah, hi, Maggie.'

There was another long pause.

'It was my first day in the classroom today.'

'Oh yeah?' he said. 'Sorry, I haven't been keeping an eye on my academic calendar, you know.'

'That's OK,' said Maggie. 'It went . . . fine. Not great. Not bad.'

'So they haven't immediately twigged you're just a schemie girl frae Govan and chucked you out on your bahookie.'

Maggie stiffened. 'Was that supposed to be funny?'

Stan wasn't sure. 'Uh, yes.'

'Well, it wasn't. There's no earthly reason I can't be a teacher here.' She thought back to Clarissa Rhodes. The tall, beautiful, elegant sixth former, who looked like a young Gwyneth Paltrow, with her clear blue eyes and shiny mass of hair, had flawlessly recited six stanzas of the Chaucer, then deconstructed them with a skill and elegance that left Maggie gasping her admiration.

'I'm not sure,' Clarissa had said afterwards when she had taken the time to meet the girls individually. 'I was thinking of discussing it at my Oxford entrance. But I've also got an offer from the Royal College of Music for the cello and Mr Bart – that's the physics teacher – he thinks I should really take this offer from Cambridge seriously.' She'd blinked her large blue eyes. 'It's hard being a teenager, Mrs Adair.'

'It's "Miss", actually,' Maggie had said, feeling about two feet tall.

'I deserve to be here,' she said now to Stan, but it was as much to convince herself as anything.

'Course you do, love,' said Stan then. 'We just miss you, that's all.'

'I miss you too,' said Maggie. 'Tell me the gossip.'

Stan thought for a while. Gossip wasn't really his thing. He thought of it as a totally female thing. Football for blokes, gossip for girls, and he wasn't about to feign an interest now. 'Your dog got sick,' he said suddenly.

'Muffin? What happened?' Suddenly Maggie felt a homesick wrench.

'Oh, Dylan and Cody were feeding him turkey twizzlers. And he took up and spewed all over the carpet. It was hilarious.'

'Is he all right?'

'Well, he ate the sick,' said Stan.

A bell rang loudly.

'I have to go,' said Maggie. 'We've a dinner meeting.'

'Whenever I bring up spew, you always have to go,' said Stan.

Maggie paused. 'I do,' she said.

'Yeah yeah yeah,' said Stan. 'Right, I'm off to find the bleach.'

And he hung up. Maggie had been hoping for a bit more interest and support on her first day. But she supposed other people's lives were still going on.

She made her way to the headmistress's office where they were having a small reception so all the teachers could meet, along with the staff of their brother school over the hill. She wondered if the crazy man from that morning would be there. Well, be nice to see a familiar face. She felt as nervous as . . . who was that terribly awkward girl in the first form? Simone. Yes. She dipped into the staff toilets to rub a piece of lipstick on, and smelled smoke as she got in there.

'Claire? *C'est vous*?' she said.

The French mistress appeared from the cubicle she'd been hiding in.

'Ah, no. Well, of course. Yes. We must go to a boring cocktail party and still they say, no, you must not smoke. But for sure, teachers always smoke. It is unusual and cruel punishment.'

'It's horrid, Claire. And it's bad for the girls.'

'Ah, *oui oui*, OK. She threw her butt down the toilet and came over and inspected her perfectly made-up face in the mirror.

'*Mon dieu*, I shall rot in this place.'

'You look beautiful,' said Maggie, truthfully.

'And what about you, you have a boyfriend?'

Suddenly Maggie wasn't desperately keen, for some reason, to talk about spew-obsessed Stan and his grumpy ways. She couldn't see him coming here and making small-talk with Claire, who was wearing a beautiful white blouse under a grey cashmere sweater which somehow didn't look boring at all, but perfectly chosen and fitting. What would they talk about? Would Stan sneer as they went through the courtyard? What would he eat? She felt disloyal, even as she said, 'Oh, kind of, you know?'

Claire nodded her head fervently. '*Bien sûr*, I understand.'

Maggie smiled.

'He is married, yes?'

'No!'

'Very old and very rich?'

'Don't you think we should go?'

Maggie was glad she was with Claire as she walked into the office. The place was full of teachers and the noise level was high. Sixth form girls were helping the staff handing round canapés and drinks. Maggie wasn't sure this was a good idea.

Giving the girls access to alcohol and the potential to overhear teachers' gossip. There was loud chatter and several animated conversations were going on. Maggie saw Miss Starling bending the ear of an elderly looking chap with whiskers who was either half-deaf or just politely nodding at random intervals. Dr Deveral was deep in conversation with a rather charming older man, dressed tweedily in the Oxford style, with a waistcoat and patches on the elbows of his jacket. On seeing Maggie, she beckoned her over.

'Yes, Margaret. Let me introduce you to some of the staff from across the way. This is Dr Robert Fitzroy, headteacher of Downey Boys, just over the hill. It's a stunning Georgian building, you must make an effort to visit as soon as possible.'

'Nice to meet you,' said Maggie, unsure about what to do, but gratefully accepting the outstretched hand. She was a little wary of the English tradition of kissing strangers.

'Of course, you're Veronica's social experiment,' said Robert, smiling kindly.

'Of course she isn't, Robert,' said Veronica, a little pink spot appearing on her cheeks. 'She's a much valued new member of staff.'

'So, do you speak any of your beautiful languages from up there?' said Robert. '*Ciamar a thathu?*'

Maggie decided his face wasn't that kind after all. 'No,' she said.

'What about lallans?'

'I know some Burns,' she said.

'Some Burns! Well, that's a relief.'

'Robert,' said Veronica, reprovingly.

'I'm sorry, my dear,' said Robert to Maggie. 'I'm just making a comment on the state of comprehensive schooling, that's all. I'm so pleased you're here.'

'There are plenty of good comprehensive schools,' said Maggie, angry and prepared to be outspoken.

'My school,' said Robert, 'has two computers per boy, and fifteen acres of football pitch. Don't you think every child deserves access to those kinds of facilities?'

'I think one computer is probably enough for anybody,' said Maggie.

Robert raised his eyebrows. 'A socialist on our hands.'

'Robert, stop being annoying,' said Dr Deveral, with more charm than Maggie had seen before. 'Maggie, do ignore him, he's teasing you.'

'All right,' said Maggie. But it hadn't particularly felt like teasing. She looked around to see if there was anyone else she could talk to. Her gaze fell suddenly on David McDonald, who was standing on the periphery of some sports masters and mistresses who appeared to be demonstrating rounders pitching. He looked bored. But as soon as he saw her his face broke into a wide, slightly manic grin and he raised his glass. Then, seeing she didn't have one, he strode over.

'Hello! Where's your wine?'

'Of course,' said Veronica, looking round for one of the sixth formers, who stepped forward immediately. Maggie took a glass of white and hoped she wouldn't be asked to comment on the vintage.

'Margaret, this is David . . .'

'We've met,' said David, grinning broadly. 'Both fans of early morning walks.'

'Oh, good,' said Veronica.

'I think we should introduce compulsory cold early-morning walks for the pupils,' said Robert. 'What do you think? Blow the cobwebs away before classes.'

'Well,' said Veronica. 'One, they're hard enough to shift as

74

it is. Two, they'd probably take us to the European court of human rights. And three . . .'

'Boys and girls out together in the early morning is just asking for baby-shaped trouble,' said David, draining his glass. 'What about those cold showers, Robert?'

'Well, yes, that too . . .' started Robert, as David guided Maggie away.

'He's a dinosaur,' said Maggie.

'Oh, he's all right. Just old-fashioned. Bit set in his ways. Thinks school was better when there was a lot more whacking in it. The parents love him.'

'I'm not surprised – he looks like he walked out of the pages of the *Daily Mail*.'

'The boys love him too. He's all right. Anyway, if you're that dead set against the *Daily Mail*, what are you doing teaching in a private school in the south of England?'

'I wanted to learn some good techniques to take back to Govan.'

'Is that all?' asked David.

Maggie looked at her wine glass for a moment.

'And well, I just . . . I wanted a change. To see a bit more of the world, I think. I mean, I was teaching at the same school I went to, having to make small talk with my old teachers, can you imagine?'

David made an appropriate face.

'It just seemed a good opportunity. Robert's right in a way. The school I was in was kind of getting me down.' She looked up. 'Why are you here?'

'Holding the line against the philistines,' said David, gesticulating rather wildly with his wine glass. 'Against a world full of texters and magazine addicts and people who think punctuation is for pussies and only care about trainers and would beat you up if you liked poetry. Hearts and minds.'

75

'Hear hear,' said Claire, who was standing nearby.

'And also, I'm on the run from the French Foreign Legion.'

Maggie smiled. 'Really?'

'We had a misunderstanding.' He whirled off to get some more drinks.

'What a very peculiar man,' said Maggie to Claire.

'The boys they love him,' said Claire.

'I bet they do.'

'I can't believe the teachers are downstairs getting pissed,' said Alice to Fliss, as they mounted the stairs of their tower to prep. It was still light outside. Fliss was used to going to bed when she liked, pretty much. Her parents would try and pick their battles, and bedtime was no longer one of them. This was inhumane. Prep till seven-thirty, then television till nine, lights out at ten! Surely they could sue someone over it.

'This is why they send us to bed so bloody early,' said Alice. 'So we don't stumble on them completely half-arsed, throwing up on the lawn.'

Fliss laughed. 'And copping off with each other.'

Alice looked at her thoughtfully. 'Have you ever been pissed?'

'Course,' scoffed Fliss, although in fact, apart from the champagne they were allowed at Christmas and a few slugs of an alcopop Hattie had once lowered herself to letting her try, she hadn't at all. Hat was so bloody perfect all the time, far too busy with her sports clubs and guiding to get caught up in any kind of 'nonsense' as her father called it. So there wasn't any illicit vodka swilling all round the house, like Fliss had heard other girls talk about. Some even claimed to be going to nightclubs already, though she wasn't sure if this were true.

'What about . . .'

'What?'

But Fliss knew what was coming next, and wasn't looking forward to the question. She thought she'd better lie.

'Have you ever . . . snogged a boy?'

'Of course,' said Fliss, fiercely jumping in.

She thought back over the last summer. She'd had the biggest crush on Will Hampton, the eldest son of their near neighbours. He was tall and slim with floppy brown hair, was going up to Oxford in the autumn and went out with one of the local girls who was emo and gorgeous, really skinny with her huge eyes outlined in black liner. Fliss used to hang around the village shop just in the hopes that she'd catch him going in to buy *The Times* (she'd vowed to take *The Times* when she was older, even if boring old Mummy got the *Mail* and Dad liked the *FT*) and he'd grin and say hello to her and that would be enough to last her the whole day. Once, he'd patted Ranald.

Her hopes were high when her parents had his round at Christmas for a couple of glasses of wine, but he showed up for five minutes then scooted off to a party in town. How she'd wished he'd turn round to her, in this totally stupid dress her dad had wanted her to wear, and ask her to come with him. Of course he hadn't. Still, at least he hadn't asked Hattie, that would have been too mortifying. Hattie pretended she didn't care that she wasn't asked. Everyone would like to be asked somewhere by Will Hampton. But *this* Christmas . . . surely she'd be out of this dump by then.

Apart from that, opportunities for snogging were pretty limited, although Fliss was absolutely riven with curiosity. She'd read *Cosmo* and so on, but they were terribly graphic. And everyone had chattered at school when Faith Garnett had reportedly tongue-smashed one of the jockeys up at the pony club and Faith had briefly been the most interesting and popular girl at school as they'd all queued up for details (sloppy and a bit wet was the consensus), then some of the girls had started saying nasty things and it had ended up with Faith in floods in the toilets surrounded by concerned onlookers and Miss Mathieson giving them all a strict talking to on the perils of gossip, most of which had gone completely over Fliss's head.

'Oh,' said Alice. 'Have you got a boyfriend?'

Fliss would have given anything to be able to answer 'yes' to that question: 'Yes . . . he's going up to Oxford . . . his name is Will Hampton.'

'No,' she said. 'I'm too young.'

'I've been asked out a lot,' said Alice. 'Most people think I look older than thirteen. When I'm not wearing stupid effing knee socks.'

'I know, it's harsh,' agreed Fliss vehemently. 'You do, you look loads older.'

'Thanks,' said Alice. 'I think I have a mature face. Though it's ugly.'

'No, you're beautiful!' said Fliss. 'I'm disgusting.'

'You're beautiful,' said Alice immmediately. 'I'm so disgusting.'

'You're not, you're gorgeous,' said Fliss.

Alice started getting undressed for bed with a sigh. 'We're never going to meet boys here. What do you think, Imogen?'

Imogen was still studying, her face towards the wall, her back towards the room. She just shrugged. Alice turned to Fliss with a merry look.

'God, Imogen, do you have to be so noisy all the time?'

Simone trooped in from the bathroom in her big pyjamas and slippers.

'What about you, Simone?' said Alice, sitting on the bed.

'What?' said Simone, colouring again. Fliss thought what a shame it was she was carrying so much weight; there was a very pretty face in there. If only she wasn't so heavy.

'Got a boyfriend?'

'No,' said Simone shortly, taking her book and climbing into bed.

'Well I was only *asking*,' said Alice. 'You don't need to be so touchy.'

'Sorry,' said Simone, in a miserable voice.

'Maybe she likes women,' whispered Alice to Fliss quietly. 'Better watch out for yourself.'

'Stop it, Alice,' said Fliss. And the bell came, ringing for lights out.

Back at the drinks party Veronica eyed two women sidling in, both wearing wildly unflattering trouser suits. One was carrying a clipboard. Not, thought Veronica to herself, the most elegant of accompaniments to a drinks party. Neither of them was smiling. Veronica checked her hair (perfect, as ever – not a strand would dare defy her kirby grips) and glided over towards them.

'Liz, Pat,' she said. 'Thanks so much for coming to join us.'

'We just found our way,' said the older of the two women. She had very short hair, unflatteringly layered along the side of her head, clear glasses, pale lipstick and a couple of chins too many. Veronica didn't want to see what the stretched seat of her trousers must look like. 'It's not easy to get here.' She said this in an accusatory tone.

'No,' said Veronica. 'I think when it was built it wasn't particularly easy to get anywhere, so it didn't really matter. And I've always thought our location and views are so worth it, don't you think?'

'All right for some,' said the other woman, who had grey hair that looked like it was standing as a rebuke to other, lesser women who dyed theirs.

Veronica's heart sank. She knew the school had to be inspected, she'd just hoped she'd get some people sympathetic to what they were doing here, not ex-local government class warriors. She gave the second lady, Pat, a cool stare. 'You are here to examine the school's facilities? So of course you're hoping everything will be as good as possible?'

'Yes, good for the kids whose parents can afford it.'

'I realise that,' said Veronica, bristling. 'But that's the world as it is. And you're here to see that we're doing as well as we can for the girls here, isn't that right?'

The first woman grunted, and looked around to see where the girls were with their canapés. She beckoned them back and took a handful, cramming them into her mouth. Veronica privately thought that if one of her girls ate like that in company she'd have taken them outside and had a quiet word. Then she started considering her strategy. What a shame that scholarship girl was so timid this year. That's what they needed to be pushing; how Downey House could be a force for good in poorer communities and bring out potential that would get squashed elsewhere. She must keep an eye on that girl.

And that outspoken Scottish teacher should impress them too. They could share the chips on their shoulders.

Veronica smiled at Pat and Liz and asked them if they'd like more wine. They would, of course.

'Betjeman,' said David disconcertingly.

'What?'

'We should add some Betjeman for the Christmas concert. He's fallen so far out of fashion; we could remind people just how good he is. It's a great poem. Got bells, vicars.'

'I know the poem,' said Maggie, impatiently. 'I come from Scotland, you know. Not classical Mesopotamia.'

'But you've heard of classical Mesopotamia,' said David, with an engaging grin. 'Everyone in Scotland is a genius anyway, it's a well-known fact. So. Your predecessor, incidentally, was a ninny, who never wanted to get herself involved in cross-school work. Or work of any kind in fact. Are you like that?'

'I'd have to check with Miss Starling,' said Maggie, thinking that being involved in the Christmas concert would be such a huge treat for the girls and really fire their enthusiasm. At Holy Cross they'd had talent shows at Christmas, which had usually become sexy dancing and rap competitions. They were good fun, rowdy affairs but not the same thing at all. And it would have to be with the younger girls; the older ones had mock exams coming up and wouldn't have time for rehearsals.

'Ah, the fire-breathing Miss Starling,' said David. 'Moral guardian of our humble state. Although you know she's all right really.'

'Miss Starling? Are you serious? She's terrifying.'

'She's a poppet.'

'A *poppet*?'

'A poppet,' said David decisively.

Maggie glanced at June Starling, who appeared to be giving short shrift to some messy looking women with sour faces. Their trouser suits looked shabby and cheap next to Veronica's immaculate twinset. With sinking heart Maggie knew she probably looked more like the women than the head. She really must reconsider her wardrobe. The girls had all looked like off-duty models in their home clothes from the first day, so there was no point trying to compete on the casual end of things. Could she look classic without looking like a gran? It would be nice to stand out a bit for . . . for any men that might be around, not that she was looking.

'What are you thinking?'

Maggie spluttered a little into her drink. 'Nothing. I just . . . she doesn't seem like a poppet at all.'

'I would have thought you were quite hot on not judging a book by its cover.'

Maggie smiled. 'I know. Just settling in I suppose.'

'Well, watch this.'

David left Maggie hovering by the punch and sidled up to the group.

Oh, thank goodness, thought Veronica to herself. That young English teacher from over the hill was something of a maverick, but a good example. There weren't anything like enough smart men going into teaching these days. Too many nebulous accusations from a Childline-savvy generation. She'd have liked to poach him, actually, but there were too few male teachers these days to risk a tall skinny one with quick dark eyes and a wide grin – she didn't want anyone flunking their A-levels because they'd gone puppy lovesick for a master, and, equally, she knew how beautiful and eloquent her eighteen-year-olds were, because she'd worked incredibly hard to make them that way. Best not tempt fate.

'David,' she said, graciously. 'Would you like to meet Patricia and Elizabeth? They've agreed to survey the school for Centrum Standards.'

'Oh, that's great!' said David.

Pat and Liz smiled a little.

'Where are you from?'

'Reading,' said Pat.

'I live in Hackney,' said Liz. 'Everyone else has moved

out, you know, like "white flight", but I believe it's important to stay in local communities.'

'I couldn't agree more,' said David. 'In fact, maybe you could come over to the boys' school one day and talk to them a bit about where you live? Share a bit of experience about your environment?'

'Reading is very mixed too,' said Pat, eagerly. Liz shot her a dirty look. 'We might be too busy,' she said. 'We have a lot to do. We're always really incredibly busy.'

Pat took the opportunity to refill her glass for the fourth time.

'Well, if you can,' said David. 'It's been a real pleasure to meet you.'

'Thank you David, that's a very interesting offer,' said Veronica, slightly irritated that it took a man to get a smile out of these two self-professed feminists.

'Anytime,' he said. 'June, I was just talking to your very nice new English teacher Margaret, and we were thinking of putting some of her girls up for the Christmas show.'

Dear me, thought Veronica. I hope that one doesn't run away with itself. But it certainly was time they had a good turn-out again. Mrs Ferrers had always had lots of excuses as to why she couldn't quite put her girls up this year.

Miss Starling sniffed. 'Maybe,' she said. 'What were you thinking of?'

'Christmas poetry and prose set to music,' said David. 'Lots of Dickens and Eliot and so on. Huge fun.'

'I think Eliot is terribly elitist,' said Pat.

'Good,' said David.

'That sounds suitable,' said June Starling, ignoring Pat completely. 'I expect you'll be wanting our auditorium.'

'You do have the proscenium arch.'

'We do,' said Veronica, smiling at him, and wondering

how many good kudos points they'd get for doing it. 'Well, the third formers don't often get a chance to join in . . . that sounds wonderful. As long as you don't distract our Miss Adair too much.'

'I promise,' said David.

'You know, many of our schools now prefer to use "ms",' said Pat.

'Or first names only, to foster a sense of equality,' said Liz.

'Good God,' said David, beating a hasty retreat.

'See?' he said on his return. 'It's all arranged. She's lovely.'

'You did that on purpose,' said Maggie.

'What?'

'Pretended to ask those two boots over to your school.'

David's face turned serious. 'No I didn't. Why would I do that? I think it's good for the boys to be exposed to all sorts of people.'

Maggie bit her tongue so she didn't say anything sharp.

'Not to worry,' she said, as Claire came up to them and started to moan about being trapped by the agony of the non-French French master from Downey Boys.

'His accent, it ees *atrocious*. Like un tiny petit horse who can't stop being sick.'

Maggie and David looked at each other and grinned. Great, thought Maggie. An ally.

Simone lay awake, listening to the waves outside crashing against the rocks below. She couldn't sleep, her heart pounding. The day had been confusing from start to finish. She didn't know what she was supposed to eat here. She didn't know what on earth the girls were talking about; St Barts, and the South of France and eventing and dressage and how many dogs they had. She'd understood completely, though, the looks they'd given her as she'd entered each new class. English had been followed by maths, at which she shone, even though the class moved at a much faster pace here.

She liked that and the skinny, slightly odd Miss Beresford who taught it in a quick, humourless clipped style, as if the laws of mathematics were the only important thing in the universe and everything else was ephemeral. Simone would have loved to agree with her. But she couldn't. Everything else *was* important. Having a friend. That was so important. Fliss and Alice were horrible, but she was so envious of how quickly they'd turned up and decided they liked each other. Both pretty – one dark, one blonde – and both so *thin*. Why did it work like that? Why did you only get to have friends if you were thin? She'd thought maybe Imogen, the other girl in the dorm, might be easier, with her thick glasses, but she didn't want to chat at all, just get back to her books. Based on what she had on her desk – molecular biology, introduction to canine anatomy, and the hundreds of postcards of animals pinned up – Simone had asked her shyly if she wanted to be a vet. Imogen had nodded vehemently. And that had been the end of the conversation.

Another nightmare had been the afternoon. Simone had been shocked to see on her timetable that there were four periods of PE a week. Back at her old school they'd been slashed down to one, and she'd always got her mother to give her a note. Her and Krystal Fogerty who was nearly sixteen stone and boasted about how when she left school she was going to get to go straight onto disability because she had obesity syndrome. They'd sit it out in the changing rooms and normally Simone would go to the vending machine for them – until they took the vending machine away.

Here, it was PE nearly every day. And half days on Saturdays girls were expected to take part in organised events of one kind or another – either sport *again*, or drama or music. Simone usually liked staying in and watching television all day on Saturdays.

So she'd got changed into the school PE kit; short skirts of the kind that had been outlawed at her school for years, as they made all the boys howl like dogs. They'd had to get the age sixteen size to fit her, so it came nearly to her knees at the front but stuck out over her bum at the back, displaying, she was sure, all the cellulite on the backs of her legs. The polo shirt made her breasts look absolutely massive, and her mother hadn't thought to buy her a sports bra, so she was terrified of having to do any painful running.

All the other girls looked so neat and fresh with their skinny legs bare under the skirts, their small breasts perky under the fresh white shirts as they tied numbers on their backs. Simone started to sweat with nerves. This was bound to show up on her shirt. Now she felt even more anxious. Everyone thought fat girls sweated a lot, and now this would prove it. She wiped her damp hands nervously on her skirt. Oh God, please, please let them not pick teams. She couldn't bear that.

Miss James, the games mistress, walked in, stern and muscular looking.

'Hello,' she said to everyone. 'Sit down.' The girls perched around the changing rooms in twos and threes. Simone sat on the edge, folding her arms over her stomach to stop other people looking at it. Fliss and Alice were sitting together with their hair tied up in identical high ponytails.

'Now,' she said. 'Downey House has a sports tradition to be proud of. We fight hard and we fight fair. Those are the rules of the school, and I want you to work just as hard here as you do for your university entrance or anything else you do. Fulfil your potential.'

She peered round fiercely for a moment.

'Because I don't like it when we get our arses kicked.'

For a second there was a stunned silence at a teacher swearing. Then a murmuring at the release of tension. Miss James was obviously all right.

'OK' she said. 'I've no idea whether you're a bunch of tigers or pussies. So . . .' Then she went round the room and numbered them one, two, one, two. 'The ones are playing the twos,' she said. 'Have you all got that or do I have to run through it again for the mathematically challenged?'

Sylvie, an inordinately pretty girl with golden curly hair and round blue eyes, blinked and looked as if she was about to raise her hand, then put it down again.

'OK then. If you don't have your own stick, grab one on your way out.'

Simone was a one. She made her way out as slowly as possible so nobody could walk behind her and look at her rear. The other girls had glanced at her but so far there'd been no remarks or unpleasantness. At least, not so she could hear. If there'd been boys here, they'd have already been doing whale imitations all over the floor.

'You,' said Miss James. Simone was looking out on the huge playing fields. It was quite a sight. There was a running track, several netball courts, hockey fields, a lacrosse pitch and equipment for track and field events. The grass ran on for what seemed like miles, down towards the cliff edge, where there was a wooden fence. And beyond the cliffs was just the sea, choppy waters all the way to France. It was beautiful. Simone was struck by the skyline, absolutely nothing like the single grey asphalt multi-purpose pitch with weeds growing up under the stones that graced St Cats.

'You!' said Miss James again. Simone realised she was being spoken to.

'Good morning! Glad to have you with us!'

Some of the girls giggled. 'Sorry, miss,' said Simone, staring at the grass. She couldn't believe she was getting into trouble with the teachers. The one thing that never happened to her was getting into trouble with the teachers.

'I want you in goal,' said Miss James. 'Think you could be useful there?'

It wasn't really a question. Simone opened her mouth to say that she'd never played hockey before, then thought better of it, donned the blue vest she'd been given and marched off to the far end of the pitch.

'OK,' Miss James was saying. 'Any volunteers for centre-forwards?'

It was pretty obvious how to play, Simone realised, watching the girls attack the small solid puck-like ball. You pretended you were going in to whack the ball, then you whacked the others' legs instead. It was clearly vicious. Simone shivered in the freshening wind coming off the sea. Fortunately most of it was taking place up the other end of the pitch for now, but she was dreading it coming her way. She had no idea what she was doing.

Miss James was right amongst the throng, sizing people up, seeing who could play and had serious potential, who hated pulling their weight and who slacked. She'd felt sorry for the bigger girl, who obviously felt horribly self-conscious. Trying not to be cruel she'd put her as far out of the way as possible, where she might even manage to get over her nerves. But really. What were parents thinking of, letting their children get so heavy? Didn't they know it was cruel?

Simone realised the play was hotting up as the girls in the green vests were coming her way, amongst them Alice, but not Fliss, as of course they'd been sitting next to one another. She stiffened with nerves.

'Goal! Goal!' some of the girls down the end were shouting, as the action moved closer and closer to Simone's end. She felt her heart in her throat. Suddenly, there was Alice, right in front of her, whacking the ball towards her with all her might. Without thinking, Simone launched herself and her stick at it – and the ball bounced off the end of her stick and back out into the field. A huge cheer went up from the girls in the blue vests as Miss James blew her whistle. Simone went pink, entirely taken by surprise, even as Alice said, 'Well, of course she's going to block the goal', in a nasty tone of voice, especially as the teacher said 'Well done'. Simone swallowed. She was so used to steering clear of sport. It must have been a fluke.

But, as the game progressed it became obvious that her goal-keeping skills weren't a fluke. That, ungainly and lumbering as she could be, she was good at anticipating when the ball was going to come thudding towards her, and from what angle. The blue team won by some considerable margin, largely due to her efforts. All the way back to the changing rooms the girls talked to her, asked her where she'd played before, and were friendly. Simone couldn't believe it, it felt like a totally new sensation. When she told them she'd never played before they were even more flatteringly surprised and one, a big sporty girl called Andrea whose parents lived in New Zealand, and who had scored all the goals for the blue team, announced that if they let her pick a team, Simone would be on it. Simone felt herself almost bursting with pride.

Back in the changing room, though, her heart sank as she

followed the girls into the showers. They weren't communal, but the girls sashayed up to them with only small white towels and, it seemed to Simone, so much confidence. Even though they kept squeezing non-existent bulges in the mirrors over the sinks and saying loudly, 'God, I am *so* fat' whereupon the rest of the girls would chorus, 'No you're not, you're *soo skinny*', and another one would take up the mantra. Simone wondered if she could take two towels in, and waited till everyone had dived off to break before she started to get dressed. There was no one to wait behind for her, even if she was not a bad goalie.

Chapter Six

The first few weeks of the new term passed in a blur. Maggie found every day her nerves at facing her classes grew less and less. It was such a refreshing change having classes filled with conscientious students, anxious to learn – often she discovered lesson plans were too short, as she had factored in her traditional disciplinary time.

In a funny way, though, she missed the boys. She missed their smart-alec remarks, their easy laughter; the way they bounded in like mischievous puppies, clouting one another with their schoolbags. She didn't miss their aftershavey, sweaty boy smell, but she did even miss the way they teased the girls. The lairy, shouty nature of it had always offended her at the time, and of course she'd had her fair share of girls in floods of tears; with late periods or worse. But now it was so much harder to get a sense for the emotional temperature of the forms. Girls' whispering was harder to monitor than boys' fighting, and whether they were sharing confidences that would make them intimate friends for ever, or planning to completely exclude someone else from the lunch table could be hard to ascertain.

And that was what was difficult. She could hear it in the elaborately elongated vowels the girls used when they were talking to her. The little remarks when she tried to introduce a contemporary poet, particularly a Scottish one. Obviously her strictness with Felicity Prosser hadn't had quite the desired effect. She was finding these girls intimidating, she couldn't help it. And on one level that was obviously showing, and they were taking advantage. Odd, how a rowdy class of forty kids shouting didn't bother her, but a silent one of fourteen was so unsettling. Plus their horrible assumptions. When reading about a character buying a lottery ticket, they'd all fixed her with large eyes.

'Have you ever bought one of those?' Sylvie Brown, her blue eyes wide and her golden hair cascading down her back, had asked her innocently.

'No,' lied Maggie. She bought one every week; she and Stan used their birthdays.

'My father says they're a stupidity tax,' announced Ursula confidently. Alice was watching Maggie closely.

'Would you say they're a stupidity tax, miss?' she asked slyly.

Maggie found herself slightly stuttering for words, and was sure the girls had noticed. And Stan wasn't best pleased to hear that he would have to buy the weekly lottery ticket from now on. Maggie didn't want to get caught out by someone from the school at the village store.

The weather grew colder. Now, some mornings, Maggie was waking with frost on the outside of the window pane. She'd thought it would be milder here, but out exposed at the edge of the country there was a real chill to the wind whistling through the eaves. Also, the central heating was on as low as was possible. She wondered if this was a money saving exercise, but Claire had assured her Veronica believed it was good for the girls not to get too stuffy, and good for the complexion too, and she'd had a cashmere throw for her bed sent over from a friend in Bruges, would Maggie like one too?

Maggie pushed her younger form on through more contemporary poetry that she thought they might like, and the compulsory Shakespeare, where she had to take the expanse of daunting-seeming blank verse and shape it; mould it into something digestible, alive and relevant to younger minds – to all minds she remembered a lecturer saying once. It could be a slog, but it was a highly satisfying one, as the girls finally caught the rhythm and intent behind the beautiful words. The work wasn't a problem; the girls were smart, and diligent. But their attitude to her was . . . she sighed. Her problem.

Three weeks in, Veronica summoned her to her office. Maggie swore to herself, wishing she didn't feel so nervous. Veronica had spoken to her casually a few times, of course, but Maggie usually sat at meals with Claire, who was great fun and by some distance the youngest member of the staff, or took her lunch upstairs.

A couple of times when it had been sunny enough she'd taken her lunch out to the moor – the girls weren't allowed to leave the premises unsupervised until the fifth form, by which time they never wanted to go outside, just hang around the common room complaining about the curfew and pretending they were desperate for a cigarette. So Maggie would take a sandwich and stroll across the lavender-scented moors and find a sheltered spot overlooking the sea where she could gaze out and try and forget her petty frustrations; her overwhelming sense of not fitting in. Sometimes great freighters rolled past on their way to Ireland, but she never saw David out walking Stephen Daedalus again. She could have gone out early in the morning, but now with lesson plans and catching up on the marking she should have done instead of watching *Lost* the night before, mornings were too fussed. Plus, she was a bit embarrassed. She didn't want it to seem as if she was out looking for him.

She was, though, she admitted to herself one day, staring out across the white-crested heads of the waves at a long vessel loaded with Maersk crates, a little lonely. She missed Stan. Their nightly phone calls were degenerating into short recountings of their days, with a lot, she felt, being left unsaid. The silences were growing longer, the calls shorter. She had promised to go and see him at half-term but wasn't really looking forward to it and was half considering, if the situation didn't improve a little, accompanying the girls staying behind to London for an outing.

And her sister's emails, whilst friendly, were a little short. She still hadn't been forgiven for giving up on aunt duty. 'Cody and Dylan are fine,' Anna would write, and Maggie could almost feel the tightness behind the words. 'Dylan has been excluded from nursery and Cody has nits again.' Then she would relent a little and tell her about a zoo they'd visited, or how Stan had come round and played football with them and they'd pretended to be Celtic winning the European Cup and then all gone out for KFC then gone home and watched *Dr Who*, which had had Dylan up all night fretting, and Maggie would feel a huge tug of longing for home; a desire to say sod it all, you stupid posh girls.

She didn't mean to tell any of this to Dr Deveral, however, and sat rather nervously outside her office, as Miss Prenderghast smiled at her sweetly. Miss Prenderghast smiled at everyone sweetly, though, whether you were there for an award or there to get kicked out for ever. Maggie was aware, somewhat uneasily, that there was a probationary period in her contract, and she was still in it. Surely Veronica couldn't be about to tell her to go home? That she wasn't suited to this school? Maybe there'd been complaints. Suddenly she felt her heart beginning to race. OK, Miss Starling didn't seem to like her, but she hadn't really given her a fair chance from the start – she thought back to the previous week when Miss Starling had stopped her in the corridor and called her into her classroom.

'I hear you and Mr McDonald are doing a *performance*,' she'd said in the same tone of voice she might have used to announce, 'are planning to bring in poisonous *snakes*.'

'Yes, Miss Starling,' Maggie had said. 'I was just coming to discuss it with you, see which classes would be best. I thought Middle School 1 . . .'

'That class,' Miss Starling had said, whilst methodically arranging the exercise books on her desk. Miss Starling always seemed to be tidying something. '. . . is best suited to total disruption, mild hysteria, and attempting to destroy the confidence of whichever mite is unlucky enough to get the leading role. I don't approve. However, as it seems you got someone else to ask me in public . . .'

'That wasn't my idea,' said Maggie, instantly regretting it. Now she sounded like she was trying to weasel out of responsibility. Also, she really ought to have talked it over anyway, days ago. 'I'm sorry,' she'd added. 'I should have . . .'

'Well, it's done now,' Miss Starling had said, with a glance that made it clear that Maggie could leave. 'At least don't turn it into one of those dreadful PC Winterval shows you see at other schools,' she'd added disdainfully.

'No,' Maggie had said, and was then cross with herself for not standing up for her background. Although the semi-stripper dancing the fourth years had done last year at Holy Cross to the tune of *Santa Baby* and the howls and stamping of the boys probably wouldn't have done the trick.

She worried whether Miss Starling had complained to Veronica. Talked about trampling on her toes, or getting in the way? Maybe Miss Starling didn't think she was up to it. Maybe the girls had slagged her off to their parents and they'd made a complaint? Maggie steeled herself as Veronica came to the door.

'Maggie. Hello,' she said, with a small smile. Maggie followed her into the room with some trepidation. Veronica sat down on the red velvet upholstered couch and indicated that Maggie should do the same. Miss Prenderghast brought in the teapot on a tray, biscuits nicely arranged. Maggie tried to ignore them; she knew Veronica would no more eat a biscuit than perm her hair.

'So, Maggie,' said Veronica, leaning forward. 'How are you finding things?'

Maggie swallowed. 'Well . . . I mean, I really like it,' she said. 'I think it's a really good school. It's so nice to work with some great materials.'

This was true. For example, Maggie had always had a weakness for stationery. At Holy Cross she'd always had to sign in and out of the stationery cupboard and keep to a strictly rationed budget to make sure she didn't steal any staplers from the workplace. Here, although Miss Starling had eyed her beadily, seeing her face light up with the brand new equipment and wide range of teaching aids, pens, computers and AV, no one tried to intimate that she was about to pillage the place and set up a secondary concern. Here, nobody had to share a book (at Holy Cross it had been one between three, sometimes) or complain about their pens running out. Oddly this had the effect of making Maggie feel guilty.

'And what about our girls?' asked Veronica. 'Are they great materials too?'

Maggie felt herself colour. 'They're good. Most of them.'

'But? I sense a but.'

'Oh, nothing. I just wonder if they're perhaps a little complacent.'

Veronica twisted her pearl earrings. 'How so?'

Maggie thought of Felicity and Alice. Right from day one – when she had, she knew, shown a heavy hand with punishment – they had taken against her; chatted and made remarks whenever they felt themselves unobserved and in general showed a thorough lack of respect; turning up late, and usually sniggering. Felicity's work was poor too, which was strange as, according to her old school report, she was an extremely able pupil. From which Maggie could only conclude that she was doing it on purpose. To annoy her.

'I mean, they've just got such a sense of entitlement,' finished Maggie crossly. 'Sorry. That probably sounds really chippy.'

Veronica smiled to herself. 'A little.' Maggie glanced down.

'Felicity Prosser probably thinks she's the unhappiest girl in this whole school,' said Veronica.

'You're joking.'

'No. I could tell straight away. Her sister has done very well here. A little intense for my taste, if you know what I mean, but very much a success. I don't think Prosser minor wanted to come here at all.'

'Well, that's clear enough.'

'I'd keep her away from that little minx Alice Trebizon-Woods. I've had her two sisters through as well and they're all attention seekers of the highest order. Parents in the diplomatic corps, hardly notice them. But you might do all right then with Felicity – and all of your Middle School 1.'

So, she had heard. Maggie felt her ears burn.

'I know you can do it,' said Veronica gently. Maggie bit

her lip, in case she started to cry. Veronica spotted this immediately and swiftly changed the subject. 'Well, I wanted to mention two other things,' she said. 'Firstly, there's another girl in MS1 I want you to keep an eye on.'

'Simone Pribetich,' said Maggie without hesitation, glad for the change of subject.

'Yes. She's one of our scholarship girls. Very smart, but needs dragging out of herself. Miss James is doing wonders with her in sport, but it's not enough. She could do with a friend. I know you can't work miracles, but she's very bright and I'd hate for her to waste her potential.'

'I'll try.' Maggie was incredibly relieved. Veronica had referenced the situation, but didn't seem to think there was anything to worry about.

In fact, Veronica had expected this to happen. Downey's girls often hadn't met people from other backgrounds who weren't staff of some sort. Maggie needed to learn to cope. But she shouldn't be doing it alone.

Feeling slightly better, Maggie waited to hear what the other thing was. It must be the show. She and David had emailed a couple of times about it. She got a little surge of excitement whenever one of his emails pinged up. They were always chatty and beautifully written, and they'd narrowed the choice of extracts for the show down to four, which Mrs Offili, the music teacher, was now looking at how to stage.

'Secondly, you, Maggie. You know this isn't prison. You are quite welcome to get out and explore a bit, meet friends and so on. Go and visit your family.'

Maggie was surprised Dr Deveral had been so observant.

'Thank you,' she said, 'but they're so far away. And I have seen something of Claire and . . .' she felt a little embarrassed saying his name out loud, '. . . David.'

Veronica arched an eyebrow. She'd thought as much. 'Do you have . . . and forgive me for stepping outside the professional arena for a moment, but do you have a boyfriend?'

Maggie nodded, feeling obscurely embarrassed at Veronica even having to use such an adolescent word.

'Why don't you invite him down at half-term? He can't stay here, of course, but I can recommend a good B&B in the village. Teaching is a demanding job, Margaret, as you are currently finding. We all need to relax sometimes.'

Maggie had returned to her rooms with conflicting thoughts. After all, getting Stan down here was the right thing to do. He could see she hadn't run away from him for a life of champagne and fun and whatever else he seemed to think she was doing down here.

On the other hand, she thought suddenly, would Stan fit in around here? Could she trust him not to make inappropriate remarks all the time and, well, *embarrass* her? She imagined Claire, with her immaculate outfits, listening to Stan discuss his latest triumphs in Championship Manager, but it was difficult to picture.

Veronica watched her walk across the forecourt. Actually, Maggie was settling in much better than she had expected. Miss Starling had reported that although a little 'trendy' for her tastes (Veronica suspected anything that wasn't simply memorising lines would be a little trendy for June Starling, particularly given they were studying poetry that didn't rhyme), but committed and hard-working, which was the most important thing in a young teacher. Finesse could come later; they were all there to help. Oh. She remembered what she'd forgotten to mention. Maggie was wearing a blue and white striped shirt that looked like it was half of a pair of pyjamas, and a grey skirt that wasn't quite the right length for her. She *must* have a word with her about her dress.

'I can't believe they take away your phones.'

Fliss was raging, and Alice was agreeing with her.

'I mean, it's completely fascist. One hour a day? That's just, like evil and against your rights and things.'

'Yeah,' said Alice, whose mother could never remember the time difference and thus rarely rang.

'You know in Guildford, I'm allowed to go shopping on my own. Here you're not even blooming allowed out unless there's six of you and a teacher! Until upper fourth! It's prison.'

Alice was trying to do her prep, but Fliss was deliberately ignoring hers, so Alice pushed it to one side. Egging on Fliss was more fun anyway.

'And then they fob us off with stupid common teachers.' Fliss stuck out her bottom lip.

'We need to do a trick,' said Alice.

'A trick?' said Fliss, as they drank Orangina in the dorm. Imogen was working quietly. Simone was nowhere to be seen.

'Yeah, you know. A good practical joke that everyone will piss themselves about.'

'I know some good ones,' said Fliss. 'What about putting cellophane over the teachers' toilets?'

Alice sniffed. 'Old hat,' she said. 'We need something amazing.'

'Flour bombs?' ventured Fliss.

'You've got to think big,' said Alice. 'I shall put my brain to work. And who should be the victim?'

'Well, not Miss Beresford,' said Fliss, thinking uncomfortably back to a conversation they'd had earlier that week, when the stern maths mistress had unfavourably compared the marks she was getting here with how she'd done at her old school. It was hard to make a protest about how much you hated somewhere when you actually had to get in trouble and endure the consequences. Miss Beresford had exhorted her not to let herself down. Fliss wanted to burst into tears and claim it wasn't fair, her parents were letting her down, but she thought she was unlikely to meet with much sympathy, and she'd have been right. Miss Beresford came from a poor background and, although she enjoyed teaching maths here, thought some of these little madams didn't know they were born.

'No, she has no sense of humour at all,' agreed Alice. 'Why else would you be a maths teacher?'

Fliss couldn't think. She'd seen Alice's maths books though. She'd scored 94.

'What about that horrid old bitch Miss Adair?' Fliss was still stinging from Maggie's putting her down.

'Ah, Miss What Not To Wear,' said Alice thoughtfully. 'You know, I think she might be just right. She's so keen for everyone to like her, she'll probably laugh it off and not get us into trouble at all. Plus she's totally green.'

'Yeah,' said Fliss. 'Great. What shall we do?'

Alice smiled. 'Leave it to me,' she said.

They turned their attention to a parcel sitting on Simone's bed.

'Can you believe how much stuff she gets?' said Alice.

Fliss couldn't, especially when she was lucky to get the odd postcard. There was barely a couple of days went by without a large box arriving, with tinfoil-covered packages and cake boxes.

'Does she think that you have to pay for the food here?' said Alice. 'Honestly, there's so many empty cartons in the bin. It's really starting to smell. We'll get mice. You're not even supposed to have food here.' She went to her bed by the window. 'God, it smells. I hate it. I'm going to tell her.'

'No, Alice, don't.'

'I'm serious!' Alice looked crossly out the window. 'We all watch what we eat and I'm on like a total diet, and the place is a rats' nest of cakes. It's not fair. And she eats too much anyway.'

'Alice, don't be mean, please.' Fliss didn't mind being horrible to teachers and grown-ups, and whoever else it would take to get her out of here. But picking on another girl she didn't like.

But Alice had that glint in her eye as Simone came in. She'd been trying to use the old payphone down the hall and couldn't get it to work. She couldn't believe that her mum had used the guideline 'we discourage the middle school girls from having mobile phones' as an actual gospel law of the school. She was the only girl without one, not even for emergencies. As usual her mum's phone was engaged. She always had a million people to talk to. Just not her.

'Hi Simone,' said Alice. Simone looked up. Alice didn't usually do much more than grunt at her. Fliss was a bit better, but not much.

'Look, Simone,' said Alice, getting down from the window. 'Can we have a word?'

Fliss didn't like being dragged into this like it was a communal decision.

'Now, we know, you're like, a compulsive eater or whatever, and that it's like a disease and stuff and we want you to know that we're not prejudiced and we really care about you and your illness.'

Alice widened her eyes in fake concern. Simone stared at her, confused and cornered.

'But we were wondering if it might be possible . . . I mean, not if it's too much trouble . . . we don't want to make things worse or anything, but if you could keep your, like, totally disgusting food out of the dorm?'

She indicated the parcel Mrs Pribetich had stickily wound a whole rope of Sellotape around.

'Is that OK?'

Simone picked up the parcel, turned around and fled.

Maggie was heading for bed. It was her turn to do rounds, just to check all the girls were in bed and tucked up. It was a cold dark night outside, with rain throwing itself at the windows, and everyone seemed quite happy to be tucked up. Maggie picked up a couple of stray towels. She quite liked saying good night to everyone; it made her feel pastoral.

In Fliss and Alice's dorm room there was much whispering going on and no Simone. Maggie switched the overhead light on.

'Where is she?' she demanded. Fliss and Alice were both in bed, looking as though butter wouldn't melt in their mouths. Alice gave her most innocent look.

'I don't know, Miss Adair. She got a food parcel and went off . . . maybe to eat it?'

Maggie gave her a hard look. 'Did she seem in a strange mood?'

It wasn't like Simone to be late for anything.

Alice propped herself up on her elbows. 'You know, we're a bit worried about her. Like, she might have a problem with food or something?'

Maggie hated to admit it, but the dark haired little minxy girl might have a point. Even in the few weeks they'd been there, she'd noticed Simone taking extra rolls at breakfast, queueing at the little tuckshop. She'd put weight on, for sure. Although there was plenty of exercise prescribed on the curriculum, Simone did no extra sporting activities on offer at the weekends or after school hours; she didn't take any walks on the moors like the other girls did on their Sunday free time after church. And there was certainly plenty of hearty good fare – Mrs Rhys, head of the catering service, was of the old school. Traditional stodge, and lots of it; toast, steamed puddings, custard, stews and roly-poly. Maggie adored the food and was having to be very strict with herself. Simone, it appeared, was not.

'Lights out,' she said sharply to the girls. 'I'll bring her back myself.'

Fliss lay awake in the dark. It had sounded like Alice was being interested in Simone and worried about her problem. But she knew she wasn't.

Maggie didn't have to go far. Just around the corner was an alcove, the underside of a spiral staircase. It was covered from plain view by a curtain, and the girls normally used it for confidences, or phone calls. Tonight, though, Maggie could tell by the movement of the curtain that there was someone there.

'Simone?' she said, quietly. There was no answer. 'Simone?' she tried again.

A voice clearly trying to disguise its sobbing said, 'I'm fine. Go away.'

Maggie pulled across the curtain. Simone had obviously thought she was another pupil, as she genuinely flinched when she saw her.

'Miss Adair.'

'That's right,' said Maggie. 'And sorry, but I'm not going away.'

There was a bench in the corner of the alcove. Maggie sat

down and beckoned Simone to do the same. Her face was smeared with tears and what looked like jam.

Maggie sat in silence for a couple of minutes until Simone's hiccupy sobs had slowed. 'Now,' she said. 'What's up?'

'I don't fit in here,' said Simone.

'Oh, neither do I,' said Maggie, remembering Miss Starling, who that morning had mentioned that Maggie seemed to be 'rushing' in the corridor, and that if she was better prepared in the mornings, perhaps she wouldn't have to. 'I wouldn't worry about that.'

'The other girls,' sniffed Simone. 'They're so confident and pretty. None of them is fat and their mothers don't send them stuff to eat and they all got to be friends really quickly and . . .'

'Ssssh,' said Maggie, looking around for a handkerchief and making do with a paper napkin, presumably packed by the ever-prepared Mrs Pribetich.

'Now look,' she said. 'Of course you're not going to feel right here immediately. These girls all went to primary school together. Their mothers all came here. That's just how it was.'

Simone nodded.

'But that's not important, is it? Do you know how many of them could have got a scholarship like you did?'

Simone shook her head.

'None of them, that's how many.'

In fact, Maggie had been very impressed with Simone's work, particularly her poems which, whilst full of terrible angst and some horrible spelling, also had a good use of language and structure for her age.

'You're just as good as them, Simone. Better, in some instances. So you have no reason to do yourself down. And

105

are you sure these . . .' She tilted her head towards the large pile of polenta cakes that had disgorged from the bag. 'Do you think these are helping, Simone?'

Simone shook her head miserably. 'But my mum sends them, and I'm just so fed up and I don't know what to do.'

'Would you like me to have a word with your mum, tell her she's not allowed to send you food for, I don't know, say environmental reasons or something. Would that help?'

Simone shrugged. 'I'm so fat though. It wouldn't make any difference.'

'You might be amazed,' said Maggie. 'And I hear you're doing brilliantly at sport.'

Simone twisted the corner of her pyjamas and didn't say anything.

'Fewer cakes, bit more sport, you'd look better in no time, with your lovely teenage metabolism,' said Maggie, adding quickly, 'only if you want to change, of course.'

'Of course I want to change,' said Simone. 'Nobody talks to me.'

'Well, I'm sure once everyone settles down that will change. It's very early in the year.'

'These things never change,' said Simone. Maggie didn't want to tell a lie and contradict her. Sometimes they did, sometimes they didn't.

'Well, listen,' she said. 'How about, when you feel like you need someone to talk to, you can come over and visit me.'

Simone gave a sidelong glance which indicated she didn't really believe her.

'Just pop in. I have lots of books. And not just set books either. I've got the new Sophie Kinsella *and* the new Lisa Jewell.'

Maggie could tell Simone's ears were pricking up. She wasn't the first girl to take solace in reading. And it would be better for her than hiding away stuffing cake in her face, that was for sure.

'The new new one?' said Simone, sniffing. 'In hardback?'

'I was saving it,' said Maggie. 'But I'll let you have first dibs.'

Simone got down from the bench. 'Thanks.'

'No problem. Will I take this away?' Maggie indicated the cake. Simone nodded.

'Right. Get to bed then before I have to report you and Miss Starling will have to see you.'

This had the desired effect. Simone scampered away.

'And brush your teeth!' said Maggie.

'I'm really going to get that sarky Miss Adair now,' Alice hissed to Fliss the next morning as they were brushing their teeth. 'Thinks she's bloody Mother McTeresa.'

'This school sucks,' agreed Fliss. 'We need out.'

Chapter Seven

The school was busy. First were auditions for the Christmas readings. The Christmas concert was a big point in the calendar. The school orchestra, jazz band and dance troupe were all expected to perform for the parents, but as the middle school girls were so new, they were given readings to punctuate the performances. Traditionally there were lots of girls interested in this, as they were joined by the choristers from the boys' school, which meant they got a chance to meet the boys – the first two years weren't allowed to attend the mixed Christmas party; neither the parents nor Veronica liked the idea. They had a party afternoon of their own in class and there was a special Christmas dinner and that was quite enough.

'I'm sure they'll just be babies,' Alice was saying, mugging heartily over 'Journey of the Magi'. 'No use to us.'

'Deffo,' said Fliss. 'I don't want to do it anyway.'

Stand up in front of her parents and the whole school? Not bloody likely. If anything was going to prove that she'd given in and was now sucking it up it would be that, and she'd never get the chance to get back before all her friends had formed a new clique without her and started treating her like she was stuck up and horsey, the way they'd always talked about boarding-school girls. That, and the fact that their parents hated them, of course.

There was a drama teacher at the school – the rather suspiciously named Fleur Parsley – who had long hair, long skirts and floated around the place (she also taught at Downey Boys). Lots of the girls had a crush on her. Maggie found her a tad emetic. As far as Maggie could tell, she spent a lot of time getting the girls to roll around the ground pretending to be animals. No wonder they loved drama and couldn't get their prep in on time.

Liz and Pat had loved Fleur's class, as Maggie discovered when the four found themselves sitting together at lunch.

'Then you took on the characteristics of multicultural animals from around the globe,' Pat was enthusing.

Fleur smiled modestly. She was very beautiful, with long pre-Raphaelite hair and an extremely slim figure, and Pat and Liz were obviously enjoying being around her.

'Well, I believe . . .' she said. She had a very affected voice clear as a bell, and liked to intimate that she'd given up a highly successful career as an actress because she was so dedicated to teaching. '. . . that the girls here should experience influences from all over the world. They can't help being so privileged, but it's no excuse for ignorance.'

Pat and Liz nodded emphatically. 'Exactly,' said Pat.

'It's a bit like doing the *Lion King*, isn't it?' said Maggie to make conversation.

'It's actually nothing like the *Lion King*?' said Fleur. Her voice tended to go up at the end of sentences. 'It's like an opportunity for the girls to experience the consciousness of different groups of animals that exist . . . and are often persecuted . . . throughout the world?'

'Oh,' said Maggie, tucking into her macaroni cheese. 'I see.'

'I feel it's important to bring a spiritual dimension to my work,' said Fleur. Pat, and Liz, who was on her second helping of macaroni, nodded vigorously.

'Well, I suppose I have the Christmas readings coming up,' said Maggie. 'I could do with your help, Fleur.'

'Oh, I'm *so* busy,' said Fleur, smoothing back her hair.

'What methodology are you using to action that?' asked Pat.

Maggie hesitated as she unravelled the question. 'Well, I thought I'd get them all to do a reading in class, then choose two girls from that.'

Pat and Liz recoiled in horror.

'You're planning to . . . humiliate the girls in front of their peers?' said Liz in horror.

'No,' said Maggie. 'But I think it's important that they can speak in front of other people, and I need to get an idea as to who can handle it and who will crumple in front of the audience.'

'I don't really, like believe in competition in art?' said Fleur, pushing her macaroni around her plate.

'I thought acting was very competitive,' said Maggie. Fleur didn't bother replying, but let a smile play around her lips.

'I'm not sure making the children *audition* . . .'

'I'm not necessarily looking for the best,' said Maggie.

'That's good, because I don't think terminology like "best" is very helpful in an educational scenario,' said Pat.

'I'm looking to see who would benefit the most.'

Pat and Liz looked at each other.

'With your permission, we'd like to sit in on that class,' said Pat.

'Of course,' said Maggie, trying to hide her disgruntlement. Actually, two complete strangers in the class would make it much harder for the girls, surely they could see that. But she didn't want to rock the boat or make things any more difficult than they were already.

The fifteen girls in Middle School Year One all felt nervous that Thursday, and resentful towards their teacher, no matter how cool they professed to be, or how much they pretended that the school concert was a complete waste of time for morons. In fact, secretly, most of them really did want the chance to stand in front of the school and get riotously applauded in front of their parents, especially if they weren't, like Astrid, so musical they'd already made it in to the orchestra.

Astrid Ulverton was such a beautiful clarinet player Mrs Offili was completely torn between wanting to keep her for school music, and urging her parents to march her off to the nearest conservatoire. Astrid's parents believed a career in music was a waste of time and kept trying to get her to work hard at sciences in preparation for medical school. Poor Astrid was a dunce in other subjects, however, and couldn't look at a textbook without making a tune of the words and rapping her fingers on the spine.

Fliss had hurriedly grabbed one of the set pieces the night before, in a thorough temper that Miss Adair was going to get the chance to make her stand up again in front of all her classmates. It was the opening of *Little Women*, which started, '"Christmas won't be Christmas without presents," grumbled Jo, lying on the rug.'

She was going to perform it in the most off-hand way possible, so that she wouldn't get chosen and could stand at the back of the choir and look sulky. Alice was doing 'Journey of the Magi', by T. S. Eliot, so she could be very dramatic and act out being an old man. She'd done it already for Fliss in the alcove and Fliss had been very impressed. The other option was a big long extract from *A Christmas Carol* which was far too boring and hard to memorise, so only the complete dweebs would pick that.

Maggie was nervous. She wasn't sure if this was a good idea, and talking to Pat and Liz hadn't helped matters. But no. It said in the prospectus that Downey House was about turning out confident, well-rounded young women. Jobs were all about talking to groups and it wasn't as if she was getting them to read out their own stuff, which she was thinking of doing with the year nines. It hadn't worked terribly well at Holy Cross. The boys tended to write stories about how their gang had beaten up another gang, and the class would bang on the desks and shout out at apposite moments and sometimes real fights would come out of it. She'd quickly abandoned the concept.

'OK, class,' she said. It was a bright and chilly late November day. She'd noticed in the mirror that morning that her cheeks were pinker than usual, probably as a result of spending more time out of doors. Her eyes were clearer too. A lot less alcohol and some decent food were really working on her looks.

'All right, class. We're going to go for it. Nobody has to memorise anything yet, we're just going to concentrate on projection and focus.'

'Miss Fleur says focus has to come from within,' said blonde wide-eyed Sylvie earnestly. 'She says it has to come from the heart.'

Pat and Liz, who were perched on their chunky bottoms on desks at the back of the class, nodded gravely.

'Well, Miss *Fleur* is right,' said Maggie, biting back a touch of irritation. 'Speak from the heart. These are lovely pieces, famous for a long time. So, do your best. I'm not looking for the loudest, or the most "acted". I'm looking for you to try hard and show the school what an engaged class we are.'

Sylvie went first, reciting from *Little Women* in a breathless chirp with slightly odd intonation. Maggie led the mandatory clapping. Next up was Astrid, who read the poem in a rhythmic monotone which rendered the scansion almost indecipherable. Third was poor shy Imogen, who was so quiet and mousy Maggie felt terrible asking her to speak up again and again. It didn't help when Pat and Liz started whispering to one another. Maggie was so furious at this rudeness she was tempted to tell them to shut up, before reminding herself that they were judging her, not Imogen, and that she really had to learn to keep her temper in check.

Just as the whole session looked like it was going to be a complete disaster, Alice, next to be called, stood up.

'A cold coming we had of it'

She started with a tragicomically grave, dramatic expression on her face. A few lines later she pointed downwards to some imaginary camels.

'And the camels galled, sore-footed, refractory,
Lying down in the melting snow.'

She stared out of the window, allowing her pretty face to suddenly look very sad.

'There were times we regretted
The summer palaces on slopes, the terraces,'

Now she shook her head wildly as if disturbed by the memories.

'And the silken girls bringing sherbet.'

Maggie had to bite her lip to stifle a giggle. She was a monkey, Alice, but she had spirit. Her overacting was ludicrous, but goodness, she was putting in the effort. She put a mark next to her name; if they didn't get any better, she might have to go in.

Alice came to:

'were we led all that way for . . .'

Then she let a dramatic pause linger . . . and linger . . .

'BIRTH? OR DEATH?' she shouted, suddenly, making Pat jump, as she hadn't been paying attention. Could work on lazy parents, Maggie mused.

'Thank you, thank you,' she said, as Alice finished the poem with '*I should be glad of another death*' before throwing herself into a great bow. The applause in the classroom was genuine and loud, and Maggie could see Alice had to work hard to stop a huge grin cracking across her face.

Next it was Simone. Maggie gave her her most encouraging look as the girl slowly got up. Alice smirked at her as she passed on her way back to her seat at the back of the class. Maggie hoped it wasn't going to be a massacre; the girls had enjoyed Alice's performance but wouldn't take too kindly to Simone stuttering along.

Suddenly, as Simone reached the front of the stage and turned to face the audience, Maggie glimpsed Pat and Liz swapping a very obvious look, Liz with an eyebrow raised like she thought she was Simon Cowell, Pat rolling her eyes to heaven. Simone could hardly not have seen it. If anyone ought to be sensitive to the girl, it should be them, with their belief in the virtues of the working classes and their supposed sensitivity to the underdog. Maggie felt the bile rising in her throat, and it was a few moments before she actually tuned in to what Simone was saying.

Simone had decided just to treat it as she did when she got called up every week by her mother to 'do something clever' in front of the aunties, something which had happened on a weekly basis since the moment she could talk. She simply steeled herself and did the best she could.

Years of being forced to perform, however, had rubbed off on her, and as she launched into the Dickens extract, she couldn't help but imbue it with some feeling. It was a book she'd always loved – her parents had bought an entire set of Dickens from a book club and she'd started working her way through them at the age of eleven.

Add to this her naturally gentle, very London-sounding voice, and by the time she reached the phrase, 'I have always thought of Christmas time . . . as a good time: a kind, forgiving, charitable, pleasant time ... when men and women seem by one consent to open their shut-up hearts freely, and to think of people below them as if they really were fellow-passengers to the grave', Maggie was completely engrossed and marked her up for it immediately. The applause at the end was distinct and heartfelt and Simone looked surprised to hear it, as she'd tried only to focus on the meaning of the words she was saying, and not how she looked. If she stopped to think about how she looked to everyone, she'd just want to curl up in a ball. The applause was a pleasant bonus.

'Well done,' said Maggie, trying to keep her tone from sounding too surprised and patronising.

The next few girls were passable, if unremarkable, and everyone was getting bored with hearing the same three pieces regurgitated again and again. Fliss sighed with the tedium and stared out of the window. A storm looked to be coming in over the sea; the grass and scrub on the clifftops was bending over. There was so much *weather* here, thought Fliss, missing the gentler environs of Surrey. Apparently in London you hardly got weather at all, all the buildings protected you from it. It would be the Christmas party in the village soon. Will Hampton would probably be in town for it. She wondered if she'd see him over Christmas. God, if only her tits would grow. Then at least she might have a tiny chance of him noticing she wasn't a baby any more. She tried to imagine herself out of this bloody itchy navy wool skirt and navy bloody ribbed tights, and into something slinky and, well, maybe even a bit sexy. Or at least that showed a shoulder or something. She would just turn up at the party and it would be like that bit in *Enchanted* when the princess enters the ballroom and everything would go a bit slow and Will would just stop whatever he was doing to stare at her, then advance towards her, with his hands out, completely amazed that he'd never recognised her before . . .'

'Felicity? Felicity Prosser?'

Maggie hated daydreaming, even while she was a chronic sufferer herself. You never knew how much they'd missed and it wasted everyone's time.

'Yes, miss?' said Fliss, as cheekily as she could manage. She was embarrassed to get picked out and even more embarrassed about what she'd been thinking. If her bad marks didn't convince her parents to take her out . . .

'It's your turn,' said Maggie. 'If you could grant us a moment or two of attention.'

A couple of girls tittered, and Fliss felt her face flush.

'Do I really have to, miss?' she asked. 'I don't want to read out at the stupid concert.'

Silence fell immediately. *Nobody* questioned the concert.

Maggie weighed up what was the best way to handle it. If she let her off, she might have full-scale rebellion on her hands. Plus, all the parents were hoping their own daughters would have parts. Plus, this exercise was about reading in public anyway. And she was sick and tired of this girl, whatever Dr Deveral said.

'Don't talk about school events that way, please,' she said briskly. 'I won't have rudeness in my classroom. You can discuss it with Miss Starling if you like, but whilst you're in my class you will try out for the concert.'

Fliss pushed out her lower lip, but wasn't brave enough to continue her rebellion.

'This is like prison or something,' she said, mooching to the front.

'Yes, Felicity, it's exactly like prison,' said Maggie, folding her arms and waiting for Fliss to start reading.

'"Christmas isn't Christmas without presents,"' began Fliss sulkily.

Oddly, her sullen tones enlivened the reading, and Maggie could easily see the petulant Amy, and the stubborn Jo, in the set of Fliss's jaw. By the time she got to Jo examining the heels of her shoes in a gentlemanly manner, Maggie was wondering whether it might be a combination of a good punishment and a good concert to actually put Fliss up for it.

'Can we have a word?' said Pat, as Maggie left the classroom to go and have tea, and the girls dashed off outside.

'Of course,' said Maggie. She was still irritated by their distracting behaviour in her classroom, but wasn't about to mention it.

'You know, when Felicity Prosser said she didn't want to be included in the concert auditioning process . . . we're a little confused as to why you still made her do it.'

Maggie looked at them. 'Because that was the objective of the class – to perform a piece to the rest. Whether you get picked or not isn't really the point.'

'But,' said Liz, 'don't you think Felicity clearly demonstrated articulacy and reasoning skills when she said she didn't want to participate?'

'No,' said Maggie, feeling the heat rise in her face. 'She said it was stupid!'

'In the comprehensive system,' said Pat, adjusting her unflattering glasses, 'we don't believe in humiliating children like that.'

Maggie bit back a retort about how that explained a lot.

'I didn't humiliate her. It was part of the lesson plan, and she actually did very well. How did that humiliate her?'

'Forcing children to do things against their will can destroy their self-esteem,' said Pat, making a mark on a clipboard.

'Young adults,' reproved Liz.

'Young adults,' amended Pat immediately. 'They are individuals too, with their own desires and fears.'

'You don't think children should have to do what they don't want to do?' asked Maggie in amazement.

'We believe in child-centred learning,' said Pat. 'You should look it up sometime.'

Later, Maggie wished with all her heart that she had just let it go and left then. She could have forgotten all about it. But something inside her saw red.

'I *know* about child-centred learning, thank you,' she said, her voice louder than she'd intended. 'I did get a first. And I also think that being pushed outside your comfort zone on occasion is what education is actually about. If you asked some of these girls to direct their own learning we'd spend the entire day kissing ponies. And whilst we're talking about humiliating children – sorry, *young adults* – I could have done without you two whispering, muttering and rolling your eyes all through some of the readings. What do you think that was doing for the girls' self-esteem? You lot thinking you're Simon bloody Cowell! It was disgusting!'

Pat looked taken aback at Maggie's outburst. Liz looked rather jubilant and made some notes on her clipboard. Nobody said anything, as, just then, June Starling walked past.

June Starling had heard a raised voice from two class-rooms over and had headed towards it as quickly as she could. Now she saw Maggie, in some disarray, red in the face, squaring up to the women from the commission. Oh, this was all she needed. Some street fighting from the outsiders.

'What's this?' she asked.

'Did you know you had a lot of dissension in the ranks?' asked Liz in an unpleasant tone. June Starling raised her eyebrows.

'Really?'

Maggie coloured up immediately. 'They're trying to interfere with the way I run my classes,' she spat out, before Liz could get any further.

'That's why we're examiners,' went on Liz in the same patronising way. 'We're trying to help you make things better.'

'But it *doesn't* . . .'

June Starling clasped Maggie firmly by the arm, as she recoiled.

119

'Oh, you remember when we were young teachers,' she said in as blithe a tone as she could manage to Pat and Liz. 'So full of passion and fire. Keep it up, you two. I can't wait to see you for the girls' cooking afternoon tea. It's entirely vegetarian, and grown on our own grounds.'

'I can't believe your grounds are big enough to have orchards,' sneered Pat, but June was already on the move again, Maggie clamped to her side. She didn't say a word to her until they got to her office.

Maggie sat down on the hard chair there, sure when she explained her side of things, Miss Starling would understand immediately. But then she turned round.

'What on earth were you thinking?' she said, her sharp tone not hiding the anger behind the words. 'Hollering at our school examiners like a fishwife.'

Maggie opened her mouth. 'But . . . but they were being really unfair. Liz said . . .'

'I'm not interested in who said what,' said June. 'I'm interested in passing an assessment that means that parents will be interested in sending children to this school where we can teach them well. And that means, ideally, the young English teacher, who should be setting an absolute shining example of the comprehensive system, and showing that different worlds can exist and integrate side by side, not screeching her head off in full view of the girls. And I know Veronica would agree with me.'

Maggie's heart felt sick. She'd been so sure that when she told her about what the women had said she'd see her side straight away. But obviously this was not to be the case.

'I'm sorry,' she said, feeling her face burn up and not feeling sorry at all.

'Let's say no more about it,' said June. That girl had a very hot-tempered streak that she needed to learn to contain.

'You'll apologise to Patricia and Elizabeth.'

'I *can't*,' said Maggie. 'I don't agree with them.'

'Margaret, you're not one of my pupils. I can't order you to do anything. But you have responsibilities in being a teacher here, and one of them is handling disputes in an appropriate fashion. I don't believe you handled the assessment today in an appropriate fashion, do you?'

Maggie shook her head. 'No.'

'Very well then.'

Miss Starling indicated that she could leave. Maggie wondered whether she'd offer a consoling word on her exit. But she didn't.

'What, no poetry today?'

Stephen Daedalus had found her first, sitting sobbing on a mossy outcrop that led far out to sea. He'd come padding up gently and licked her hand, which only made her cry more. David wasn't far behind.

'Hey, what's the matter?' he'd said gently, as Maggie had desperately scrubbed at her face with one of the tissues she carried in her handbag.

'Nothing,' she'd said fiercely.

David crouched down beside her.

'It's OK, you know. To find everything a bit overwhelming sometimes. You've come a long way.'

'It's not that,' said Maggie, and found herself pouring out the whole story.

'She didn't even want to hear my side! She didn't care, just sided with them straight away.'

David stared out to sea. 'Didn't you ever get inspected at your last school?'

'Yes,' said Maggie, defiantly. 'They thought I was very good.'

David smiled. 'I'm sure they did. And did your school pass?'

Maggie wrinkled her nose. 'Well, we didn't get put on special measures. But it was a pretty close thing.'

'And did it affect the roll for the next year?'

Maggie saw what he was getting at. 'I suppose not. But I was right and they were wrong. I thought June would back me up – or at least hear me out.'

David patted Stephen Daedalus and threw him his stick of the day.

'What you have to realise about June Starling—'

'The poppet,' said Maggie.

'The poppet,' said David. 'Now, don't get prickly. Is that she really, really, cares about the school. Above everything. It's her life's work. She isn't married, she's never had children. The school is all that matters.'

Maggie stuck out her bottom lip, unwilling to admit that he might have a point.

'Did you really shout at them in the corridor?' His face split into its characteristically manic grin.

'A bit. Maybe,' said Maggie. She felt a smile creep on her face. 'Well, they were totally asking for it.'

'Were they?'

'Yes. A bit. OK, OK OK.'

'What?'

'You are *very* irritating. Yes, I shouldn't have shouted at them in the corridor.'

'What did I say?'

'So now I have to go and apologise, do I?'

'Would it really be the hardest thing you've ever had to do?'

'Yes,' said Maggie.

'Really? Goodness, you *have* had an easy life.'

Maggie's lips twitched. 'You are so annoying.'

'That's not me,' said David, 'that's your conscience.'

'Well, I was right actually, so it's not.'

'OK,' said David. 'It's the school's conscience then.'

He stood up and Maggie, wiping her dirty cheek, accepted his hand to her as he pulled her up. When their fingers touched – his hand was warm and dry – she felt herself quiver, and told herself not to be so ridiculous.

'Come on, I'll walk you back.'

Maggie peeked a glance at him as they headed back to the school. 'You really believe all this, don't you?' she said.

'All what?'

'About loyalty to your school and all that.'

David shrugged. 'Why? Do you think I'm an old-fashioned weirdo?'

'No,' said Maggie, though she realised as she did so that yes, she did think he was old-fashioned, and he was perhaps a little bit weird.

'You do!' said David, sounding scandalised. 'You did a big pause! That means you do!'

'Well . . .'

'I'll get you for that,' he said. 'I'll set my very fearsome dog on you.'

'If you can catch me,' said Maggie suddenly, dancing away from him in the crisp autumn air.

'Oh, I can catch you.'

Maggie took off with the wind at her heels, and Stephen Daedalus not far behind. David, taken by surprise, took a moment to set off after her, but when he did he caught up with her with ease. Maggie, feeling his touch on her cardigan, let the baggy garment fall off her shoulders, as she reached the gate for the girls' school.

'I'm safe, you can't come in, unless I invite you across the threshold,' she panted.

'Isn't that vampires?'

'Oh, yeah.' Maggie was pink-faced and giggling, and David thought how young and fresh she looked. Then he banished the thought from his head immediately.

'So, do you have your Plantagenet readers for me?' he said.

'I do,' said Maggie, feeling a little foolish for teasing him as he immediately turned the conversation back to work. Her hand was still on the gate post.

'And I have mine,' he said. 'We're doing the Betjeman. *And is it true . . . and is it true.*'

'I love that,' said Maggie.

'I'll try and do it well, then,' he said, smiling.

'Thanks,' she said, and she didn't mean for the poem.

David gave her his grin, then summoned Stephen Daedalus with a whistle. From a high turret window, Miss Starling watched them, grimly.

In the end, it wasn't as hard to apologise as she'd feared. Pat and Liz had been delighted to take the young teacher under their wing and give her the benefit of their wisdom, acquired through about two years in the classroom and twenty in administration, as far as Maggie could work out. Two long lectures later and they were all friends. But Maggie made a vow to herself to steer well clear of Miss Starling.

Chapter Eight

Simone was absolutely delighted to be chosen to read at the Christmas concert, although she hoped it wasn't just because Miss Adair was taking pity on her. Fliss, on the other hand, was livid. As was Alice, although for the opposite reason.

'For goodness sake,' Fliss had said when she saw her name on the list. Hattie bounced downstairs. 'Well *done*, Felicity,' she said in that mock-parental tone Fliss hated above all others. 'Mops and Pops will be *so* proud.'

'Well, I'm not doing it,' said Felicity, fiercely. 'I know those women said it wasn't compulsory. So there.'

Hattie stopped and laughed. 'You funny thing! You have to do it now! You can't let the Plantagenets down! The Tudors will think it's hysterical.'

Fliss rolled her eyes. 'I'll get over that.'

'It's serious, Felicity.'

'*It's serious, Felicity*,' mimicked Fliss.

Hattie produced a mobile phone from her blazer pocket.

'You aren't allowed those,' said Fliss immediately.

'Prefects are,' said Hattie, 'for emergencies.' She tapped some buttons and let it ring. 'Daddy? Daddy? Guess what!'

Fliss started to move away, but Hattie grabbed her.

'Fliss is leading the Christmas concert!' She paused. 'I

know! Non-prefects can't use their phones so she couldn't tell you straight away but she's right here.'

Hattie held out the mobile to Fliss with a fearsome look, even as Fliss was backing away, shaking her hands at it. Hattie made a face and held it out further and with a resigned sigh, Fliss had to take it.

'Yes?' she said, nonchalantly. She couldn't deny it, though, hearing her dad's voice on the phone outside the normal Sunday hours, when her mother usually took over anyway and asked her whether she was eating too much jam roly-poly, was lovely.

'Is that my Flick-flack?'

'Hi Daddy,' she said, unable to keep the smile out of her voice.

'What's this I hear about you leading the concert?' He sounded puffed up with pride and his voice was louder than usual. She wondered if he was in a room full of people he worked with.

'I'm not *leading* the concert, Daddy,' she said. 'There's like, a million people doing it. The teacher only picked me to annoy the assessment people anyway.'

She could feel her dad's smile, all those miles away.

'Well, well done for being so modest,' he said. 'You know we'll be there with bells on.'

Fliss's heart sank.

'We're so, so pleased you're doing so well. Your emails are always so negative . . . we do worry about you, you know. We don't want you to be unhappy.'

Fliss felt a lump grow in her throat. She wanted to shout out that yes, she was unhappy, and they had to take her home, that she wanted to go Christmas shopping on Oxford Street with her friends and go ice-skating and she couldn't do all that because she was trapped in a horrible place with horrible food and freezing cold dorms and stupid teachers out in the middle of bloody nowhere. But right at this moment she didn't know how to tell her dad that; it sounded so petty when he was so happy.

'I miss you,' she choked out eventually.

'I know, sweetheart,' he said. 'We miss you too.'

'So why—'

But her dad knew better than to get involved in this argument again.

'That's why we can't wait to see you at the concert. And we're so pleased that you're getting on. Your marks are a bit disappointing . . . more than a bit.'

Fliss gritted her teeth. At least that was working.

'But we know you're going to buck up and do just fine.'

'Yes, Daddy,' finished Fliss quietly, handing the phone back to Hattie, who took it triumphantly.

'See. I told you so,' she said with a smug look on her face. Inwardly, Fliss decided: this was it. She was going to have to be a lot, lot worse if she had the slightest chance of ever getting home again. It wasn't fair on Ranald.

Maggie had thought about Veronica's advice, and had had a long chat with her mother, who had revealed that Stan was indeed missing her more than he'd said on the telephone; that he was still going round there for his Sunday lunch, even on his own, and that he'd been out a lot with his mates.

'Just because he misses you, of course,' her mum had said. 'We do too, darling. How are things?'

Maggie didn't want to mention that she'd had a very public dressing down from her boss and that her class had all turned against her – particularly after what was seen as vindictiveness in leaving Alice out of the school concert in favour of that fat girl, as Fliss had been saying loudly as she'd walked in the other day. 'Schemie types stick together,' someone else had offered and everyone had nodded loudly before pretending they'd just noticed her. She decided she would definitely invite Stan down, but hadn't been able to get him on the phone that Saturday, as she and Claire had gone out for tea and discussed their love lives. Or rather, she'd told Claire the whole story of Stan; Claire hadn't seemed to want to talk about her own situation too much. Romantically, Maggie wondered if she'd been involved in some terribly passionate French love affair that had gone horribly wrong and made her hide away here in the country, rather like the modern equivalent of going into a nunnery.

But all thoughts of Claire left her head when, still unable to raise Stan on his mobile, she'd gone to bed and later, much later, about two a.m., she'd received a text. The beeping woke her up.

'TX FR GRET NIGHT' it said. From Stan. She'd stared at it for a long time, her heart pounding, and a horrible sinking feeling in her stomach. This wasn't meant for her. Would it be for his mates Rugga and Dugga? But why would he text them in the middle of the night when he saw them every day at work?

With a trembling hand she called the number back, still groggy from sleep.

'Uh, yeah?' Stan sounded drunk, and a little nervous.

'Stan?'

'Wha? What time is it?'

'Did you just text me?'

There was a long pause.

'Uh, did I?' said Stan. 'Must have been a mistake.'

Maggie felt her stomach plummet into her shoes.

'What kind of mistake?' Maggie heard the steel in her own voice.

'A daft one, knowing me,' said Stan. 'Uh, it was . . . I must have meant Rugga.'

'Yeah?'

'Yeah. I saw Rugga. Call him tomorrow if you don't believe me.'He said this in a very defensive tone.

'It's all right,' said Maggie. But it wasn't, and they both knew it.

Maggie spent the next week in a blur. What was Stan doing? Was he telling the truth? He was daft as a brush when he'd had a few, that was for sure. But he wouldn't even look at another girl, would he? I mean, surely fidelity was just taken for granted, wasn't it? That they didn't even have to discuss it. After all, if it wasn't . . . but she quickly shook away any thoughts of David from her brain. No. This was nothing to do with anyone else. It was her and Stan. Is this what being apart meant?

Anna wasn't much help.

'I haven't heard anything,' she said. Normally in the hair salon Anna missed nothing that happened for miles around. 'But really, Mags, if you will move so far away . . . I mean, he's a young bloke.'

'Yeah, *my* young bloke,' Maggie said.

'Have you asked him about it?'

'Yes. He just says it's his mates, and would I stop going on about it.'

'Can you get up?'

Maggie thought about the heavy schedule of rehearsals and marking she had on. Plus she didn't think shooting back to Glasgow at the first sign of trouble was exactly what Veronica had had in mind when she'd said she should keep in touch with her family more.

'Maybe he'll come down,' she said.

'You can ask,' said Anna. She hadn't been at all as sympathetic as Maggie had hoped. In fact, she'd as much as implied that if she, Maggie, was going to head off and be hoity toity at the other end of the country, she basically deserved a boyfriend who'd cheat on her. Maggie didn't know what to think.

Feeling lonely and, for the first time since she'd arrived, really questioning whether she'd done the right thing in moving, Maggie threw herself into work. Sometimes it seemed the more she prepared her lessons for the girls, the less bothered they were. But what was the alternative?

Maggie was shocked to realise she'd been at Downey House for three months as December rolled around. Three months of bells, of teaching girls who sat in rows and (usually) paid attention; of almost no male company whatsoever. Half term had come and gone in a blur of lie-ins, marking and wandering around the local town, where the shopping amounted to an unbelievably dated department store that sold a lot of haberdashery, bras the size of barrage balloons, and day gloves; and an outlet of Country Casuals.

Maybe she should have gone home after all. Her parents were worried about her too, no matter how much she assured them she was getting plenty of fresh air and cream teas, and she missed her sister and her little nephews, terrors though they were.

Now the school was readying itself for Christmas. Even amongst the older girls, who had mocks in January, there was a palpable air of excitement running through the pupils, as great swathes of mistletoe and ivy wound their way around the banisters and the great hall. Veronica hated starting the whole Christmas folderol too early, but she did enjoy the school looking its very best.

Pat and Liz had gone away for a little while – their inspection would continue throughout the year at different points. However, Liz had gone off sick for an unspecified length of time apparently suffering from stress – Veronica had wondered whether it wasn't the set of Liz's trousers that had been suffering from all the stress, and whether the amount of chocolate biscuits Liz ate had anything to do with it – but Pat would be back at Christmas with another of her protégés. Veronica hoped they would be an improvement. The inspection was definitely not going well. It wasn't just Maggie's outburst that had had to be dealt with; Miss James in PE had insisted that if they wanted to understand her class they had to experience it, which hadn't pleased either of them – they were both very anti competitive sports; Mlle Crozier had the sixth form reading 'that disgusting old sexist', Jean-Paul Sartre, and they had been overheard discussing how to ask for condoms in Paris, something of which Veronica had thought the inspectors would have entirely approved. She tried to put them out of her head for now as she OK'd Miss Starling's request for a shorter Seniors' Christmas party this year and nothing the Downey Boys could pour booze into, e.g. punch.

Veronica wandered through the hallways. Really, this year Harold the caretaker and his ground staff had excelled themselves. The greenery gathered in from the grounds gave everything a beautiful scent, and she had ordered the large wood-burning fire in the entrance hall to be lit every morning. It was comforting for the girls, coming down from their chilly dormitories, to be confronted with the fire, the Christmas cards steadily arriving in pigeonholes every day, and warm porridge with cream, honey, maple syrup and occasionally all three, to set them up for the day ahead.

She liked hearing the laughter in the air as the girls fussed about the concert and the party to follow; to see their flushed faces as they dashed in from hockey for tea and scones by the fire. They hadn't had much trouble with the St Thinians craze – anorexia – which was endemic in some schools. Perhaps because Downey House was known for its devotion to outdoor life and health; perhaps sensitive and prone girls just avoided it. Or maybe they'd just been lucky so far, thought Veronica, who ate like a bird herself.

'Not running are you?' she enquired gently to one galumphing middle schooler, who immediately turned puce and slowed down. The gentle approach did seem to work the best.

Christmas was hard for her. Of course she could go to her brother's, but he was a nice simple chap, worked in a warehouse in Oldham, and his wife thought she was uppity because she didn't bring their spoilt children the latest trainers and PS3 games they wanted, even when she was told what they absolutely must have. It wasn't a prospect to relish. No, she was going to take that Greek islands tour with her friend Jane, who taught classics at a wonderful school near Oakham. A Swan Hellenic, lectures every day, walks in the winter sun and a little learning – it would do her a world of good. Christmas was a terrible time for . . . for people like her. Veronica tried to keep her thoughts in order. After all, who knew what her son would be doing now, and where? Veronica just hoped and prayed, as she did every year, that he was happy – he would be a grown-up man now, maybe with children of his own. Best she never knew. Best nobody knew.

'I do hope you're not chewing gum, Ursula,' she muttered gently to the dark-haired girl who passed her on her way to the post boxes. The girl swallowed audibly.

'No, miss,' she said, eyes wide.

'Good,' said Veronica. 'Good.'

*

Fliss headed to Bebo to catch up on her messages. The first one that struck her eye was from Callie, her worst behaved friend from back home.

FLISS!!! I kno you are locked to death in that school, but you have to have to have to come home for this – Will is in a band at his school and they're playing in the pub! And anyone over fourteen can get in and I think we will definitely count! It's on the 12th December!

Fliss's heart immediately started to race. The twelfth! Two days after the bloody concert, but also two days before they broke up. Would her parents let her go? Definitely not. But if Will saw her there, supporting his band – being a fan right at the beginning, before he became, like a famous singer and everything – he'd definitely definitely talk to her. And there wouldn't be Hattie or any of the other girls around because everyone would still be at school so she'd have him all to herself, practically.

She had to be there. She had to.

'What are you thinking about?' said Alice, who'd come to find her in the computer room.

'I need to get suspended,' said Fliss. 'I've had enough. I really really really have to do something so awful that I get sent home.'

Alice's eyes widened. 'A challenge, eh?'

'Don't you want to get sent home too?'

'Don't care,' said Alice. 'It would only be some diplomatic nanny. I can't even remember where they are. Cairo, I think. Cairo is *so tedious*.'

Fliss nodded as if she'd found Cairo very tedious every time she'd been there.

'But you really want to get chucked out?'

Fliss glanced at the frosty moors outside the window, and nodded enthusiastically. 'I want to go home,' she said. 'I'll miss you, though.'

'I'll come stay for the holidays,' said Alice, philosophically. 'See if this bloke you like has any mates.'

Fliss wasn't sure she wanted to introduce dark gorgeous Alice to Will, but having her to stay would be great. She'd probably be grounded and stuff for a little while – for ages, after they caught her sneaking out to the gig – but then it would be Christmas and everyone would soften up and forget; Christmas was great at their house, they all got loads and loads of pressies and got to watch telly and her mum just heated up some turkey stuff from M&S but then let them eat chocolates all day and gave them a taste of champagne – and by the new year everything would be back to normal and she'd be with her friends and at a normal school again.

'OK,' said Fliss. 'Well, I need your help.'

Maggie felt nearly as nervous at her first rehearsal with the boys' school as her girls did. She'd drilled them after school – having to get them to learn all the pieces off by heart was the first challenge, but they were making good progress. Fliss had suddenly become surprisingly good about it considering she hadn't wanted to be chosen in the first place. And Simone was stolidly professional, doing it the same way every time.

Simone had taken to coming over to Maggie's office occasionally, once or twice a week, to exchange a book from Maggie's large collection. They rarely spoke much, but it was a companionable silence as Maggie did her marking, or occasionally chatted with Claire, generally in Maggie's halting French so as to keep it from Simone's tender ears. When they did speak, Maggie saw further flashes of the sensitivities and humour that came through in her essays. Crippling shyness was such a terrible thing. Yet on stage she was perfectly fine. Most peculiar.

Maggie noticed that even though the girls shared a room, Felicity never included Simone in their conversations or little whispered private jokes; even when heading back to the dorm together they somehow contrived to leave Simone out. Maggie hated to see it and wished she could do something about it, but didn't know how.

All the girls involved in the performance were there for the readings, plus the orchestra, and they met in the great hall that doubled as a theatre. There was seating for six hundred; it was rather daunting, Maggie mused, standing on the stage and looking out. Downey House meant what it said about creating confident young ladies. She imagined the rows of parents watching her girls and applauding . . . perhaps she would be asked on to take a bow . . .

'Hello hello!' shouted a voice, startling her from her reverie. David strode into the hall on his long skinny legs, a Pied Piper leading a long line of young boys behind him. The boys looked around – they looked more confident and certainly had better skin and posture than the boys Maggie had taught, but they seemed to lack that jokey nonchalance her boys used to put on in new situations, where they would kick each other and pretend that they were twenty-five and could all drive cars. This lot probably had drivers and would be aiming for parliament by the time they were twenty-five. The girls behind her quietened down noticeably and stopped messing about.

'Right, first years all together!' said David. 'We're only going to do this twice, so no messing about. Girl readers stage right, boys stage left, orchestra in the middle, dancers do your thing, and it will all be fabulous.'

He stood looking up at Maggie on the stage and she was seized with a huge impulse to put out her hand and let him help her jump down. But she knew any hint of physical contact would be leapt on by the pupils and gossiped over obsessively, so she hopped down by herself. Nonetheless she could feel her heart beating, and checked again to see if the lipstick she'd surreptitiously applied earlier was still there.

'So, are your girls all ready then?' said David, giving her his grin. She felt her insides fizz.

'They're great,' said Maggie, loud enough for them to hear. 'It's the orchestra I'm looking forward to.'

'I wish I could conduct, don't you?' said David. 'It always looks like such fun. Just waving your arms about in a good coat and getting rounds of applause.'

'I'm not sure that's all there is,' said Maggie, laughing at his daftness.

'Yeah, course it is. Bet they earn tons of money too.'

Mrs Offili came out and shot David an affectionate look.

'Showing off your impeccable musical pedigree as ever, Mr McDonald.'

'Certainly am, Mrs O. You've seen me dance.'

Mrs Offili shook her head, although there was a smile playing on her lips, and started on the tuning up.

Watching everyone run through their parts, Maggie was impressed. But even as one of the boys, a tall, thin lad called Peregrine, was doing a spine-tingling rendition of the Carol of the Bells, she found herself glancing at David. He was totally rapt, mouthing the verse along with him and, although she was sure he'd be incredibly embarrassed if it was pointed out, actually conducting the verse. Maggie looked at his long fingers and wondered . . . No. This was nonsense. She shook her head. And wildly inappropriate. She'd clearly been holed up here for too long, and was getting frustrated. It wasn't

David's fault he was the only semi nice-looking man for twenty miles. She could see the girls eyeing him up too.

Both girls did well. Fliss really would be quite beautiful when she grew up, with her pale skin and even features, thought Maggie, however overshadowed she was at the moment by the glamorous, knowing Alice.

Everything went smoothly and well until after rehearsals had finished and David and his troupe were getting ready to leave – Maggie had slightly hoped he would linger and ask if she wanted to go for coffee, or even a drink in town, but he wouldn't – and the girls went into the changing rooms at the back of the auditorium to pick up their bags. Fliss came out looking slightly upset.

'Miss? Miss?'

'Yes, Felicity?'

'I've lost my watch. I took it off to put it on the side while I was timing myself, then I definitely left it in my pocket – definitely – but it's not there now.'

'What do you mean?'

'It was in my pocket before I came on stage,' said Fliss, looking miserable and staring at the floor. That watch had been her grandmother's. It had been left to her, and her parents had had severe misgivings about letting her take it away to school. She'd promised to look after it. Even though this would help her case to leave the school, she was still utterly devastated. Her grandmother had loved her to bits and she'd loved her too, and her little house, full of knick-knacks, and Malinkey, her gran's little Scottie, who always tried to fight Ranald. Of course Ranald would never fight back, he was far too much of a softie. Thinking about her gran, and her dog, made the tears prick Fliss's eyes.

'It was my gran's,' she said, lip starting to wobble.

'Let's go look,' said Maggie. 'It couldn't have fallen out?'

Fliss shook her head. 'I've looked everywhere.'

Simone, and Alice, who'd turned up to meet Fliss after class, were standing outside the locker room, looking dismayed. Maggie looked closely at their faces. Stealing at school was one of the most disagreeable things to deal with. It was time-consuming, unpleasant and caused a lot of talking behind pupils' backs. With a stab of guilt she wondered if, with the amount of time she'd spent out the front talking to David, she might have been able to prevent it.

The changing room backstage was quiet, as various girls from various houses sat around, looking worried. There was a passageway to a corridor exit on the side, noted Maggie, which meant it was accessible to almost anyone in the school. Alice and Simone both looked nervous. Maggie glanced at Simone. It couldn't be denied that she didn't own nice things like the other girls did. And that Felicity and Alice had basically ostracised her since she arrived. Could she do something like this to teach them a lesson?

And what about Alice? She didn't think Alice had been too thrilled about Felicity getting the part, and sharing in the glory that should have been Alice's alone. Could she be trying to get her own back? Surely she wasn't that sly?

'Hello everyone,' she announced to the silent room. All the excitement and good cheer of the rehearsals had gone; she'd also fetched in the boys from their locker room, and David stood behind her.

'We've had a report of a lost watch,' she said, firmly. It wasn't time to search the children or their belongings. She wasn't sure that was the best way to go about it anyway; stolen goods could be easily hidden, and searching promoted mistrust and implied the children had no sense of moral values at all and might as well steal. And the watch probably was just lost; the kids were so careless.

'Now, I'm sure it will turn up.' Behind her she could feel Felicity bristle. 'However. If anyone knows anything – anything at all – about this, can I urge them to come forward to Mr McDonald or myself, in strictest confidence, at the first opportunity, do you understand? Thanks!'

She glanced round the faces looking up at her, trying to catch a glimpse of embarrassment or guilt. Immediately she couldn't help noticing that Simone had gone brick red, and was doing her best not to catch her eye. Maggie's heart sank. The punishment for stealing could be suspension, or even worse. She really hoped Simone hadn't jeopardised her future for something as petty as this. It would be a tragedy if so.

'If for any reason this watch isn't just "lost" you can come and see me or Mr McDonald in our respective offices, or leave us a note. I'm sure we can clear this up without any unpleasantness being necessary. Do I make myself clear?'

There was a mumble of awkward consent.

'All right,' she said. 'Good rehearsal everyone. Your parents are going to be proud. Off you go.'

The children scrambled off to get a late tea the kitchen had made specially for them as Maggie and David looked at each other sadly.

'Say it isn't lost . . .' said David.

'I don't know,' said Maggie. 'What do you think we should do, cancel their concert?'

'They've worked so hard,' groaned David. 'And I hate this "punish the many" thing. It's so concentration camp. Kids never rat anyway.'

'I know. Bugger.'

They stood in silence for a moment.

'Do you think it was stolen?' asked David.

Maggie nodded. 'One of the girls went very red.'

'Oh no,' said David.

'I think it's my scholarship girl. Fliss isn't nice to her at all. Not bullying, but just excludes her. She just looked so horribly guilty.'

'You can't jump to any conclusions,' said David. 'But maybe a quiet word.' He sighed. 'Boys just whack each other about for that kind of thing.'

'I know. I think you have it easier.'

'Yes,' said David, moving away. 'Apart from the world wars and things. Do you think your cook would have any tea left over?'

Despite her disappointment, Maggie couldn't help feeling herself perk up.

For once, Simone skipped supper. Her face was flaming. She'd seen the way Miss Adair had looked at her. Accusingly. Like, 'you're the poorest girl in the school. It must have been you.' She'd felt the guilty blush steal over her cheeks. Fliss and Alice, too, had given her such a hard look when Fliss had realised her watch had gone. She'd wanted to shout at them that it wasn't her, that she would never do that, but she couldn't. The words wouldn't come; it was as if her throat had seized up. Now they would definitely think she'd done it; that she was jealous of Fliss just because she was pretty and popular and all of those things. Which she was.

Only Imogen was in the room, studying quietly with her back to the door. Simone undressed quickly, threw herself under the blankets and cried herself to sleep as quietly as she could.

*

140

Fliss was the centre of attention at the table, as people jockeyed for position to tell her how sorry they were about her watch and try and remove themselves from suspicion.

'Who do you think it was?' asked one of the Tudor girls.

Alice looked around. 'Well, don't think I mean anything by this or anything,' she said. 'But have you noticed the one person who's not here?'

The children had bolted their food and moved on to the television lounge by the time David and Maggie had finished clearing up and everything was dark in the cafeteria. Mrs Rhys, the cheerful cook, had left two covered plates of sandwiches, scones, cheese and fruit out, and the urn was still plenty hot enough for tea.

'It's still going to be a good concert,' said David, his hand on her shoulder as they walked over to the deserted tables. 'Don't worry about it.'

Maggie stiffened instantly when she felt his hand, and nearly dropped her scones. 'I know,' she said. 'I just want everything to be all right, you know?'

They sat down, not facing each other, but corner to corner, their heads nearly touching. She wanted to lean forward, breathe him in, but didn't dare.

'I know,' he said, and for an instant, Maggie thought he was going to take her hand, in the darkened, deserted meal hall. The space between them was charged; she was sure she could see sparks leaping between their fingers. Her heart beat faster.

It was so strange. She'd got so used to her and Stan over the years, and had worked with so many female teachers, she hadn't really thought much about other men, apart from in an abstract, Brad Pitt kind of a way. It was strange how quickly this tall, skinny dark-eyed man with the manic grin had got into her head.

There was a pause, which turned into a long, loaded silence. And suddenly, she knew. Suddenly, they were staring at each other in the deserted hall. David turned his gaze on her and she returned it. For once, the noisy school had fallen completely quiet. Maggie was aware of her breathing; and of his, and she wondered, as time seemed to slow down and take on a fluid quality, if he would be rough, or smooth, or both, and, almost as if it didn't belong to her, she felt her own hand stretching out to clasp . . .

'SIR! SIR!!! LLEWELLYN'S PUSHED MIKE JUNIOR'S HEAD DOWN THE LOO AGAIN!'

'I DIDN'T! I DIDN'T! OR AT LEAST I WAS SORELY PROVOKED!'

Six boys burst into the hall like a small angry torrent of beavers. Maggie pulled her hand back immediately as if she'd been touching something hot. David gave her a quick glance – was it annoyed? Regretful? She couldn't tell – and stood up.

'What? What's all this? No, on second thoughts, I DON'T want to know. Come on you savages, back to the prison pit where you belong.'

He turned to Maggie, and the look in his eyes was completely unfathomable.

'I'd better go and round up the rest of this sorry crew before they unleash the dogs of war all over your nice hall.'

Maggie forced her lips into what she hoped was an unbothered smile and nodded vehemently.

'Definitely. Definitely. Of course. Right. Bye then.'

Chapter Nine

The days passed, and the thief did not come forward. Although it had been the talk of the school, the chatter started to die down a little. But Simone was well aware it centred on her, and stalked the halls with her head down and her eyes red. Maggie decided she really must have a word with her, although she'd been putting it off. There had been no more cosy book swaps, either. She needed to find out what was up, she was neglecting her duty. But everyone was just so busy at this time of year.

At least nothing else had gone missing. A note had gone round the entire school, warning the pupils that there might be a thief on the loose, that valuables should be given to Matron and locked away, and that anyone with any information should come forward. No one had.

Meanwhile, Maggie had a more pressing problem on her hands. Stan was on his way. He was coming down for the week of the concert, then they could drive back up home together. The idea was he could see the Christmas show and a bit about her life, and hopefully they could spend a little bit of time together and get themselves back on track. Every time she thought about it, she felt so nervous. Partly because of what he might have been getting up to. And partly because of what had crossed her own mind. David hadn't emailed her since the rehearsal. Although disappointed, she'd realised immediately what this meant – that there was nothing going on, just her slightly feverish imagination. It must be true what they said about girls locked up in boarding schools. And it was absolutely ridiculous behaviour; getting a silly crush on some teacher across the way, who probably got crushes from every child he ever met, girl or boy, she thought firmly. It was ridiculous and completely unprofessional; they were working together, and they had to stop it getting out of hand.

She and Stan had been together seven years. That was worth fighting for. And the idea of Stan cheating on her was the real issue, not distracting herself from her sadness by a dangerous flirtation.

The train from Glasgow took a long, long time to wind its way down the entire country and finally into Exeter. Maggie was standing at the barrier and saw Stan disembark a long way down the train. He was brushing a lot of pastry crumbs from his hoodie. Maggie looked at him as if through the eyes of a stranger. He looked the same as ever – long and skinny, except with an oddly protuberant pot belly that made him look a bit pregnant; spiky, gingerish hair, pale skin. He carried a large sports bag and a copy of *Top Gear* magazine – surely it couldn't have been all he'd brought to read for a ten-hour train trip. Or maybe it was.

It seemed to take for ever for him to make it to the gate. All around were couples falling into each other's arms, running up and crying with happiness and relief.

'Hey,' said Stan, looking nervous.

'Hey,' said Maggie. She wished she was running into his arms, but somehow she couldn't make herself. It would be stupid. Starting a relationship at school meant you never got over-demonstrative.

144

She didn't know how to broach the subject, but she couldn't just dive in straight away.

'How was your trip?'

'Good,' said Stan. He burped. She smelled lager. 'You look posh.'

'Do I?' said Maggie. Veronica had very kindly mentioned that a friend of hers owned a boutique in town and offered a discount to school staff. Claire had taken her shopping, and together they'd spent rather a lot of money (Maggie was finding that without paying accommodation, food, petrol or going-out costs she was able to save a huge amount of her salary) on some new basics for her – two beautiful wool skirts, some plain white, well-cut shirts and a heart-stoppingly expensive cashmere jumper. The plain clothing accentuated Maggie's good legs and beautiful dark hair, which she had tied back more loosely, after Claire had insisted on pulling just a couple of fronds round her face.

Stan could see that she looked well. His heart sank. If she'd looked fat, or sad, or lonely or any of those things. But it was patently obvious that she was doing just fine down here without him. Better, if anything. He knew it.

They stood there a tad uncomfortably for a moment, then Maggie leaned forward and kissed him awkwardly on the cheek. Stan turned his face so that the kiss could hit his mouth, but he didn't quite make it in time, so it ended up a rather awkward mishmash.

'Ehm. So. Have you crashed my car yet?' he said, as they disengaged.

'It's our car!' said Maggie. 'And no, of course not.'

Stan heaved his bag into the boot, and climbed in the driver's seat.

'Eh,' said Maggie.

'What?'

'Well, have you been drinking?'

'I had a couple of lagers on the train, but nothing . . .'

'I think I'd better drive,' said Maggie. 'Plus, I know the way, remember?'

Stan didn't want to get out of the car and feel like an idiot, but he supposed she did know the way.

'OK' he said, ungraciously, and moved round to the passenger seat, heaving a sigh.

They left the ring roads of Exeter behind them quickly enough, followed by the motorway, and eventually left the main roads to start the climb towards the cliffs of Downey House. Early snow had stayed on the tops of the hills and the views over the sea were quite starkly beautiful. Maggie took quick glances to her left to see if Stan was taking them in or even noticing them.

'It's scenic, isn't it?' she asked eventually.

'Hm,' Stan grunted, non-committally. 'I thought you hated the country.'

'So did I,' said Maggie. 'I'm quite surprised with myself.'

'Hm,' said Stan.

Maggie couldn't believe she was feeling so disloyal, but as she parked the car – at least Stan had shown a mark of surprise when he'd seen the towers emerging from behind the hills – she was wondering if he should have come at all.

'Fuck me,' he'd said. 'It really is a fucking castle, isn't it?'

Maggie looked at it affectionately.

'Yes,' she said. 'And it's starting to feel like home.'

'Thought as much,' said Stan, ungraciously.

This wasn't going right at all, thought Maggie. She needed to get over the horrid panicky feeling she'd had when she'd got that text, and remember her priorities. She was Maggie Adair. From Govan. Who'd fallen in love with

Stan when he was seventeen years old. He was her best friend. Her lover. Her Holy Cross saviour.

She cast her eyes to the left. He was sitting in his Celtic top, looking so awkward and nervous. She felt her heart soften towards him. Of course it was a new environment. Of course he was nervous. Hadn't she been, the first time she'd rolled up the gravel drive in their small, unimpressive car? The school was designed to impress; to be the best. Stan was intimidated, and she should be careful of his pride.

'Hey,' she said, reaching over and grabbing his knee. 'You know, they're all a bunch of English arseholes.'

'Yeh,' he said, glancing down at her hand on his leg. He felt bony, warm, reassuring somehow. 'I know. I had to hear them shouting all the way down on the train. No wonder I drank so much lager.'

Maggie nodded. The smell was noticeable in the small car.

'I really need to take a wazz,' said Stan.

'We're here,' said Maggie, opening the car door. Her heart suddenly skipped a beat. There, crossing the car park and looking distracted, in a tweed jacket with a long stripey scarf blowing out behind him – he couldn't have looked more like a fey English type if he tried – was David.

'MAGGIE!' he hollered, as she emerged from the car, Stan slightly crossing his legs as he levered himself out the other side. He came striding over, Stephen Daedalus bouncing excitedly when he saw Maggie there, tail wagging furiously.

'Thank God,' said David, looking slightly breathless. 'We need you. It's an emergency.'

'What?' said Maggie.

'Forters junior has put his back out doing water polo. He can't stand up for the concert.'

'But it's tomorrow!'

'Yes, I know that.'

Maggie thought as quickly as she could. His lovely piece, ruined. Who did she know . . .

'I think I have just the person,' she said, internally rolling her eyes at how she was going to have to crawl to Alice now, and completely underscore the girl's original strongly held belief that she should have been the star all along.

'Trebizon-Woods,' she said. Stan looked at her as if she was speaking a foreign language.

'Will she learn it in time?' said David. 'You know what my lot are like, you have to hide the verses in porn mags and Yorkie wrappers.'

'Oh, she knows it,' promised Maggie. 'She may be a tad reluctant to do it for me, but hopefully sheer ego and vanity should shine through. I'll flatter her a lot.'

'EXCELLENT,' hollered David. Then he turned his penetrating gaze on Stan, who was standing and looking increasingly awkward.

'Hello! Who are you?' David stuck out his hand. Stan didn't stick out his. David shoved his back in his pocket. 'I'm David McDonald. Maggie's opposite number at the boys' school.'

'I thought there were only girls here,' said Stan, in a rather uncomfortably bleating tone.

'Oh, yes, yes, that's right . . . I work on the other side of the hill.'

'Oh,' said Stan.

'And you are?'

Maggie felt ashamed of how embarrassed she was. Of Stan, in his nylon Celtic football shirt, covered in McCoy's crumbs, with his dirty jeans, pot belly, short haircut. She hated feeling like she was seeing them through David's eyes. Partly because she also suspected that David wouldn't judge people on what they wore; it wasn't his thing at all.

'I'm Stan. I really need to go to the toilet.'

David's eyebrows arched temporarily. 'OK. It's all girls' loos up there, but maybe Miss Starling wouldn't mind if you attacked her rhododendrons.'

'David.' Maggie shot a look at him. This was not the time for dry English humour. Stan looked miserable.

'Stan's my . . .'

She was scarcely conscious of the pause until it had happened.

'Boyfriend,' said Stan, sullenly. It sounded strange coming from him. He'd seemed so reticent in the first place. 'I'm her boyfriend.'

'Ahh!' said David, looking back at Maggie and then to Stan. 'Lovely!'

Maggie bit her lip. She didn't want Stan to realise that she'd known David for a while and had never mentioned him.

'Yeah,' said Stan.

'There's a loo over here,' said Maggie. 'I'll speak to you later, David. I'll have a word with Alice and get back to you, but I'm sure it'll be fine.'

David nodded and retreated, looking rather thoughtful.

Maggie showed Stan up to her rooms quickly, ignoring the sizing-up glances from the girls she passed and trying not to think about whether or not they'd gossip – of course they would. She wondered how many men in football shirts arrived here. None of their fathers or brothers, that was for sure. Stan, whilst moving reasonably swiftly, kept stopping on the stairs to look at things: portraits of old girls, chandeliers, panelled doors. He whistled softly to himself.

Finally they reached the little suite in the East Tower. Stan couldn't stay there, of course, not without all sorts of criminal records checks and so on, but he could have a look around. Maggie had tidied up and laid a new bedspread over the bed. It didn't make it look any more like a double than it had done previously, but it cheered things up a little. She'd also added flowers, and bought some lager for the fridge.

'I'll just have a wazz,' muttered Stan. Maggie stood, staring out of the window, feeling suddenly helpless.

Five minutes later Stan came back out. He'd brushed the crumbs off his shirt and eaten some toothpaste. 'Hey,' he said quietly. Maggie didn't turn around, just kept staring out of the window. 'I didn't know there were men around here at all.'

'He's just a teacher at the school across the hill,' said Maggie dully. 'We have to work together.' She turned round to face him. She could see it in his face. He looked guilty. 'Stan,' she said.

Looking at him for the first time in a while she suddenly saw him again. Seventeen and long and skinny, pretending he wasn't waiting for her outside the dinner hall. The leap in her heart as she'd seen him there; trying to hide her French jotter, which had his name scribbled all over the back page. His slow creasing smile as his mates joshed him, but he had stayed and waited for her anyway.

The bedroom felt colder than ever.

'I didn't do anything,' said Stan sullenly, staring at the floor. 'She wanted to, but I didn't.'

'So there was a "her",' said Maggie, feeling her blood run cold. 'And you told "her" it was a great night.'

'I didn't say I wasn't thinking about it. I said I didn't do anything. And you can believe me or not.' Stan ended on a defensive flourish. Then he looked up at her to gauge her face.

'I missed you,' he said simply.

Maggie felt her prejudices about him, her worry about how he came across, amongst her new life, her worry about whether he really cared for her or whether he was quite pleased to have the place empty for a bit . . . all of that faded away as she saw her spiky-haired Stan right there; his cocky funny side gone, and all because he loved her and missed her. She felt . . . love, mixed up with feeling a bit sorry for him.

She stepped forward. She believed him. It was as simple as that. Some woman would have come on to him, and he'd have done his best to back down from it. There might even have been some snogging, but she could deal with that. After all . . . and she banished the thought of David from her mind. She put her hand up to Stan's cheek.

'I missed you too,' she said.

'Naw you didn't.' He indicated all around. 'Not now you're living in a fucking castle with *David*.'

Maggie stepped forward. 'Sssh,' she said. Stan looked at her, half suspicious, half hopeful, as Maggie stepped towards him. 'Want to go out and do something that is totally banned in a girls' school?'

After a mostly successful reunion afternoon at the local B&B, Maggie needed to get to the dorms; there was a rehearsal after supper and she had to catch Alice. She wasn't particularly looking forward to it, but there it was. Simone and Imogen were there finishing their prep. Fliss and Alice were reading about Britney Spears in a gossip magazine.

'Alice, can I see you for a minute?'

Alice heaved a sigh that was a tad too grown up for a thirteen-year-old, then brightly announced, 'Of course, Miss Adair,' so she couldn't get into trouble for it.

Maggie took her outside.

'Simone seems to be happier,' said Alice, in that irritatingly adult way she had.

'It's not about Simone,' said Maggie. 'One of the Downey boys has had to drop out, and we need someone who can perform the T. S. Eliot.'

Alice's eyes lit up, but she tried not to look too eager.

'Yes?'

Maggie rolled her eyes. 'And Mr McDonald and I thought you might like to take it on.'

Alice pretended to look as if she was thinking it over. Maggie smiled; she was pretty good.

'Well, it is a lot of extra work.'

'Fine,' said Maggie, 'I'm sure Simone would be happy to do two.'

'No! I think, I think I can fit it in.'

'Good,' said Maggie. Then she relented. 'Well done, Alice. I'm sure you're going to be very good.'

Alice nodded. 'Is that your boyfriend, miss?' she asked. Not much didn't get round the school in about ten seconds, Maggie thought ruefully.

'Is that your business, Alice?' she said sharply, deeply regretting bringing Stan up the main staircase rather than sneaking him in the fire escape door.

'No, miss,' said Alice, delighted she'd obviously struck a nerve and looking forward to spreading it round the class.

'Well, on you go then. And finish your prep before you start on *Heat*, OK?'

Alice re-entered the dorm smiling broadly to herself.

'What?' said Fliss, suspiciously. She had wondered if there was any updating on the thieving. Nothing had gone missing in the last week or so and it all seemed to have settled down.

'You know we were trying to work out what you're going to do at the Christmas concert?'

Fliss felt again the big ball of anxiety in her stomach. She was horribly nervous about doing something really terrible. On the other hand, she had to get out of this school, she had to. Get back home again, go to Will's party; see Ranald, go to a proper school. She just had to steel herself and do something really bad once. It did make her feel horribly nervous and anxious, though, and was keeping her awake at night.

'Well, you just got better back-up. I'm on too.'

Fliss jumped up. 'That's brilliant! That's great news.'

Simone overheard and shrank a little inside. When it was just her and Fliss at rehearsals, Fliss wasn't that mean to her. A little quiet and distracted maybe, and friendlier to the girls from the other houses than to her, but not horrible, and sometimes she'd even walk her back to the dorm, though she never mentioned this to Alice. Fliss was someone Simone would like as a friend. She was glamorous and quite funny, nothing like as sullen as she pretended to be in class. If she could just get to know her, Simone thought she could really talk to her. If she could just get to know anyone. Simone sighed and went back to the letter she was sending her parents. They didn't have a computer, so she couldn't email and Skype like everyone else. On the other hand she did get a lot of letters in the post, which made the other girls jealous. She'd told her mother to stop sending cake, and thankfully she had.

'I am having a good time here,' she wrote out carefully. 'Everyone is very friendly and I get on well with everyone.'

Well she couldn't write the truth. Even isolation was better than being plucked out and sent back to her old school.

*

153

The dress rehearsal for the concert went badly, which, as much as David said it was tradition, shook Maggie up a little. Lights didn't cue at the right time, the orchestra was all over the place, and Simone lumbered on at completely the wrong point, bursting into tears when this was pointed out to her for the second time. Alice was word perfect already, but Fliss was suddenly strangely jumpy and nervous. The weather had turned frightfully cold, and David said Stephen Daedalus could smell snow and was refusing to leave the house. Maggie wondered if he was right. It didn't snow much in Glasgow; too built up and too near the sea, and when it did it hardly lay on the ground before it got dirty and snarled up with cigarette butts and footprints.

Stan had spent his days holed up in her rooms watching television. In vain she'd tried to interest him in taking walks around the local area; visiting the beautiful, windswept beaches, or the quaint villages. He'd been happy to go to the local pub every night and eat their microwaved lasagne and drink the local beer whilst complaining it wasn't Eighty Shilling.

Oddly, though, Maggie was finding she didn't mind. It was just Stan, doing what he did. It was comforting. And they had fun together, taking part in the pub quiz with Claire (the English league football round stumped them all), chatting about her friends and family and what everyone was up to, then retiring to the B&B which, perhaps through enforced intimacy and the fact that Stan couldn't eat in it, meant they were making love more often than ever.

It was only now that Maggie realised how lonely she'd been. All the silly fantasising about David was clearly just that, the imaginings of a lonely woman who'd let her imagination run away with her; no better than the girls she taught. This was where she belonged, sipping beer and laughing at Stan's impersonation of his boss at the distribution plant. She must just stop thinking about David, that was all. And she could tell Stan was happy too. It wasn't so unlikely that other women fancied him, after all.

It did snow, huge choking flakes through the night. The girls woke with yelps of excitement and a festive atmosphere ran through the school quicker than lightning. Mrs Rhys took the nod from the grounds manager, and decided to make bacon and eggs rather than the weekday porridge (or gruel, as the girls referred to it). Some of the parents who were coming to the concert were staying a couple of days, to take the girls home from school in the car, though most would take the London train on which the school had a block booking. Though many girls had gone home at half-term, some hadn't seen their mum and dad for twelve weeks and were quite beside themselves. There was a flurry of nerves and packing and huge excitement as the delicious smell of cooking sausages wound its way up the stairs.

Veronica went to her office early, a heather-coloured cardigan from Brora pulled tightly round her shoulders. This was not ideal at all. The snow would affect the roads, which would mean the parents would be late, the concert would overrun horribly and everything would be out of sync. She hated disorder. Not only that but the inspectors were coming back to watch the concert. She shook her head. This wasn't *High School Musical*, the film every single girl in the school had suddenly gone mad for last year and even got up a petition to go and see. It wasn't a performing arts college. The quality of the music teaching was one thing, but turning her girls into a troupe of showboats was extremely far away from her original aims.

She leafed through her paperwork. Very few girls were staying over the Christmas break; just one whose parents were diplomats in a country currently going through some upheaval, and an Australian fourth former, Noelene, who got horribly unhappy in the winter months. Veronica couldn't understand the parents sending her so very far away. Getting an English education was one thing. Getting it whilst your parents were sunning themselves by the pool was quite another.

There was a knock at the door, interrupting her train of thought. Miss Prenderghast popped her head round.

'It's Patricia from the Inspector's commission – with a new inspector too,' said Miss Prenderghast. She lowered her voice. 'It's a *man*.' Veronica raised her eyebrows. The men in this line of work tended towards the very pernickity, finicky types brandishing a large manual of health and safety practices. Not, frankly, ideal.

'All right, Evelyn, thank you. Send them in please,' she said.

Pat bustled in, all frenzied seriousness as usual, as if someone had just deliberately said something to upset her.

'Merry Christmas,' said Veronica, conscious of the fragrant holly and mistletoe lining the fireplace. Pat raised her eyebrows.

'Do you know, many schools prefer to inclusively celebrate Winterval now? So that no child feels left out?'

'Christmas leaves no one out, Patricia,' said Veronica, wondering what would constitute a safe nicety.

Her eyes moved upwards to look at the man who followed her in. He looked quiet, neat and tidy in a grey suit. Quite young for an inspector; not yet forty, she would say.

'Veronica Deveral,' she said, holding out her hand. The man seemed to look at it curiously before he took it.

'Daniel Stapleton,' he said. Then he shook her hand quite forcibly, staring into her face.

Veronica sighed inwardly. Were any of these inspectors quite normal? He probably learned 'keep eye contact' on some money-wasting training course. 'Welcome to Downey House,' she said.

'Thank you,' he said, his voice sounding a little trembly and nervous.

'Coffee?'

'Yes please,' he said, glancing nervously at Pat. Pat nodded and said, 'Miss Prenderghast, do you think we could maybe get a couple of sandwiches?'

Veronica despised anyone treating her highly organised administrator as some sort of domestic servant, but Miss Prenderghast was already heading off to the kitchen as Pat took the seat nearest the fire.

'Now, for the concert tonight, we have several quality target initiatives that we'd like to see pushing the envelope . . .'

Sylvie ran into the common room, where the girls were talking nervously about the concert and the party, in particular what they were going to wear. Everyone was asking Fliss and Alice what the boys in the orchestra were like, what the readers were like, and in particular who was the tall boy they'd seen walk in in full high-collared dress uniform?

Besides that, of course, the main topic of conversation was Miss Adair's chav boyfriend. There had been great excitement when he'd been spotted in the main halls wearing a football top! The girls were full of excited speculation as to whether he'd ever been arrested and whether or not he was a football hooligan. Ursula and Zazie, a Moroccan girl from a wealthy family who spoke perfect French and English and had a usually mischievous sense of fun, had both expressed amazement that someone as old as Miss Adair would have a boyfriend at all, rather than some ancient husband stashed somewhere.

Fliss had found her nerves all shot; she'd hardly slept the previous night. But she and Alice had talked it through; they were going to do it. She was going to do it. In front of everyone. She was going to ruin the concert and go home. Then she'd sneak out to Will's band and then ... well she didn't know what would happen after that, but it didn't really matter. No more stupid classes. No more stupid Miss Adair on her back all the time. No more stupid having to share a room with Imogen and fat Simone. No more having to listen to Hattie's boring stories about being a prefect, blah blah blah. She'd be back where she belonged. And once Mum and Dad got over being a bit pissed off they'd be pleased, she was sure of it. Pleased to have her back, just her on her own, no stupid sister. It would definitely be worth it. But oh my goodness, the nerves. She tried to concentrate on what the other girls were asking her – about Jake, the lanky pretty boy from the boys' school, who was reading the Betjeman. Not her type. Her type was only Will. Will. Even saying the name made her heart flutter, and steeled her resolve.

Anyway, here was Sylvie tearing in. She was meant to be dancing, but was looking as scatterbrained as usual.

'I've lost them!' she was saying.

'What?' said Alice.

'My earrings! I have special silver earrings that go with my Dickens outfit. And I can't find them! But I'm sure they were in my desk drawer.'

The noisy common room went quiet. It was common knowledge that Fliss had lost her watch. Most of the girls had hoped it was a mistake or a one-off. Now it looked as though there was a serial thief amongst them.

Sylvie was nearly tearful. Normally nothing troubled her, so to see her upset was very unusual. She looked around.

'I know they were there because I tried them on last night for rehearsal. So it was someone who's been around the dorms since. I didn't lose them. So if it was one of you . . .' Her voice choked up. 'I hope you're proud of yourselves.'

Simone, crouching in the corner with one of the books Maggie had lent her, stiffened. Then Alice picked up what Sylvie was saying.

'Yes,' she said. 'I know not everyone has lots of money at this school. And people shouldn't be judged on how much money they have. But if you don't have much, you shouldn't take other people's things. I'm not accusing anyone. I'm just saying.'

The whole room went silent. Simone felt every eye on her.

'Anyone got anything to own up?' said Alice. Nobody said anything. 'Anyone?'

Simone felt herself get to her feet. Her face was flaming, a bright, bright red colour she could feel. She wanted to make it clear; to show people and tell them that it wasn't her, she wasn't a thief; all the girls in her old school had gone stealing all the time and she'd thought it was disgusting. But the words wouldn't come out. Her throat was completely choked up.

'Just . . . shut up!' she half-screamed at Alice in a high-pitched tone. 'SHUT UP!'

And she pushed her way through the girls and left the room.

All the girls were hanging out of the windows as the first cars started to pull up, snow on their roofs, into the allocated car spaces. Sixth formers were out in padded jackets to direct the traffic, along with the grounds staff. The forecourt was lit up with fairy lights, and a huge Christmas tree stood in the middle of the cobbled quad. The school looked as beautiful as it possibly could, thought Maggie, waiting for Stan to make his way up from the village. He'd taken the car, although walking would obviously have been slightly healthier for him, but she didn't want to argue.

She was wearing a new dress that she'd bought. It was a deep, Christmassy red, that reflected well against her dark hair and brought out the pink in her cheeks. Pulled tight around her waist, and with a pair of magic knickers on, she looked good – pretty, but not so vampy that any of the girls' families would feel uncomfortable around her.

The girls were in uniform for the concert, but were doing their best to bend the rules for the visit of the boys' school, so there were ribbons in the hair, illicit skirt turning-up and barely traceable make-up everywhere. Yelling and running, normally completely *verboten* in the inner sanctum of the school, was breaking out all over. Usually very conscious of the feelings of the pupils who did not have parents coming, Veronica found this difficult, but didn't forbid it. Just because some were unhappy didn't mean you had the right to make everyone so.

Finally, quite a while after the scheduled six p.m. start, the heavy, old red curtains of the packed theatre opened, and Veronica walked out.

'Welcome everyone,' she said, 'particularly those of you who have come a long way. We've been very proud of our girls this term and I know that next year, as we move towards the summer, they will work harder than ever.'

There were some theatrical groans at this, as the students knew they were far enough away from their austere head-mistress to risk a little gentle heckling.

'But Christmas is a festival. Wherever you are from, and whatever your beliefs.'

Pat's head, from where she was sitting in the audience scoffing Haribo, popped up at this.

'Northern European countries have always celebrated the depths of winter, the very nadir of the year, with celebration, dancing, warmth, food and light. We in the Christian tradition also celebrate the birth of the infant Christ, but there are many winter traditions that surround us, and all exist to wish us peace and prosperity at this cold time of year. So on behalf of my girls, and Dr Fitzroy, who has so kindly lent us some of his boys to make up the orchestra and some of the readings, may I wish you peace and joy from all at Downey House.'

The applause was loud as Alice, looking beautiful and very meek – Maggie mentally shook her head – came out with Lars, a cellist from the upper school. The idea was to interplay the poem with a strange, eastern melody and it worked beautifully. Maggie felt a shudder go up her spine as Alice, having been told to downplay her reading, came to 'This birth was hard and bitter agony for us' and the refrain was subtly echoed in the music. There was no doubt Mrs Offili had done a wonderful job.

After that, there was dancing from the older girls, and the choir, which was nearly of professional standard, all sang except for the back-row altos, Maggie made a mental note, who were standing far too close to the boys and four of them were red-faced and sniggering about something. They weren't in her group, but she might have a word with Miss Starling.

Backstage, the mood was giggly and tense amongst the soloists. Astrid was in a world of her own with her clarinet, tapping out melodies in the air when she was meant to be putting make-up on (the girls took this performing privilege very seriously). Clarissa Rhodes, school star, was singing a version of the Carol of the Bells which, it was rumoured, had made Mrs Offili cry. As usual, she didn't think she was good enough and was nervously checking the sheet music.

Alice had bounced off the stage to a mass of warm applause, and was making a terrible job of hiding her delight. Now her part was over, she could content herself by basking in how much better she'd been than everyone else. Simone was in a corner by herself. Nobody had offered to put her eyeliner on, or a bit of lip gloss. She looked terrible; her eyes were red and dark-rimmed from lack of sleep; her hair was a mess and if anything she'd put on weight again.

Fliss was also standing alone, her heart beating at an alarming rate. She'd have been nervous about performing anyway, but this hadn't really sunk in until she'd peeked out of the red curtains and seen how many people were out there; hundreds and hundreds. She couldn't even see her own mum and dad.

'There's still time not to do it,' said Alice, who was hoping very much that Fliss would. They'd cooked up the plan together in the alcove late at night. 'I wouldn't tell anyone.'

Fliss shook her head. 'No,' she said. 'I have to do it. I have to get home. And this is the best way that doesn't involve hurting anyone.' She glanced over at Simone. 'Or stealing stuff.'

At the sound of the 'stealing' word, Simone had raised her head, then she buried it again. Maybe the best thing she could do would just be to tell her parents that she didn't want to go back to Downey House, that it hadn't suited her after all, that she'd been wrong. But then they'd send her back to St Cats. There wasn't a solution. She was trapped.

She tried to focus on her piece. Her hands were shaking. She mustn't forget it. She mustn't.

The Tudor first years finished their pageant – a series of rhyming couplets they'd written themselves about Christmas down the ages. It was good, thought Maggie. She should have done something like that. It was sure to have impressed Miss Starling.

'Hello,' said a voice in the wings. 'Nervous?'

Maggie turned round to see David standing there, looking tall and handsome in a velvet jacket which should have looked odd and dated but actually rather suited him.

'No,' she started to say. 'Actually . . . yes. For them, of course.'

'Of course,' said David. 'You look very nice.'

She felt herself blush; she hadn't thought he'd pay attention to things like that.

'Thank you,' she said. She'd managed, whilst Stan was there, to mostly wean herself off thinking about him. But she did wonder, once again; was this man gay, single, or what? It wasn't a conversation they'd ever had.

They stood in silence for a while, watching Clarissa sing the Carol of the Bells. At first her high voice rang out accompanied only by a single bell. Then, as the choir came in on the ding-donging, Maggie felt the hairs on the back of her neck rise. Finally, the entire orchestra and choir together sang to the rafters the triumphant, 'Merry merry merry merry CHRISTMAS'. It was stunningly beautiful.

'Wow,' Maggie said breathlessly. She realised, with sinking heart, how aware she was of David right next to her. Maybe it hadn't gone away at all. Maybe it was just lurking, to catch her out.

'Yes,' he said, turning to look straight at her. She caught her breath.

Then suddenly the quiet intimacy of the moment was lost completely as the horde of the choir pounded off through them like a flock of clumpy-shoed gazelles, to cheers from the audience. It was hard to find a quiet moment in a school. Maggie checked her programme and realised she should be herding on Felicity.

'I have to go,' she muttered, almost apologetically, feeling her heart pound.

'Of course; me too,' said David, looking very awkward.

Maggie darted off in the direction of the dressing room. 'Come on, come on,' she chided Fliss, who was standing there looking slightly ill. 'Don't worry, you're going to be great.'

Felicity was the last act on before the interval, after which there was the senior ballet and play to get through, with Simone's monologue opening the second half. They were running late, though not ruinously so.

'Come on. You're not too nervous are you?'

Fliss couldn't work out why Miss Adair was being so kind to her, even offering her a glass of water. Everyone at this school was horrid, except for Alice. That was why she was leaving. She was going home. That was it.

'You'll be wonderful,' said Maggie, surprised Fliss was so pale and terrified. Most of the girls had reasonable poise in front of their peers; part of a class that had told them since birth they were more than good enough. But here she was, practically having to throw her on stage.

There was a silence from the auditorium now, just an expectant rustling of programmes. Fliss closed her eyes.

'OK,' she said. Then she walked on to the stage.

The lights were so much in Fliss's eyes at first she could scarcely see a thing. In a way that was quite good. People looked further away; she couldn't distinguish who was who. But it did make her realise the scale of the occasion.

She stepped up to the microphone. It was set to Clarissa's height, far too tall for her, and no one had brought it down, so she had a very awkward moment fumbling for it. Maggie, watching from the wings – David had vanished – felt embarrassed that she hadn't arranged for someone to fix it for her. Oh well, sympathy would be on her side. She would deliver Jo's speech and just as it ended the orchestra would join in with some jaunty American turn-of-the-century melodies to play the audience out into the main hall where there was exceedingly weak mulled wine for the grown-ups and sixth formers, and squash for the rest.

Fliss gave up her struggle with the microphone stand and decided just to hold the mike instead. She bit her lip and stepped forward. 'Eh,' she said. Immediately the microphone let out a howl of feedback. People were starting to sit up and take notice. There hadn't been much in the way of hopeless amateurs so far. Everyone was too good. For the bored younger brothers and sisters in the audience, as well as those members of the school not involved, a little diversionary failure couldn't come soon enough.

'There's a few things I want to say about this school before I start,' said Fliss, but her voice was wobbly and not quite close enough to the mike.

'Speak up!' shouted a voice from the back.

Suddenly Fliss saw red. 'This school is crap!' she yelled into the microphone. 'The food is crap and the teachers are crap and you're all being ripped off!'

A thrill of delighted rebellion rushed through the younger (and some older) members of the audience.

'First of all, there's the COMPLETE unfairness of the mobile phone locking scheme. That is a complete attack on human rights. And some of the teachers can barely speak English. Our English teacher is almost impossible to understand. Why should we have to suffer through that?'

Maggie had a quick intake of breath and moved towards the stage.

'Not to mention the horrible PE changing room where there's still communal showers like this was 1980 or something.'

Some of the fathers' eyebrows were raised at this.

'SO . . .' And at that, Fliss ripped open her shirt. The entire audience gasped as the buttons popped off and, underneath it, saw she was wearing a white T-shirt, crudely scrawled with the words DOWNEY HOUSE SUCKS.

Fliss, realising she'd captured the attention of the audience, stepped forward to continue the litany of injustice, before ending it on a chant she hoped would be taken up by the entire school – DOWNEY HOUSE SUCKS! – until someone ran on stage to drag her off. That English teacher most likely. That should do it.

Sure enough, Maggie, who'd hardly been listening until her name came up, so conscious was she of where David was, now made to run on stage. Mrs Offili was already on her feet to start up the orchestra in order to drown out the noise. But right then, Fliss took one last step forward to emphasise her point . . . and dropped out of sight completely.

The orchestra didn't sit in the orchestra pit for the first half of the show; they went on the stage, so that the proud parents could pick out their daughter, the second bassoonist. They would go down there once the ballet started, but for the moment it was empty. Which could be seen as good luck, mused Veronica later, as she tried, and failed, to see an upside, as it meant Felicity Prosser broke only her own ankle and didn't injure anyone else.

The kerfuffle and yells which broke out as Felicity dropped from the stage were enormous and what had happened ran through the school at the speed of light. Most of the parents assumed the girl had been drunk, and wondered how alcohol was obtainable on the premises – and to such a young girl too. Veronica ordered the orchestra to play on and for the interval to continue as planned; of course, there was only one buzz in the air.

Maggie was third on the scene, to find David and Mrs Offili already there ministering to a white-faced Felicity, who had tears streaming down her face from the pain.

'What the hell!' she started shouting at her, her own shock and worry about her pupil coming out too clearly in her voice. 'What the HELL was that?'

David turned round from where he was looking at Felicity's ankle. 'I think we need to get her to a hospital,' he said. 'I can drive her if you like.'

Maggie felt herself instantly reproved, and bristled. 'She needs to get to a hospital because she was pulling some ridiculous stunt and it's her own fault. What on earth were you *doing*, Felicity?'

Fliss couldn't breathe for the pain. The pain in her leg and the shocking and terrible recriminations she felt raining down on her head from all the people in the hall. There was a ring of people around her as all the curious individuals came to nose about. She could hear her mother's voice saying loudly, 'Where is she? What happened? What's happened to her?' and the crowd parting to let her through.

Suddenly what had seemed like such a good, rebellious idea in the dorm with Alice seemed like the worst idea ever.

What had she been thinking? Making an idiot of herself in front of the whole school? And now, her ankle really, really hurt. She felt cold inside, worrying if something was really wrong with her.

The handsome English teacher from the boys' school was looking at her in a concerned way and had covered her up with his jacket, which wasn't too bad until he prodded her foot, and Miss Adair was shouting at her, but that was nothing unusual. For a second she wondered if she could make herself faint, but as her mother and outraged-looking sister pushed through the crowd she realised there was no making about it, and she dropped clean away.

The next thing she knew she was on a bed in the sanatorium. The first person she saw was Matron who told her she was going to be fine, but she needed to go to hospital to get her ankle seen to.

Her parents and Hattie were there too, looking confused. 'But why?' her mother was saying. 'Why?'

Miss Adair was right behind her, still looking furious, as was Miss Starling. The teacher from the boys' school looked concerned. Fliss wondered if he'd carried her into the sanatorium.

She looked down at her swollen throbbing ankle.

'I just wanted to go home,' she said, tears pouring down her cheeks.

The father of one of the pupils, a surgeon, came and gave his professional opinion on Felicity's ankle – that he believed it was indeed broken – and she was packed off to casualty in Truro.

Veronica was in two minds. She should perhaps call off the show. On the other hand, there were a lot of parents who'd paid a lot of money and come a long way to see their children perform, and she didn't want the antics of one to ruin the evening for the rest of them. And she disliked quitters. She came to a decision.

'Ladies and gentlemen,' she announced in the grand hall, where quite a few parents were getting stuck into the mulled wine. 'I do apologise for the behaviour of one of our younger girls. She's very new here. But all our other wonderful girls and boys are here and ready to perform for you, so if you'd like to retake your seats . . .'

There was a general mutter of approval, particularly from parents who hadn't yet seen their own offspring, and a loud tut from Pat, who was, no doubt, Veronica reflected, judging how much she could escalate the incident in her own report, for health and safety reasons.

Simone, trapped in her own misery backstage, had hardly noticed the commotion, only that everyone had disappeared and left her on her own, which was hardly unusual. Now they came back in dribs and drabs whispering excitedly – 'She was drunk! She called everyone a bastard!' to one another so she gathered something had gone terribly wrong with Fliss's piece. It would probably make her more popular than ever, Simone found herself thinking meanly.

'Simone,' said Maggie, somewhat wild-eyed. She was ashamed of her outburst before, shouting at a sad, injured girl in front of David. 'Do you think you can go on and do your piece without managing to jeopardise the entire school?'

Simone nodded behind her owl glasses, not quite understanding.

'OK, on you go then.'

The orchestra had just about calmed down enough to play a Grieg interlude, introducing the Dickens as Simone walked on. The audience was now upright and expectant, hoping that she would do something equally unexpected.

'Marley was dead, to begin with,' said Simone, launching into the speech she'd rehearsed a thousand times in her head.

And she was good. Very good. Not even her mother standing up and filming in the middle of the front row, in direct contravention of instructions, as well as of the people behind who wanted to see, could stop her. She was clear and her London accent added a veracity to the words, and as she came to a close, the senior girls, who were dancing a piece based on the book, fluttered on like a clutch of Dickensian fairies, in tasteful rags and smocks, to hear her intone how 'the candles were flaring in the windows of the neighbouring offices, like ruddy smears upon the palpable brown air. The fog came pouring in at every chink and keyhole . . .'

The applause was massive and heartfelt, particularly from the staff and those pupils who didn't want to see the school made a laughing stock of by a pushy middle-schooler. Maggie found herself grinning with relief, before she went off to check with the hospital. And Veronica couldn't help being quietly pleased and surprised at her awkward little scholarship girl. Would she yet surprise them all?

Maggie had called the hospital – Felicity's parents had taken her in their car, and Matron had followed on behind. All would be fine. The corridor was empty and quiet, as the audience was entranced by the seniors' ballet (some of the fathers perhaps a little more than they ought to have been). She wondered briefly where Stan was and what he made of all this. Then out of the shadows stepped David.

Maggie felt her heart flutter. Oh, this was ridiculous, she had a huge disciplinary crisis on her hands, and, who knows, the parents could take it into their heads to sue the school, and where would they be then?

'Is she OK?' asked David. Maggie nodded; Matron had responded briskly that they were putting her in plaster and she'd be right as rain.

'Her parents will take her home whilst we sort out what to do.'

'Just a little bit of teenage rebellion,' said David.

'Just a bit,' said Maggie. 'Quite a big bit though.'

David looked at the floor. 'Look, Maggie, I think . . .'

He seemed awkward and looked up again. He was standing right underneath some mistletoe.

'Ah,' he said, noticing it, but not stepping away. 'The thing is, Maggie . . . God, this is bad timing. Well. Uhm. Too late now. Uh, I really like you.'

Maggie stopped short and looked straight at him. Her heart was pounding in her mouth. Surely not, with Stan here and everything. She couldn't. He couldn't. It wasn't right. It wasn't even legal on school grounds.

But suddenly she thought she wanted to kiss David McDonald more than anything else in the world, even as she could hear the orchestra play the Coventry carol next door.

David tried again. 'There's something I should have . . . it's very important that our relationship remain professional.'

Maggie felt her heart drop like it was in an elevator shaft. Of course it was. Of course. What an idiot she was. David was looking at her, but it was hard to read his expression. Almost as if he found this painful too.

'I think it's for the best, don't you?'

Inside Maggie wanted to scream, NO! No! I want you! Instead, she just nodded her head and said, 'Quite! I'm sorry, I didn't realise we'd gone beyond the normal bounds . . .'

'No,' said David, shaking his head vehemently. 'No, of course we haven't.'

Without being able to consciously help it (or so she told herself), Maggie found herself glancing upwards at the mistletoe, and then back towards David. He seemed to move towards her – was he? Did she? She found herself compelled to move forwards. Her gaze was fixed on his dark eyes. Was she really going to move straight into his arms? What if they were discovered? The school really couldn't have any more scandal tonight. But to feel his lips on hers suddenly seemed more important than any rule; any job she could possibly have. She felt drunk with longing; she wanted him more than she'd ever wanted anything. Shocked by the power of her feelings, she stepped forward. It felt as though the music dropped away; the snow outside rendering everything silent and still.

'David,' she breathed.

'David!' she heard.

It was a loud, friendly voice and it came from a blonde woman who'd just entered the passageway. She was pretty and fresh looking.

'Hello!' she said cheerily, putting out a hand to Maggie as she came forward. She came up to David and took his hand.

'I'm Miranda.' She turned to him. 'Ooh, look, mistletoe. Do you think it would be *dreadfully* naughty to kiss in school? This is where I learnt after all.'

'Hi! I'm David's fiancée,' she added to Maggie, as if the ring on her finger and her stance of ownership could have left anyone in any doubt.

172

Chapter Ten

It was not the happiest of Christmases. Glasgow was covered in a grey sludge which, Maggie felt, reflected her own state of mind. She felt so stupid, so ashamed and so damn cross! OK, she'd never mentioned Stan, but – a *fiancée*? So, David probably had lots of girls crushing on him every year without a *teacher* embarrassing herself. Was she, a woman with a boyfriend, really going to snog another, engaged teacher, in the school when all the parents were there? Thinking about it made her shiver with horror. What on earth had she been thinking? What was wrong with her?

Stan thought she was sad because she was realising how much she missed Glasgow and all her friends. He was being incredibly nice to her. Maggie had thought guiltily that maybe he suspected something was up, but, no, he hadn't mentioned David – he'd hardly mentioned the school at all, just arranged nights out at the pub with their friends and lots of trips round to her mum and dad's. She was grateful for the distractions and touched at Stan's kindness – long distance relationships really were difficult. Maybe it was time to see if he'd like to come and work closer by. Stop her getting fixated on someone like a teenager who still had posters up in her bedroom.

And it was nice to get looked after by her mum and dad,

and watch telly late, and play with her nephews and come and go as she pleased without having to worry about being on show all the time. That was the thing about Downey House, and she'd never anticipated how much of a burden it could be; to eat communally, work communally; to see the same faces all day every day was quite wearing, more so than she'd realised. It was nice, after all, to slump around the house in pyjamas, playing music loudly and watching television with Cody and Dylan.

'I thought we'd go out on New Year's Eve,' said Stan, as she sat polishing off the Quality Street in front of the *Doctor Who* Christmas special they were watching for the fourth time.

'Oh yeah,' said Maggie, not really paying attention. 'Is Jimmy having another party?'

'Neh, thought we'd go out for dinner, something like that.'

'OK,' said Maggie, surprised. Going out for dinner wasn't a very Stan thing to suggest. He was improving.

New Year's Eve was, as ever, utterly freezing and bitterly wet. Maggie started regretting their plan almost immediately as they waited for a bus, having tried and failed to catch a cab into town. The restaurant was filled with large groups of noisy people shouting and bursting balloons at one another whilst wearing party hats, and the frazzled waiter moued apologetically as he showed them to a cramped table for two buried in the corner. Stan immediately ordered a bottle of champagne, which was very unlike him. Maggie gave him a sharp look. They were doing a little better financially as Maggie's job paid more than her old one, and she was spending a lot less. But still, this was a bit recklessly extravagant, and they should really . . .

'Maggie. Maggie!'

Stan had to say her name twice before she responded. When she looked up she saw he was kneeling on the floor.

Oh my God! Why hadn't she noticed he was wearing his only suit?

'God, I meant to do this at the end of the meal, but I'm sweating like a pig, and I don't think I can hold it in, so . . .'

Maggie stared at him. What was he doing? Oh God. This was the last thing she'd been expecting. The other, red-faced, drunken people in the restaurant had started to look round, after someone caught sight of what was going on. She shook her head in amazement. Well, David wasn't the only person who could be engaged after all.

'So, my lovely Maggie . . . you've had your time away, and I've missed you horribly and we've had our ups and downs, but I really really want you to be mine for ever, so, uh, will you marry me?'

Somebody woo-hooed in the restaurant, but everyone else had fallen suddenly, eerily silent; even the waiters had stopped scurrying around. Stan looked up from where he was kneeling, and fixed Maggie with his kind blue eyes.

'Well?'

Fliss was, in the end, only rusticated. That meant, as Hattie had pushily explained, that she was suspended but without it going on her permanent record. It was only for the last three days of term. The school saw her broken ankle as quite punishment enough and had given the lightest penalty. Had she managed to deliver more of her speech, it had been made extremely clear to her in a conversation with Miss Adair, Miss Starling and Dr Deveral, which her parents attended – a meeting Fliss would never be able to think of again in her life without feeling the most deep and intense shame – then things could have been a lot worse.

Of course she had not made it to Will's Christmas party. Or any Christmas party. Her mother was more sympathetic, but her father's disappointment was clear to see in his face. She hated making him so miserable. Hattie, of course, was triumphant and made a show of being extra helpful by bringing her books and extra study guides to help her catch up. Only Ranald, licking her face every day like he couldn't quite believe she was home, gave her any succour.

Now, her cheek and rebelliousness felt a bit stupid and immature. Getting bad marks on purpose? Fliss thought, with a creeping sense of contrition. Did she really do that? What must the teachers think of her, even that horrid Miss Adair.

After a muted Christmas – the grounded and incapacitated Fliss opened her new clothes without much pleasure, knowing her opportunities to wear them were severely limited – and oddly stilted visits from her friends, who were full of the new shopping centre, and the new boys at the school and teachers whose names she didn't know, she was staring out of the window at the sleet driving into the orchard, whilst failing to take her usual comfort in rereading *What Katy Did*, when both her parents entered her room at the same time and sat down. Fliss looked up at them nervously. Being grounded was one thing. Getting another lecture on how badly she'd let everyone down and how she'd disappointed them was quite another.

So she was surprised when her mother took her hand.

'Felicity,' she said. 'Your dad and I have been talking. We didn't . . . we didn't realise you were so unhappy.'

'I wasn't unhappy all the time,' said Fliss, grudgingly. She'd had a lot of time alone in her room to think about things. She glanced at her father, but his eyes were downcast.

'We've talked about it, and we've decided,' continued her mother. 'We'd like you to see out the year. And then, if you still really hate it . . . well, we can talk about it then.'

'I want you to give it a proper shot,' said her father, his voice sounding gruffer than usual. 'To see it through. None of the best things in life are easy right off the bat, Felicity.'

'And we paid the fees up front,' said her mum, like that was important. 'I've spoken to the school. You can go back on your crutches with your plaster, they can manage that. You will apologise to everyone involved in the concert for the upset you caused. Then it will never be spoken of again. But if you as much as breathe out of line . . . I'll be furious. I want you to try, Fliss. Try your absolute hardest, OK?'

Fliss nodded, grudgingly. She'd expected a lot worse. Her book was easier to read now, after her mother had kissed her on the cheek and both parents had gone off to the RSPB Christmas ball. Till the summer. She could wait.

'If I have to listen to that BLOODY' – Joel, trying out the word in case it counted as swearing – 'Dickens garbage one more time do you think I am going to be a) a little bit bored, b) extremely bored or c) so bored I'm going to have to kick myself in the head?'

'You should be proud of your sister,' said Mrs Pribetich. Simone had been made to perform her extract in front of every set of relatives and friends her mother could muster to showcase her privately educated daughter.

The relief of being home, where nobody watched what she ate, or made sly remarks (apart from Joel, and she could cuff him) or accused her of being a thief, almost made her want to cry. She revelled in the very smell of home; of food cooking and her mother's perfume. Seeing her own bedroom made her sink down with relief.

But her parents' pride in her and her accomplishments was so strong.

'Shy, but with excellent imaginative and intuitive skills,' Maggie had written on her report card. The fact that Simone's spelling and punctuation were behind, thanks to years of noisy undisciplined classrooms, she'd put aside with the aim of trying to boost the girl's confidence. She still didn't know how to broach the subject of stealing. She'd have to do something about that in the new year.

'A pleasure to teach,' Miss Bereford the maths teacher had added. Mrs Pribetich had brandished that report at everyone from the postman upwards. So Simone swallowed her feelings and tried her best to smile and take things in good humour, even as her mother tried to get her to wear her school uniform to church.

It was only towards the end of the holiday that Simone's nerves started to bunch up again in her stomach. She was eating more, she realised. Packing her suitcase was torture. Even the thought of having to walk into that dorm again; to hear the whispers and giggles of the other girls instantly silenced as she entered. Of another lunch or supper sitting alone at the end of the table, excluded from the conversation. The thought of it made her queasy. The night before she was due to catch the train she went upstairs to finalise her packing, taking a packet of Hobnobs with her as she went.

Her father came in to find her weeping over her new chemistry textbook.

'Hey, what is it, *scumpa*?' He chucked her gently under the chin, which made her cry even more. 'It's not the school, is it?' he said, sitting down on the bed. Simone wanted nothing more than to throw herself in his arms and tell him everything; about the teasing, and remarks, and the loneliness; the huge, massive, crushing loneliness.

But what for? He'd sacrificed a lot to come to this country; to see his children do well. In Romania he could be an engineer. Here he could drive a cab. He had sacrificed his own hopes and ambitions for her. She couldn't tread on his dreams, even though she knew at some level how much he hated her being away from him and thought the fancy school would carry her even further away.

And to go back to her old school. How would that be better? How would that help anything at all?

'It's nothing,' she sniffed. 'I'm glad to be going back. I'll just miss you all, that's all.'

Her papa took her in his arms and gave her a long squeeze.

'We miss you too,' he said, patting her back and rubbing his own eyes. 'We miss you too. And we love you, *iubita*. You're making your mother so proud, you know? You're making all of us proud, even that *obraznicule* brother of yours. Never forget that.'

Veronica usually saw in Christmas with the minimum of fuss. She liked to keep busy. Jane was a good companion in this respect; she minded her own business and chose to discuss history rather than pry into anything personal. Veronica wondered about Jane herself, and her own preferences, never voiced, but she wouldn't dream of raising it. And the weather was clear and bright and warm in the Greek islands, where they ate moussaka and visited the ruins and in the evening put cardigans on their shoulders and strolled through villages, looking for the most authentic tavernas. It had not, flighty teenagers notwithstanding, been a bad year, on the whole. Applications were up, and the new English teacher, whilst hot-headed on occasion, certainly seemed enthusiastic and worked hard; two qualities, Veronica often felt, that compensated for the occasional practical deficiency, though June Starling didn't always agree. Now, she only had this wretched assessment to get through and everything would be clipping along quite nicely.

Maggie took a deep breath. They could sort out the geography later. OK, her new job had its tough moments – and she wouldn't mind never seeing David McDonald again – but she didn't want to give it up straight away; there was still so much to learn she could bring back later. Stan could even find something in Cornwall; he liked the pubs well enough. Anyway, it was something they could discuss. And they had plenty of time; there was nothing wrong with a long engagement.

Gosh, she also found herself thinking. Here I am. Being proposed to. How extraordinary. She was even more surprised at not having guessed it was coming. After all, they had been together a long time. But they'd had such a difficult year. She looked at Stan's scruffy, loveable face.

As the restaurant diners, almost as one, leaned closer, she let a huge smile break out.

'Of course,' she said, only a tiny part of her mind wondering if this was quite right. 'Of course!'

And the room let out a huge round of applause.

Chapter Eleven

The weather was sharp and cold as the cars rolled up for the spring term. Faces were solemn; this term there was sport outside in the freezing cold; mock exams for the older girls. Maggie examined the little shiny half-carat ring they'd chosen in Laings on her finger for the thousandth time and vowed that there was going to be no more nonsense of the Felicity/Alice variety – she was going to split up the troublemakers and put everyone's nose to the grindstone. She didn't care that they sniggered at her and that the girls didn't accept her. She was going to make them work. It was a broad syllabus and she wanted to prove to Veronica, to Miss Starling, to the assessors and everyone else that she was capable. No, better than capable: a good teacher.

Claire was the first to pounce when she arrived in their little suite of rooms, amazed at how pleased she was to be back there again.

'*Qu'est-ce que c'est?* What ees that on your finger!!!' she exclaimed, as soon as she heard Maggie arrive. Maggie beamed and stretched it out. They had phoned her parents, Stan's dad, and everyone they knew as soon as Stan had got up off the ground, looking as pleased with himself as if he'd just won the lottery. Everyone's happiness was so strong and palpable she'd found herself getting swept along in the champagne, and the hugs and the planning. She needed to have a conversation with Stan about maybe him moving to Cornwall for a couple of years, just while she got the experience she needed at Downey House, then they could go back to Glasgow, she'd find a school that needed her and everything would be just fine. All the talk was of where, and when, and what it would be like and who would come. They hadn't set a date yet, there was too much to discuss and they only had a few days before Stan was back at work and Maggie was already making plans to go back south.

'But it won't be for long, love, will it?' Stan said hopefully, tucking into pizza on their last night together.

'Well, I think I need to be there a bit longer than three months,' said Maggie, carefully folding up her new soft grey jersey dress, just like one Claire had, that she'd picked up in the January sales. 'I need to get a good reference, then I can work anywhere. I should stay for at least two years.'

Stan made a grumpy face. 'You don't want to get married for *two years*? I thought you girls were always desperate to get down the aisle.'

'Well, we could do it next summer. This summer is probably too early anyway, everything will be booked up. And it will give us longer to save up.'

Stan looked at her. 'Yeah? You want a big do?' He didn't seem the least bit put out by the prospect.

'I don't know,' said Maggie. 'We could just slip off to Vegas if you like.'

'Yeah, get married by Elvis. In a cadillac,' said Stan, his eyes gleaming. 'Neh. It would break your mother's heart.'

He was so thoughtful, she thought.

'Stan,' she said. 'Are you sure you couldn't look for work in Cornwall? They have newspapers there too, you know. And fish suppers.'

Stan looked perturbed. 'But I like it up here. All my friends are here. And my family. You're the one that wants to go down and ponce about amongst English folk.'

'I know,' said Maggie. 'But I thought you'd like us to be together.'

'Yuh,' said Stan. 'That's why I asked you to marry me. Come home. Let's get a wee house in Paisley. It'll be good.'

'I know,' said Maggie. And it would. It would. She just . . . 'I just think I should see this job out, OK? It's a great opportunity for us. For setting up our future.'

'I miss you,' said Stan.

'I know,' said Maggie. 'I miss you too.'

'And that school of yours is full of mad folk. What about that weirdo, the bloke teaching English?'

'David's not weird! He's just different.'

'I didn't think they let blokes like that teach in boys' schools.'

Maggie looked at him in exasperation. 'I'm going to pretend I didn't hear that.'

Stan smiled. He liked winding her up.

'Was eet *romantique*?' asked Claire, as they sipped tea together and watched the cars draw up.

'Well, it was in a restaurant,' said Maggie. 'And there were about a hundred pished folk watching. But it had its moments.' She smiled to herself at the memory.

'*Bof*.' Claire had finally confided in Maggie that she was having an affair with a married man but she wouldn't tell her where. She often vanished on weekends and in the holidays, and came back slightly sad, if suntanned, and with a fabulous new pair of shoes every so often. Maggie was convinced she'd winkle it out of her sooner or later, but for the moment, Claire was content to dive on Maggie's romantic news.

'So what are you going to do?'

'Well, nothing yet,' said Maggie. 'I think I'd like to have a long engagement.'

'Oh yes, like Monsieur McDonald.'

Maggie stopped with her teacup halfway to her mouth. Claire had known? Why hadn't she mentioned it? Well, she supposed it wasn't really her business. She had never discussed David with Claire; was too afraid of a giveaway blush if she so much as thought of his name.

'Oh yes, I met his fiancée.'

'She works in Exeter, I theenk,' said Claire. 'Does not visit very often. I sometimes think that he is lonely. The other teachers at the boys' school, they are very old, don't you think? Apart from Monsieur Graystock, *bien sûr*.'

Maggie hadn't met the classics professor, but had heard Claire mention him. She'd spied him from afar at the concert; he was tall, aristocratic and distracted looking, and she hadn't given him much thought. But then, Maggie had never had much thought to spare for the other teachers at Downey Boys.

'So why aren't they married?' she asked.

'*Je sais pas*,' said Claire, shrugging. 'I heard she wanted him to move to the city, but he does not want to go and move Stephen Daedalus . . . it is true,' she said, wrinkling her nose. 'The English and their dogs.'

Maggie would have added something about the French and their mistresses, but didn't feel it was entirely appropriate. But that was interesting about David. Pulled in different directions, just as she was. She instantly dismissed all thought of him from her head. That was pointless, and supremely silly. And she was an engaged woman now, with someone at home who loved her very much.

'We should get changed for supper,' she said. 'I'm sure the girls are going to be *thrilled* to see us again . . .'

'And a hardworking term too,' said Claire. 'I am going to be *slavedriver*. I want those *petites rosbifs* to stop just one time from mangling my beautiful language until it sounds like peedgeons fighting. Do you think it can be possible?'

'Definitely,' said Maggie, as the two friends headed for the stairs.

Fliss was nervous as they pulled into the gravelled forecourt once more. She had promised her parents she'd behave, but was worried about how her teachers would be with her – particularly the hated Miss Adair, who hadn't shown the least bit of sympathy over her ankle. She'd promised faithfully to raise her marks; they could hardly get any lower. She swung her plastered ankle out of the side of the car, and waited for Dad to help her out. She was only limping slightly now, with a stick, and it didn't hurt at all, except when it was itchy. Would the other girls shun her for messing up the Christmas concert?

She needn't have worried. From the moment Alice spotted her from the dormitory window, and ran down with a scream of excitement, Fliss was enveloped in a mass of girls eagerly asking her what it had been like at hospital, asking to sign her plaster, and, mostly, sighing over the romance of fainting and being carried to the san by dashing Mr McDonald, just like Kate Winslet in *Sense and Sensibility*, or Keira Knightley in *Atonement*. Fliss was very peeved she couldn't remember a bit of it.

'Are we really sure she hates that school?' said Fliss's father as they drove away, scarcely noticed by their popular offspring, both completely submerged in chums.

'Let's just see at the end of the year, shall we?' said her mum.

*

At least there was a heavy workload this term, thought Simone, the only person pleased at the prospect. She could bury herself in books and nobody would notice. The fuss about stealing seemed to have died down for now. Maybe those things really had just gone missing after all. She would ignore the accusatory glances, ignore everything except concentrating on work and passing exams. She was going to make her dad so proud. Even prouder than he was already. Remembering her family's love provided a small candle of warmth inside her.

'Yes?' Veronica looked up at the door, as Daniel, the new assessor, knocked and slipped into the office without Pat. She was surprised, yet again, at his youth and wondered why he'd chosen this job.

'Hello,' she said pleasantly. 'Tea?'

'No, thank you,' he said. 'I think Patricia is on her way.'

She nodded. Then they both spoke at the same time.

'So,' she said.

'Well . . .'

They both smiled.

'You go,' he said.

'I was just wondering what brought you into this line of work?' asked Veronica. 'Sorry if that's a personal question.'

'No, not at all,' said Daniel. 'I'm really a teacher, I'm just on secondment.'

'Oh yes? Where do you teach?'

'I teach history in a grammar school in Kent. But this offered some travel, a chance to look at practice in independent schools. See what good ideas we can come away with.'

'That's not always how assessors see it,' said Veronica, smiling wryly.

'It's how I see it,' said Daniel firmly. 'And I was looking

forward to seeing the famous Downey House . . . and meeting you. You've quite a reputation.'

Veronica knew and disliked this, even though it was good for the school.

'It's not about me,' she said. 'It's about the girls.'

Daniel smiled and nodded.

'Sorry I'm late,' said Pat, breezing in without knocking, and not sounding sorry at all. 'Terrible traffic.'

Veronica refrained from commenting on the fact that there was never any traffic on the quiet country road that passed by the school.

'Shall we begin?' she said.

Maggie took a deep breath. All right. So things hadn't gone brilliantly with Middle School 1 last year. But it was time for a new start for all of them. Then she winced. Oh no, she still had to deal with Felicity. She'd had her punishment, but Maggie still had absolutely no doubt that Alice Trebizon-Woods had been involved at some stage, and now she really had to split them up.

'Alice, Felicity,' she said, feeling the eyes of the class on her. It hadn't escaped her notice that Felicity had been lionised for her act of defiance. 'Felicity, I know you paid the price for your little prank at the Christmas concert' – a ripple ran through the room – 'but nonetheless. I don't want you two sitting together any more.'

'But . . .' started Felicity, before remembering crossly that she'd promised her parents she'd behave herself and that that was her new route home.

'Uh-uh,' said Maggie, stopping her. 'I don't want to hear it. I want heads down this term. We have a lot of work to get through, and I want everyone applying themselves. And I mean everyone, including you, do you understand?'

'Yes, miss,' said Fliss in a small voice, making a token attempt to hide the resentment in it. She picked up her books and moved to the only spare seat in the room, inevitably next to Simone, who gave her a half-smile and nothing more.

'Right. Class,' said Maggie. 'We're going to ease into the new year gently with "The Crystal Set". Here, pass copies back.' She felt herself stiffen. Why did she feel like such a martinet with this class? Such a grumpy, chippy drudge?

'Miss!' said Sylvie suddenly, out of the blue. 'Is that an engagement ring?'

Maggie glanced up. She'd forgotten that kids didn't miss a thing, and was still very conscious herself of the new ring on her finger.

'Yes it is, Sylvie,' she said, a half-smile crossing her lips. Their campaign of animosity forgotten, all the girls craned their necks to see it, apart from Fliss and Alice, who were sulking.

'Are you getting married, miss?' Sylvie sounded amazed that someone her age could possibly have met a chap.

'That's what being engaged means, yes, Sylvie.'

'Where are you getting married, miss?'

'What's he like?'

'What is your dress going to be like?'

'Was he that skinny bloke that looked like one of the Arctic Monkeys?'

The questions came from all over the class.

'All right, all right,' said Maggie, trying to hide her pleasure. 'I am marrying my long term boyfriend, who lives in Scotland, and yes, he came to the Christmas concert, which he found quite the eye-opener.'

There was a little bit of laughter at this.

'We aren't marrying for a long time, so we haven't made any decisions about the wedding, and I'll be staying on for the moment. OK? But thank you for your good wishes. Now, heads down please – Simone will you start reading?'

'Just as the stars appear . . .'

Maggie was still conscious of Felicity and Alice gazing daggers at her. But it was a chink, surely.

Term continued to improve. There was more snow on the ground, and it was the season for tough cross-country runs, which most of the girls despised, but it gave them pink cheeks, resistance to bugs and a healthy appetite, so Miss James maintained the practice in the face of the annual onslaught of suggestions for figure skating, trampolining, salsa dancing and the like.

The senior girls were taking their examinations for Oxford and Cambridge and starting to worry about boards, but for those further down the school, worries mostly centred around the sports team trials.

And Maggie found she was feeling a little happier. She enjoyed the teaching more now she was focusing fully on that. OK, so maybe she wouldn't – couldn't – ever be fully accepted here, in a world that was so different from that she knew. But if she and the girls could see past their mutual antipathy, they would find that she could teach them success-fully. Perhaps, she thought, in her gloomier moments, she could be like Miss Starling. Respected, if not adored like Mrs Offili, or even Miss James, however much they complained about her.

Stan didn't manage to get down to see her, but the weight and suspicion had lifted from their conversations; devoid of the jealousy and insecurity Stan had felt before Christmas, and the mistrust she had had, they could chat lightly about their days, without focusing too much on when and whether Maggie was going to leave.

'After all,' Stan had said, 'you'll be wanting a babbie after that. So, it makes sense.'

'I'm only twenty-five,' Maggie protested. 'There's lots of time for all that. Let's put some money by first, then we'll be set up.'

'Are you saying I don't make enough money?'

'No, it's not like that . . .'

So they'd move on to other topics less likely to bring sensitivities out in the other.

'Getting married are we?' June Starling had said, without much in the way of enthusiasm. Maggie wondered if June had ever had a boyfriend. It seemed hard to imagine it; June Starling seemed to have been born forty-five years old. Perhaps, thought Maggie tragically, she'd had someone who'd been killed and it had soured her for romance ever since. Or maybe it was just because she was mean.

'Will you be leaving us, or . . .?'

'Oh no,' said Maggie. 'I'm staying.'

She wondered whether this were true.

Daniel took to taking tea with Veronica every time he came in for an assessment day.

'Is this because you appreciate my company, or because you're digging for dirt you can write up later?' she'd asked him, only half in jest, but he'd put his hands up and apologised and promised to stop coming.

'I didn't mean that,' she'd said. In fact, he was easy company, and certainly more pleasant to spend time with than Pat and Liz. He set out his plans for teaching and changes in it, as well as showing her pictures of his family – he had a pretty teacher wife at home in Kent, two boys and a beautiful baby girl, Eliza, whom he adored and could rarely wait to get back to. Veronica wondered if he was casting about for a job. If he was, she'd have to see what she could do.

Still stung by the memory of the way she'd behaved the previous year, Maggie wasn't consciously staying out of David's way . . . all right, perhaps she was. It was some weeks before she ran into David, down in the village shop as she was picking up, to her shame, some Maltesers (she disliked using the tuck shop, and it was going to be stopped for Lent anyway) and a clutch of gossip magazines. The shop was run by a friendly couple, who sold practically everything and were good at not passing over contraband to the girls. She was putting her change away when she heard a familiar friendly voice behind her ask for six panatellas and some dog treats.

Scooping up her magazines as if they were pornography (which they probably were to him; and how could she expect to teach *Clarissa* to her fifth formers next term if she kept putting off starting it?), she wished she'd put on lipstick as she turned round, determined to seem bright and breezy.

'Hello,' she said, so brightly it sounded to her ears fake and forced.

David looked a bit taken aback. So he should, she thought, crossly. She couldn't possibly have imagined all of it, could she? Mind you, could she? What had they done, really, when you thought about it? Nearly hold hands once? Have him say 'I like you, but . . .'? As the days went by, and the reality – that she was marrying Stan – fell more into place, she wondered if she'd made the whole thing up in a Cornwall/new-job-induced frenzy.

'Oh, hello,' he said. Then, as if he couldn't help it, his irrepressible grin broke out. Her heart skipped, and she told it firmly to stop.

'I wasn't buying cigars.'

She smiled back at him.

'I wasn't buying gossip magazines.'

'You *weren't*?'

'Why are you trying to make me feel guilty? Since when do gossip magazines give you *cancer*?'

'An occasional treat,' said David.

'Me too,' said Maggie. She thought of her stuttered hellos to Miranda at Christmas, his pretty blonde fiancée who was something high up in a shipping company in Portsmouth.

David had been warning her to back off, and she wanted to assure him that she'd got the message.

'Did you have a nice Christmas?' he asked now, leaning down to give Stephen Daedalus a treat. The dog was already licking Maggie's hand, delighted to see her again.

'Great,' said Maggie, pleased at the opportunity to mention it. 'Stan and I are getting married!'

There seemed to be a brief instant before David's grin spread over his face again, as he held the door to let her out before him.

'That's wonderful news!' he said. 'A wedding. What a wonderful thing.'

'Two weddings,' said Maggie. 'If you count yours.'

'Yes,' said David. 'Uh, I hadn't realised you hadn't met Miranda before. She's away a lot.'

'She's great,' said Maggie, determinedly light of tone.

'Yes, she is.'

It was a lovely cold sunny afternoon and Maggie, wrapped up warm in a red beret and scarf, had been planning on walking back to the school. It did seem absurd for them to be heading the same way and not go together.

'Are you heading back?' asked David. Maggie nodded.

'Perhaps,' he said, 'we could enjoy our occasional treats on the way.'

Maggie smiled. 'I'd have thought a pipe was more your style.'

'I did try it. Bit affected,' said David. 'I felt as if I should be keeping lookout for the hound of the Baskervilles.'

'But cigars . . . are you celebrating something?'

David shook his head as they struck out for the cliff path, leaving the pretty pastel village behind them.

'Nope. Except for it being Saturday . . . do you mind?' He took out a book of long matches.

'Not at all,' said Maggie. 'I rather like it actually. My granddad used to smoke the little stubby ones. I missed the smell when he died.'

'Of throat cancer,' said David.

'Old age,' said Maggie. 'He was ninety-three.'

'Excellent. Now, what about your treat?'

'Would you like a Malteser?'

'I'm not sure they go.'

'Oh. Would your dog like one?'

'Definitely not. Stephen Daedalus?'

The dog came flying back in order to chase a stick David threw for him in the air. I do not fancy this man, ordered Maggie to herself, as he unfurled his long body and ran, thin as a reed and looking like an over-excited teenager, with his ridiculous cigar between two fingers. But at least they seemed to be over their awkwardness. In fact, it was as easy as ever to be with him, as he chatted about books he was reading, gave her some pointers on getting in to *Clarissa* and made her laugh telling her about the camp adult pantomime he'd unwittingly taken his nephews to, then spent two hours afterwards trying to explain the double entendres. He is fun, Maggie told herself. Good company. A little peculiar, like Stan said. But fine.

*

Everything went smoothly until the middle of February, when the entire area was hit by a freezing patch. The snow came down full force and made the road impassable for two days until the plough had reached them, something that had caused much hysterical excitement amongst the girls, with the more impressionable genuinely believing they would be reduced to eating corpses and barricading the cellars against wolves. Once this hysteria passed, however, it was business as usual – until Astrid Ulverton's clarinet went missing.

Chapter Twelve

Maggie and June Starling had discussed the missing items before, of course. It was so sporadic and so difficult to prove – teenage girls were notorious for losing anything that wasn't nailed down – and in the end they had decided not to launch into serious further action with either Fliss's watch or Sylvie's earrings. Things did get lost, and as they weren't allowed to search lockers without good reasons for their suspicions, they had merely appealed for the culprit to come forward, without much hope of success.

This was different, however. Everyone in the school knew Astrid was married to her clarinet. It was worth a lot of money, and Astrid rarely let it out of her sight. It slept on her nightstand like a favourite teddy bear and the usually strict rules on instruments in the dorm were occasionally bent for Astrid in those difficult times when inspiration struck and she was trying to get down a new tune – her roommates, Sylvie, Ursula and Zazie, were fairly tolerant on the issue.

But Astrid had left her clarinet on the bed and the door open whilst going for a shower the previous evening. The dorms were just off the common room, with plenty of girls from the first two years popping in and out. It could have been anyone. But one thing was for sure; it hadn't dropped down behind a bed or been mislaid.

Astrid was red-eyed from crying as she stood in front of Miss Starling, Maggie by her side. Veronica had been alerted but didn't want to interfere at this early stage.

'And you've looked everywhere?' said Miss Starling, sternly. 'You can't possibly have lost it?'

'I couldn't have,' said Astrid stoutly. 'I know exactly where I put it. I never leave it alone.'

'What on earth would someone want with a clarinet?' wondered Maggie. 'It's not as if they can play it without giving themselves away.'

'It's not about that,' said Miss Starling. 'It's about power, and upsetting people. Do you have any enemies, Astrid?'

Astrid looked as if she was going to burst into tears again.

'I don't *think* so,' she said. In fact it was true; nearly everyone liked Astrid. Her talent was too natural and extraordinary to attract jealousy.

'We're going to have to interview them all,' said Miss Starling after she'd been dismissed. 'Scare the heebie-jeebies out of them. Threaten the police. We should be able to see after that . . . I hope. I hate stealing,' she said, thumping the desk to emphasise her point. 'Of all the shady, underhand, sly things to do, it's the worst. I hate to think of a Downey's girl even being capable of it.'

Maggie nodded, seeing the teacher's dedication to the school. 'Shall we get just the Plantagenet girls, or do we want Wessex, Tudor and York as well?'

'Anyone who could have been through that common room,' said Miss Starling. 'So just the locals, I suppose. First years first, they're by far the most likely. Let me see Felicity Prosser too, and that other girl who lost something.'

Maggie nodded, and went off to tell the year-group, with sinking heart.

*

Now the novelty of her being back and her injury had worn off, and since she couldn't join in the sports or walks or drama, Felicity was bored. And she was having to apply herself to being good, which was, as Alice kept pointing out, much duller than before. So when the investigation was announced, she was quite excited; partly because something different was happening and, because of her watch, she didn't think she was going to fall under suspicion. It was quite interesting to see trouble when she wasn't allowed to be part of it any more. Staying on the right side of Miss Adair had been tiresome.

The girls were sent in one by one to face the inquisition. Miss Starling favoured long silences that the girls could then fill, hopefully in an incriminating fashion. Even the most innocent of girls would find their conscience pricking, wondering, if only for a split second, if perhaps they *could* have done it in a moment of madness. Simone was trembling with fear as she entered.

'Hello,' said Miss Starling sternly. Maggie had briefed her that Simone was a likely candidate – she'd been in the vicinity of each incident and had good reason to despise the classmates who'd done so little to welcome her, even oblivious Astrid. As she did so, Maggie felt a quick stab of guilt that she had failed in her pastoral role towards Simone, who seemed more pasty and miserable than ever. They'd had a few late-night tea and reading sessions, but Maggie had never quite found the words to get Simone to open up to her, and it had always been easier to chat about books than about how she was actually feeling. Now, seeing the miserable girl in front of her, she felt more of a misfit in this school than ever – she couldn't get on with the posh kids, but couldn't help the normal ones.

'Now you understand that we are talking to everyone?' Maggie began tentatively. Simone nodded, not trusting her voice. She had tried to work out what would be the best way to behave so that they realised she was innocent, but she didn't know how. It was like when she was being teased by Estelle Grant. It didn't matter what she said, whether she answered 'yes' or 'no' to the question 'are you a retard?'. They were going to tease her and taunt her regardless, and talking just made everything much worse. The only way she'd found to get through those sessions was to act like a tortoise: retreat entirely into herself and try and wait it out until everyone left her alone.

'Did you take Astrid Ulverton's clarinet?' said Miss Starling, peremptorily.

Simone shook her head, still staring at her lap.

'Speak up child,' said Miss Starling. 'Did you take it, yes or no?'

Simone wasn't going to get the words out and didn't even try; she shook her head again, tears forming at the corner of her eyes.

'It's all right,' said Maggie, playing good cop. 'Simone, if you have something to tell us, it's always best to get it off your conscience.'

There was a long silence. Simone simply couldn't speak. Miss Starling looked at Maggie over the top of her spectacles.

'You can go for now,' she said eventually to Simone, who scurried out.

'Well, I don't like the look of that,' she said to Maggie when Simone had gone.

'She's horribly shy,' said Maggie, looking worried. 'I thought she might be improving, but ... it's taking her longer to settle in here than I thought.'

Miss Starling shot her a sharp look. 'Yes, it can take people a while to settle in,' she said, leaving Maggie wondering exactly who she was talking about. 'Well, anyway, if she's stealing she won't have to worry about being here for much longer. Now who's next?'

'Alice Trebizon-Woods.'

Miss Starling sniffed. 'She'd tell you black was white, that one, and not bat an eye.'

Maggie privately agreed, but didn't want to mark her down in front of Miss Starling, and certainly Alice, with her large brown eyes and butter-wouldn't-melt manner made a very convincing job of knowing nothing about the thefts.

'I feel so bad for Astrid,' she said sincerely. 'That clarinet is her life.'

Maggie wondered why, despite the fact that she agreed with Alice, she still found her manner so irritating.

'We all do, Alice,' she said. 'That'll be all.'

There was nothing for it. Veronica detested these situations, but there was no way to get to the bottom of things otherwise. She would have to order a search, and if that didn't work they'd have to consider getting the police in. Parents would be furious if they didn't think absolutely everything possible was being done. They didn't encourage pupils to bring expensive items to school, but it was impossible to stop them, and most of the girls had laptops and mobiles. With a heavy heart, she gave Miss Starling the word. It was more work for the teachers too, and stress as they tried to tell who amongst their girls was the bad apple. She hoped fervently that it wasn't Simone, the scholarship girl, but the omens didn't look good. Which was a shame; she looked set to do very well in all her courses, with a particularly excellent showing in maths and physics; exactly the kind of girl who ended up a credit to the school.

Wednesday afternoon was put aside for the search. This

was normally a time for school sport, and the fact that it was being set aside annoyed Miss James, who disliked being regarded as a second-class subject. When the girls found out, however – Miss Starling and Maggie had to pounce on the dorms shortly after making the announcement at lunch, obviously requiring an element of surprise – they didn't, on the whole, mind. They were tired of chilly lacrosse, the dreaded cross-country runs, and changing rooms that never seemed to heat up properly.

It was a terribly freezing day; unseasonably cold even for February, with icy winds blowing down from Siberia; the type of wind that found its way inside your clothes, that blew icy swirls of sleet around you and made you lean into it as you walked.

The girls were to go and sit on their beds as the search took place. Every girl's locker and wardrobe was to be taken apart; their beds and bags thoroughly rummaged through.

It was an unhappy affair; Maggie felt like a jailer, and the girls all felt under suspicion, which they were. One by one the dorms were completed until, with heavy heart, Maggie entered Simone and Fliss's room. She was crossing names off a list and started nearest the window. Alice's clothes were much more neatly folded than her own, Maggie found herself thinking. Next was Fliss, who gave Maggie her usual pout, but none of her usual cheek.

'If you can find my watch I'd be very grateful,' she said, and Maggie nodded silently.

'We're doing everything we can,' she said. There had been no point in searching the bed of sad-eyed Astrid, but for the sake of propriety they'd had to do it anyway.

Finally they came to Simone's. She barely looked up as Miss Starling bent down and looked in her bedside cabinet.

There were lots of books, and chocolate wrappers, which Miss Starling handled with some distaste.

'You know the rules on eating in the dorm?' she asked sternly. Simone nodded.

'It's dirty and it's dangerous,' she said. 'You could be encouraging rats, anything.' The other girls in the dorm looked slightly nauseated. It must be secret eating still, thought Maggie. Once again she regretted bitterly being so caught up in shows, and Stan, and David, and getting along at the new school, that she'd left behind the one pupil who really really needed someone. She had failed, it seemed, in so many ways. One student injuring herself, another . . .

Her regret deepened even further a minute later as Miss Starling, her hand under Simone's bed, made a gesture of surprise, then pulled out, one by one, Astrid's clarinet, Fliss's watch and Sylvie's earrings.

There was silence in the room.

'Felicity,' said Miss Starling. 'Is this yours?'

'My watch!' shouted Felicity in delight, hobbling over. 'Thank God. I hadn't told my mum yet.'

She frowned, looking at Simone, whose mouth was hanging open. 'Uh, maybe it could have fallen under the bed by mistake?'

'Unlikely,' said Miss Starling, in a tone as cold as the weather. 'Someone get Astrid Ulverton and Sylvie Brown for me, please, would you?'

She made the girls identify their objects, which they did, quietly, unable to look Simone in the eye, and then sent them on their way.

'Simone,' she said to the girl, who was sitting there, red in the face. 'Could you come down to my office please?'

Numbly, Simone followed the two teachers out of the

door. They walked slightly ahead, glancing at each other, then admonished her to sit and wait whilst they went inside.

'I'll just call Veronica,' said June Starling when they got to her office.

'Yes,' said Maggie. 'Oh, it's such a shame. It really is. I feel so responsible. If I'd got more involved with her earlier . . .'

June regarded her over the tops of her spectacles. 'I heard you let her come and visit you in the evenings and borrow your books.'

Maggie twisted uncomfortably. 'Oh, that was nothing. I should have talked to her more. It's my fault. I should have—'

'I suspect it was rather more than nothing to Simone. It was kind. Unfortunately,' she continued, shuffling her papers, 'in some cases, kindness is not enough.'

She picked up the phone to call Veronica, who had been anticipating the call all morning and suggested with a heavy heart they come and see her. She was disappointed in her young teacher. She'd been given special responsibility to keep an eye on their new pupil, and clearly hadn't done so.

As they left the office to cross the great hall, however, Maggie noticed immediately what took June Starling a second or two to process. Simone had gone.

At first, they only searched around the corridors, not wanting to sound the alarm or to get anyone. But it became clear, very quickly, that Simone was not in the building, and no one had seen her.

'I'll call the police,' said Miss Starling.

'I'll go after her,' said Maggie immediately. 'She must have run out. It's perishing out there, it's below freezing. She doesn't have a coat or anything.'

June nodded. 'Take Harold.' She meant the head care-taker. 'And make sure you wrap up too.'

'I've got my phone,' said Maggie. 'Call me immediately.'

Miss Starling got on the telephone to make the arrange-ments as Maggie dashed to her room to find her coat. Simone couldn't have got far, she wasn't sporty and the weather was cruel. And Maggie knew the crags quite well now. She also grabbed Simone's coat from her dorm, ignoring the concerned faces of the girls inside, so that the girl would have something warm to put on when they caught up with her.

Harold joined her at the doors, looking worriedly at the sky. It was cold as all hell out there, and the clouds were so low it felt as if it was getting dark already, although it was just past three o'clock.

'Reckon more snow's coming, miss.'

'I'm sure we'll find her in no time,' said Maggie, hurrying ahead, and hoping that was true.

Simone was nowhere to be seen around the road, and the coastal path seemed the obvious route to follow.

Once on top of the cliffs, the full force of the wind hit them in the face. Visibility was decreasing all the time, with the first light flakes dusting them from above. For the first time Maggie felt a sense of genuine fear. Someone could seriously get into trouble out here. She moved over to the cliff's edge and peered over. Surely she couldn't . . . she wouldn't have . . . she was such a careful girl, surely she wouldn't do anything so madly impulsive?

Once again she scanned the horizon. There was no sign of another living soul . . . except one. A dark figure heading towards her. At first Maggie's heart leapt, but then she realised that it was a man's outline, not a teenage girl's. Her heart rose slightly, however, when she realised it was David, rain or shine, out walking Stephen Daedalus. She waved her arms so he would see her through the rapidly thickening snow and walked towards him.

'I thought I would be the only person mad enough to be out on a day like today,' said David. 'Of course it's my dog that's mad, not me . . . what's the matter?' he said, as he saw her face.

Rapidly Maggie explained. David's face grew worried.

'She's out without a coat? In this?'

'Well, there are people searching the school, but she does-n't seem to be there.'

Harold had made it as far as the headland now, and was turning back, shaking his head.

'I'll call in the teachers from our school, co-ordinate a wider search,' said David.

'The police are on their way,' said Maggie. 'Is there time?'

It was a proper blizzard now. The temperature seemed to have dropped even further. David sighed as they crossed over the cliff path, checking through the gorse on the other side.

'SIMONE!' they yelled periodically, though their voices were swept away on the howling wind, which seemed to rip the very breath out of them. 'SIMONE!!!!'

'I can't see any sign of her on the beach,' said Harold, returning to them. Maggie felt her fingers grow cold in her pocket. 'Has someone headed for the village?'

Maggie checked her phone. There was a text message from the school. No one had seen her in the village, and the police were on their way with their dogs.

'Dogs!' she exclaimed excitedly. Her fingers had felt numb as she'd tried to read the text, and she wanted desperately to plunge them back into her pockets.

'What?' said David. 'Oh, what do you mean?'

'Can Stephen Daedalus do tracking? I just remembered, I've got Simone's jacket in my pocket. Could he smell it and find her?'

David looked excited. 'I don't know, but it's worth a shot.'

He bent down. 'Now. Stephen Daedalus. I have a very important job for you.' He took the coat from Maggie's out-stretched arm. 'Can you find her? Can you, boy?'

Stephen Daedalus wagged his tail and looked at them expectantly.

'Sniff this! And go find her! You know you can do it! Good boy!'

The dog sniffed excitedly, then looked up at them again, as if to say, that was nice, but what's the next game?

'Go find her,' shouted David. 'Come on! You can do it!'

Stephen Daedalus took one more sniff of the jacket.

'It's not going to work,' said Maggie, who was feeling that standing still was a terrible idea, for Simone, and for them in this unholy weather. 'Come on, let's just keep going.'

'Hang on,' said David. He slowly drew the coat away and handed it back to Maggie. Then he stood up.

'On you go,' he said. 'On you go, good dog.'

And suddenly Stephen Daedalus sat upright, sniffing the air. Then he turned tail and plunged into the undergrowth.

Maggie and David looked at one another.

'Shall we follow him?'

'His father was a hunting dog,' said David. 'And do you have any better ideas?'

Harold had already set off in swift pursuit.

Later, when she looked back, Maggie couldn't remember how long they'd spent following the dog through the moors. All the world had become white and cold, with the sky and the ground hardly demarcated at all.

Harold had a torch, their only source of light as the darkness swept across the crags like a wave. Perhaps it wasn't even that long, but it felt like days following the trail, as David took her hand and helped her up difficult inclines, or across iced-over streams. They were further and further away from the school, its warm lights mere dots on the horizon; ahead was the Irish Sea and little else.

None of them dared to say what they thought might be true; that the dog had no idea where it was and could render them as lost as Simone. Maggie tried to check her phone – fumbling with her gloves and dropping it on the ground – but they'd gone out of range of a signal, so they had no way of knowing whether she'd been found or not. There was no sign of the police.

Finally, as the night was becoming truly black, with no moon visible behind the clouds to help light their way, and all of them terribly puffed from rushing after the dog, Stephen Daedalus stopped short of a copse, and started to bark loudly, the noise startling all three of the search party.

Maggie, who had felt her brain go dull in the everlasting white-out and was full of horrible fears she couldn't express, suddenly got an adrenalin rush of energy as they all hurried forward.

Under the overhang, barely protected from the howling wind and snow, curled up in a ball and shivering uncontrollably, only her thin school shirt protecting her from the howling gale, was Simone.

'Good dog! Good dog!' David was shouting in a completely hoarse voice as he launched himself forward, first with Simone's coat, then his own. Maggie and David sat on either side of the girl, all of them huddling together for warmth as Harold, who knew the moors so well, dashed back for help. Even Stephen Daedalus came up and sat across them all, and his panting warmth was extremely welcome; Maggie made sure Simone's hands, frozen into claws, sank into his thick fur.

'Leave me alone. Leave me alone,' was all she was saying, as she rocked back and forward.

'Don't go to sleep,' David was telling her. 'Don't go to sleep, Simone. Stay awake. We'll sort all of this out.'

Maggie was colder than she'd ever been in her life, but took some comfort from the three of them huddling together.

'Should we try and get moving?' she said to David, who looked unsure.

'I think we should heat her up first before we start moving,' he said. Maggie agreed, remembering that she'd read somewhere that they should take off their clothes to provide body heat, and reflecting dimly through her frozen brain that this was the kind of thing she'd ideally once have liked to do with David without a) Simone, b) a howling storm or c) Stephen Daedalus. This meandering train of thought, however, was interrupted by a huge noise that rose above the storm, as a floodlight bathed the area and the copse; the snowflakes ploughing through the light beam.

'We have you on our heat sensor,' came a voice over the loudhailer. 'Please stay where you are.'

Stephen Daedalus quivered and buried his nose in David's knees. But David and Maggie's hearts leapt: Harold must have got back in time after all. Because what they could hear was a helicopter.

Chapter Thirteen

After being briefly checked over at the hospital and declared fine, both Maggie and David were free to return to the school. From the corridor, watching David be charming to the nurses as he buttoned up his clean blue shirt, Maggie called Stan on her mobile, even though she knew it was forbidden.

'WHAT?'

Maggie squeezed her eyes tight shut. She didn't want to have to explain it again.

'What do you mean you lost one in the snow?'

'It wasn't quite like that,' she implored. 'And everyone's fine now. It'll be OK.'

'It'll be OK when you drive to Exeter Airport and catch the next flight home to Glasgow.'

'I can't, Stan. I have to stay and face the music. Simone was my responsibility. And I failed her.'

'That bloody school failed you!' said Stan. 'They let the pupils treat you like dirt, and now they blame you for some maniac running away!'

'It's not like that,' said Maggie. 'Honestly, Stan.'

She caught David out of the corner of her eye looking at her enquiringly, as if asking if everything was all right. She tried to make a reassuring expression at him.

'I have to go,' she said.

Stan let out an exasperated sigh. 'So, I don't know when I'm seeing you, then, is that right? You've half died on a mountain but, you know, the *school* is more important.'

'It's my job,' said Maggie simply, and hung up the phone. She had a sneaking suspicion Stan was right. Maybe she should just go home. She was probably going to get sent home anyway, after this fiasco. But Stan couldn't, didn't understand . . .

'Are you all right?' said David, coming out of the treatment room. Maggie bit her lip in case she betrayed her feelings.

'The kids get under your skin, don't they? Can you imagine what having your own would be like?'

Once again she was grateful to him for striking the right note, even as she knew she had to face the music alone.

'Terrifying,' she said, and they went outside into the freezing night, where Harold was waiting for them, in the battered old Land Rover that even a snow storm could scarcely stop.

Simone was being kept in overnight as a precautionary measure. After being wrapped in silver blankets, she'd been heated up in an extremely hot bath, but so far there were no signs of hypothermia or frostbite; just a touch of exposure. The doctor did say, however, that it was lucky they'd found her when they did.

Maggie had offered to stay with her, but no one was allowed to stay overnight. Matron would be over first thing to collect her. Her parents would be driving down through the night from London.

It was well after ten by the time Harold drove them up the familiar driveway; but every light in the school was burning, and the girls were outlined at the windows.

Veronica was standing in the great hall, where the fire had been lit – outside of Christmas, an unheard of concession. An exhausted Maggie entered, head bowed, ready to take whatever Veronica could throw at her – could it be as bad as dismissal, she wondered, to lose a vulnerable pupil? Stan would be seeing her sooner than he thought. And the girls here would hardly miss her, after all.

So Maggie wasn't expecting the round of applause that rose up from the line of girls waiting on the great stairs.

'What?' she said, looking round. David, standing just behind her, smiled to himself.

Miss Starling stepped forward. 'It was very brave and clever of you to go out as you did, and to think of using Stephen Daedalus. No one could have predicted that Simone would bolt as she did.'

Maggie felt her cheeks flare. Praise from Miss Starling was not something she was used to.

'I'm so sorry the situation got so out of hand,' she said. 'It's my fault. I should have realised she was so unhappy she was stealing . . .'

Veronica stepped forward too, shaking her head. 'No, it wasn't. Simone wasn't the culprit at all.'

Maggie's eyebrows shot up.

'It was Imogen Fairlie. She shared a dorm with Simone, Felicity Prosser and Alice Trebizon-Woods. She'd felt ignored and was trying to be the centre of attention, then when the searches started, lost her nerve and panicked. We've spoken to her parents. This isn't the first time, apparently. They're going to take her home.'

'Oh,' said Maggie, her heart suddenly going out to silent, no-trouble Imogen. What a dreadful cry for help – another one she seemed to have missed completely. 'Does she have to . . .?'

'Yes,' said Veronica, firmly. 'There are some things I simply can't tolerate in a Downey girl. Making a bid for attention is one thing. Cowardly letting another girl take the blame is something else altogether.'

Veronica noticed David hanging back.

'And thank you,' she said directly to him. 'From all of us.'

David looked embarrassed. 'It wasn't me,' he said. 'It was Stephen Daedalus. And Maggie, of course.'

'We were all very lucky you were there,' said Veronica simply. 'Now, please, both of you, come to my study. I think we all need a night cap.'

She turned round to the girls on the stairs.

'I certainly know I owe Simone Pribetich an apology. Please look in your consciences and see if you think you do too. And now, bed, everyone! It's an ordinary day tomorrow and I don't want to hear another sound out of any of you.'

For once, though, Dr Deveral's word was not taken as law, as the girls dispersed, chattering excitedly like birds.

Maggie had a long hot bath, accompanied by some of Veronica's excellent whisky, and slept in late the next morning, not even hearing the bell. Ordered by Miss Starling, the catering staff had made a large cooked breakfast for everyone. Maggie went to the san at eleven.

Simone was sitting there alone, without her parents, who had got trapped in the snow and had to spend the night in Devon.

'Simone,' said Maggie, 'I'm so sorry all this happened to you. But why couldn't you just tell us it wasn't you? I was there, wasn't I?'

Simone looked down. 'Nobody believed me. Everyone thought it was me.'

'Well, everyone was wrong,' said Maggie. 'Me included.'

'I'd have thought you might have understood,' said Simone. Maggie knew what she meant. They came from the same world. They knew what it was like out there.

'I know,' she said, feeling ashamed. 'I should have. I'm sorry.'

Simone shrugged.

'Do you want to come to class? I know the girls would like to see you.'

Simone looked white. 'Do you think?'

Maggie nodded. 'Definitely. They're not all bad, you know.'

Simone gave a half-smile.

'Come on,' said Maggie. 'I think it would do you good. Even if your parents do want to take you home.'

Simone thought about it for a moment, then consented.

Miss Starling was letting the Plantagenet girls watch a video of *Love's Labours Lost*. She hated letting the girls watch DVDs, thought it morally corrupting, but you couldn't swim against the tide for ever, and she had her own class to teach.

When Maggie opened the door, however, all thoughts of the video were gone. The girls stared at Simone, who instantly wondered if she'd made a mistake and that this was a really bad idea. So did Maggie. Acceptance from other children was an impossible thing to force. Maybe her running away made her even weirder in their eyes. Plus, of course, they'd have to get over their distaste for her to even say anything.

She paused the video, and for a time everyone was quiet. Then, suddenly, little Fliss Prosser, her supposedly worst pupil, stood up.

'Uhm,' she said, looking at a loss for words for once. 'I just wanted to say. And I don't speak for everyone or anything, but, err. Simone. I'm really really sorry I thought you were stealing. It was a mistake, and I'm dead ashamed. Right.'

And she sat down again, cheeks pink. Maggie was impressed. She didn't think Fliss had it in her.

Then Astrid stood up too.

'I'm sorry,' she said. 'I should have known you wouldn't take my clarinet.'

All the other girls mumbled apologies in agreement after that, and Sylvie stood up and asked Simone to tell them what it was like being lost in the snow. Maggie looked at Simone and asked if she would tell the story, and then, the most surprising thing happened. To Maggie's complete astonishment, at first falteringly, but then with more of the confidence that she'd shown at the Christmas concert, and the humour she'd suspected from their meetings, Simone began to tell the whole story: about how she couldn't decide whether to bolt or hide when she was waiting outside Dr Deveral's office; how she'd run and really quickly realised she had no idea where she was because she'd missed so many of the cross-country runs; how she'd thought Stephen Daedalus was a wolf come to eat her, and the helicopter sounded like an alien spaceship, which was when she really did think she'd died and that the scientologists were right after all.

Listening to this Maggie realised something with amazement; Simone was funny. Hearing the girls crack up, and her good comic timing and pauses, the entire class saw a new side to the previously timid girl. At the end of her account, when she said precisely what Maggie had been thinking – that she was slightly hoping Mr McDonald would go bare-chested with her so that at least she would know what it was like before she died, Maggie was laughing too, and there was a large spontaneous round of applause as

Simone took her seat back next to Fliss, who even put her arm round her and gave her a squeeze. 'Brilliant,' she said audibly. 'Much better than my ankle.'

'I think so,' said Simone. 'Though the next person is really going to have to cut off a leg or something, to get Mr McDonald's attention.' The class cracked up again, except for Alice, who donated a rather wan smile. She knew, more than anyone, that she owed Simone an apology, but was finding it rather hard to choke the words out.

'OK, OK everyone, settle down,' said Maggie, but she found it hard to hide her delight. More than just Simone, she could feel a mood in the class; a relaxing; a genuine sense that they were all working together, were all on the same side.

'And more of *Love's Labours Lost* later; I think we'll take a quick look at a poem more germane to our current situations – quickly please, Fliss and Simone, could you turn to page 271 in *Poetry Please*, and start reading "Stopping by Woods on a Snowy Evening".'

And without hesitation or fuss, thirteen girls immediately did so.

Amazingly, Simone's parents, once they'd got over the terrible shock, were persuaded (almost entirely by Simone herself) that the whole thing had been a very minor, and not at all dangerous misunderstanding. Veronica, mindful of the school's reputation, and the possibility of their suing, did not discourage them from this apprehension.

It may have helped that their first view of Simone, as she came downstairs, was of her surrounded by other girls, arm in arm with Felicity, both of them being interrogated for more details of their run-ins with Mr McDonald. Simone, carrying her bag, said something and everyone laughed. Mrs

Pribetich looked on in pride. This was exactly how she'd always imagined Simone being: happy, pleased, surrounded by other, nice, girls. She wouldn't, she reflected, have wanted to take Simone home now if she'd had a leg gnawed off by the school's own timber wolf. Simone and her father might think she didn't have a clue as to what was going through her beloved daughter's head, but she certainly did, and had been equally certain that her instinct was the correct one. Which didn't stop her screeching, 'FETITZA' over the tops of everyone's heads.

Suddenly, though, Felicity thought, Simone's mum didn't look so weird. She looked just more colourful; a bit exotic. Maybe even a bit more fun than her own stodgy parents. She swallowed this thought at once; it was disloyal.

Simone didn't care and went straight up to her parents and gave them a huge hug.

'I'm so pleased to see you,' she said.

'And you,' said her father, gruffly. 'What happened to you? Are you all right?'

'I'm fine,' said Simone. In fact, she looked better than fine. She looked happy. There was a rosiness to her cheeks and a bit of a sparkle in her eye, for the first time in a long time.

'We were so worried, *fetitza*,' said her mother. 'Even Joel was upset.'

'Where is he?'

'He wanted to go with his friends to some warcraft thing,' said her father, who had even less idea about Joel's hobbies than she did.

Simone had special dispensation for a sick day, but as she wasn't feeling particularly sick – the lucky effects of being fourteen, Matron had said, exhorting her to watch her chest and not go swimming – she went into Truro with her mum and dad, and they bought her a new pair of jeans at Gap and

215

took her to Pizza Express for lunch. Simone had rarely been happier.

And even after her parents returned to London, and the big thaw finally arrived, flooding the games fields in the far corner of the school grounds, and turning every trip outside into a muddy morass, things were still looking up. Both Fliss and Simone were signed off games for the foreseeable future and were spending PE sitting on the sidelines, sewing up netball vests, which was horribly dull, but gave them quite a lot of time to chat.

Fliss, to her amazement, was discovering that Simone, the kind of person she'd never have looked at twice for having as a friend, was actually funny, kind, and really good to spend time with. All the time Fliss had had her down as a shy waste of space, she was, whilst shy, using the time to observe people and places around the school and was, in her own way, every bit as cheeky as Alice. Sitting together in English also helped, and soon they were sharing homework, as Fliss had so far to make up her marks after her disastrous first term.

Alice didn't like the new situation at all. In fact, she hated it. It was bad enough being one of three. Being one of three to a big fat boufer was just stupid. Plus, she missed the old Fliss, whom she could coax into bad behaviour. The new one was a total goody-goody. She hadn't forgotten about the trick she'd promised to play. She was just going to have to make it pretty darn spectacular. That should get the focus back in its rightful place.

Stan seemed far more worried than Simone's parents, which was touching in a way, but also slightly irritating to Maggie, who was still on a high from being treated as a heroine, rather than the disciplinary she'd expected. Stan took the tortuously long train down the next weekend.

'What for?' asked Maggie, as she went to pick him up, the tip of her nose pink – the only relic from her expedition.

'What do you mean? You could have been killed. I want to have a word with that headmistress of yours.'

'It wasn't her fault,' said Maggie. 'Simone unpredictably ran out, then I ran out. Anyway, everything ended up fine.'

'Yes, by luck,' said Stan. 'And of course that poncey English teacher was involved.'

'And we're lucky he was there,' said Maggie. 'Come on. I've got two free days and I don't even want to look at marking. Shall we go and visit a tin mine?'

They did so, but it wasn't an entirely comfortable experience, even though they did hold hands. Finally, they arrived, slightly chilled from the still-frosty air, in a local tea room with steam rising onto the floral-curtained windows.

'This is the best bit of sightseeing,' said Maggie. 'Shall we have scones?'

Stan sat down. 'Thing is, Maggie, I've been thinking.'

'Yes?' said Maggie, looking round for the waitress.

'I know we were talking about you staying here for another year maybe, for your career, before you come home?'

'Yes?' said Maggie, uncertainly. Two lower sixth formers, on a weekend pass, had arrived just behind them – Carla's tea shop was very popular. They had sat down self-consciously, still trying to look nonchalant in the outside world, but Maggie could tell they were craning their necks desperately to try and overhear Miss Adair and her fiancé.

'Well, after everything that's happened . . . Please. I'm sick of asking. But won't you think about coming home? Nobody would blame you for leaving now.'

'They'd think I was a coward,' said Maggie, ordering tea and two rounds of scones with jam and tea, hoping they could keep this light.

'You're obviously not a coward,' said Stan. 'You should be getting some sort of award. Anyway. If you came home, you could find a job locally and we could think about buying a new place to live. You know, before the wedding.'

Maggie hated feeling so torn. Of course she wanted to go home with Stan one day; he was her partner, wasn't he? Her other half? She watched him as he piled jam on, ignoring the butter and cream as semi-nutritional by-products. At least she'd remembered not to get the raisin scones.

'But,' she said, then stopped and lowered her voice. 'You know.' And as she said the words, she knew they were the truth. 'I love this job, Stan.'

There was a long pause after that, as Maggie reflected on it.

'More than you love me?' said Stan finally, stirring sugar into his tea and not looking at her.

'Of course not! We've been through this! But I made a commitment and want to follow it through; why is that so hard to understand?'

Stan stared at her. 'Because we're getting married and I don't want you at the bloody dog-end of the country, getting half-frozen to death. Why is that so hard for you to understand?'

Suddenly, the atmosphere between them, which since the New Year had been so joyous and exciting, seemed to turn sour. It felt, on this issue at least, as if there was nothing more to be said. They seemed to be at something of an impasse. They ate their scones and drank their tea in silence, as quickly as possible. Maggie was acutely aware of being watched by the girls, no doubt vowing they would never be in one of those couples that sit silently in restaurants. Well, thought Maggie mutinously. They could see how they liked it when they got there.

'Shall we go?' she said, as soon as she'd swallowed her last mouthful. Stan merely nodded, but as they left, reached out to take her hand in a conciliatory fashion. She took it. They were friends again, but no closer to a resolution.

As they trudged up the wet lane, she heard a commotion from the local meadow. Glancing up, she saw David and his fiancée. They were throwing a frisbee for Stephen Daedalus, and David was laughing his head off. The weak winter sunlight reflected off Miranda's blonde head.

That's what I want, Maggie found herself reflecting wistfully. When was the last time Stan and I just had a really good laugh?

'Gaw, they must be proper freezing,' said Stan, who of course had refused to wear a scarf or a hat. 'Nutters.'

Just as he said this David caught her eye and waved. Both of them came over, leaning across the ancient stone wall that divided the field from the old cart track road.

'Hello hello,' he said cheerily. 'How are you, Stan? The heroine's consort.'

'Hardly,' said Maggie, rolling her eyes, and giving Stephen Daedalus a quick rub.

'It's amazing what you guys did,' said Miranda, widening her eyes. 'I couldn't believe it when I heard. It was on the radio and everything.'

'Yes, you can imagine how thrilled the head is about that,' said Maggie. '*Not* very. It was all Stephen Daedalus anyway.'

'How's our young Simone?' asked David.

'Oh, she's good. Between her and Felicity Prosser, they're having quite the time being the ones who got most snuggle-up rescue-time with you,' said Maggie, realising the light tone she'd meant to bring to the comment sounded a bit silly when she tried it out loud.

'Christ,' said David. 'Back to the boys for me. Or does that sound even worse?'

'It does,' said Maggie grinning, and grateful to be rescued.

'Darling, let's go in, I'm freezing,' said Miranda testily.

'Yeah,' grunted Stan. Maggie had rather been enjoying a little sunlight, however pathetic, and David looked disappointed, but immediately deferred to Miranda's wishes.

'Absolutely. Fancy scones in the village?' he asked the whole group. Maggie found herself full of regret that they had to say no, they'd just had some, and it was all she could do not to turn her head as they waltzed off towards the village, David pontificating on something as usual.

'He's a right weirdo,' said Stan as they went on. 'Can't shut up.'

'Some people are just like that though,' said Maggie, as they came to their hotel, feeling thankful that Stan had never had a suspicious nature. 'They can't help it.'

'Can't bloody put a sock in it, more like,' growled Stan. 'What's wrong with a bit of peace and quiet anyway? Won't want to hear much from you when we're married.'

'You're joking.'

He took her in his arms. 'Course I'm joking, you dimwit. Come here.'

And his kisses tasted good, of tea, and jam. But still, nothing was decided.

Chapter Fourteen

Easter was shaping up to be a much quieter term, thought Veronica, then she admonished herself firmly for thinking so: she'd made that mistake before. She looked with some pleasure at the daffodils ranging over the hills. That was spring down here; every single day something new burst into life, and the landscape changed all over again. Not at all like the dark grimy northern city where she'd grown up. She was reflecting on this when there was a knock on the door again. It would be the assessment team. They were finishing up. Liz was back, after her three months off for stress, and this would be their final session before they went to write up their report.

She hoped it would be a good one. Daniel had seemed much more sympathetic to her aims . . . In fact, she was surprised to see, Daniel was standing at the door on his own, Miss Prenderghast smiling apologetically behind him – she definitely had a soft spot for the young man.

'I thought you weren't due for another twenty minutes,' said Veronica, indicating the pile of applications she'd been working through. They were always over-subscribed, but this year their over-subscriptions seemed a little down. She'd have to go through the figures properly with Evelyn.

'No,' said Daniel. He looked nervous, as ill at ease as he

had done the first time he'd arrived, now over three months ago. 'I wondered if I could have a word about something?'

'Of course,' she said, stepping back and welcoming him in. Perhaps he was going to finally ask her about a job. She'd be delighted; as always she was looking for good teachers, and despite the crush factor, it was good for the girls to have some men in the profession. Stopped them going into a frenzy when they hit university, and John Bart, the fiftyish physics teacher, didn't really cut it, with his head in the clouds the whole time.

'Can we sit down?' he said.

'Of course. Would you like tea?'

Daniel shook his head, although his throat was very dry. He fingered the papers in his lap. 'I just want to ask you something,' he said.

Veronica looked up, alerted by his tone of voice. 'Yes?' she said, quite briskly.

'Was your name ... was your name originally Vera Makepiece?'

Something happened to Veronica then. It was as if her entire self shifted a little. Her eyes went wide and she found that, despite years of rigid self-control, she seemed to have lost the ability to control her expression. She went to stand up, then sat down again ... it was most peculiar; she, who always knew what to do, suddenly didn't know quite what to do.

Nobody knew this. Not Jane, not Evelyn. Nobody. She hadn't been Vera Makepiece for over thirty years.

'What do you mean?' she asked, realising too late that a giveaway quaver was instantly noticeable in her voice.

'Were you born Vera Makepiece?' Daniel asked again. His voice had a tremor in it, just like her own.

Daniel looked at her with his large, grey, serious eyes, so

like her own. And somehow, instantly, she just knew. She knew. All the little chats; all the early morning cups of tea. They were all for a reason. He was gathering clues about her; trying to figure her out.

She fell back in her chair, completely unable to speak. Daniel's face worked, and he looked like he was going to lose control completely.

'Who ... who are you?' Veronica asked finally, after Daniel had managed, with a trembling hand, to pour her out a glass of water from the crystal carafe, refilled each morning, that sat on her desk.

There was a long silence, then Daniel let out a great long sigh, as if answering this question was going to take a huge load off his mind. He himself couldn't believe it. Several nights over the last few months he'd woken up bathed in sweat after dreaming of this moment; or hadn't been able to sleep at all, tossing and turning as Penny slept peacefully beside him, until the baby woke them both. He'd had a rough idea for many years but had never found the courage to do something about it before – but when the secondment place had come up, he'd felt it was meant to be. Now, sitting here, in front of ... her ... he wasn't so sure.

'I was adopted in Sheffield in October 1970,' said Daniel, simply. 'My given name was ...'

'James,' said Veronica.

'Yes,' said Daniel. 'I'm James.'

There. He'd said it, and got it out. Years of prevaricating, until finally he'd met this woman, this headteacher. And he could see she was quite intimidating and didn't suffer fools gladly. But he'd liked her, and been incredibly pleased when she'd seemed to like him too. How she would respond now ... well, he hadn't thought much further than this

223

moment. His time here was nearly up anyway; if it all went badly, he could go back to Kent and forget all about it.

He realised he was kidding himself, of course. He could never forget.

'Ohhh,' said Veronica. Now she was giving up all pretence at reserve, or containment, or having any control over her emotions whatsoever. She made another attempt to stand up, and this time succeeded. 'Ohhh. Are you my . . . are you my . . .'

But the word 'baby' would not, of course, come out, and suddenly Veronica glanced at her hands. Tears – tears she had not shed for so long, and had sworn never to shed again – were dripping through her fingers and down onto her papers. When was the last time she had cried? She didn't have to ask herself the question. The last time she had cried was when she had held a little creature to her bosom, and the large lady had come and taken him away. After that, nothing, nothing on earth could hurt her enough to make her cry again.

Daniel didn't know if the tears were a good or a bad sign. He could feel himself wanting to cry; could feel himself as a little boy, asking his adoptive mother over and over again, 'But Mummy, you wouldn't leave your big boy, would you?' and his mother, who was a kind and patient woman, had held him and said, no, but they were very lucky, because they'd got to choose him, and he was the best one there was, and that they would never leave him.

'I'm so sorry,' said Daniel, 'to land this on you . . .'

There were agencies he could have used to act as a go-between, but he hadn't felt comfortable with the ones he'd met – they'd been very nice, but he hadn't liked them poking their noses into his private business. He was very like his mother in that respect.

'I just got confirmation through the post this morning . . .' Daniel raised his pile of papers, uselessly, as if Veronica would want to read them and check his credentials, 'And I didn't . . . I couldn't wait.'

Veronica shook her head. She couldn't fall apart. She couldn't. With near superhuman effort, she managed to page through to Evelyn and tell her to cancel her engagements for that afternoon.

Then she retook her seat and stared at Daniel in tearswept disbelief. Daniel was desperate for her to say something – anything – so he could get the least bit of a handle on what she was feeling. After all, he'd had years to plan this. His biggest fear, however – that she would simply say, 'Oh yes? The baby I had? Well, jolly good, nice to meet you' and send him on his way – was thankfully not being realised.

'Please,' Veronica said eventually, recovering some of her composure and making ample use of the large box of tissues she kept in the office for over-emotional teenage girls. 'Please. Tell me. Was the family . . .'

'My parents are great,' said Daniel carefully. 'They said you were very young.'

Veronica swallowed hard. One of the reasons she could empathise with the girls in her care was remembering how frightened, how young she had been then.

'I was,' said Veronica. 'I had no choice. And then, as time went on . . . I didn't meet anyone else I could form a family with. I couldn't have got you anyway. And then it was too late, and it would seem cruel, and I got a grant to go to university.'

She leant across the desk, her eyes suddenly burning with intensity, and gazed straight at him. 'But I never stopped thinking about you. I promise.'

'Thank you,' said Daniel, trying to swallow the lump in

his throat. Had she really? The idea that she would have thought about him all this time was . . . well, was what he had to hear. That his mother – lovely though his adoptive mum had been – that his real mother had loved him too. He managed to swallow, and went on. 'My parents said you were very young and very frightened.'

'And my father was very strong-willed,' murmured Veronica. 'But you know. If it had only been such a very short time later, I would have kept you. Feminism came late to Sheffield, you know. It's so hard to explain to people now how much the world has changed.'

'Tell me about my dad,' said Daniel.

Veronica felt the knife twist in her heart.

'One day,' she said. 'You understand this has come as such a shock to me?'

Daniel nodded. They would have time, hopefully. There was no one named on the birth certificate.

They sat in silence, Veronica letting her gaze wander over his long nose, short grey hair – the similarities were unmistakeable now she looked at them. The thought struck her; thank goodness she had never found him attractive.

'So, you planned all this . . .'

'Actually, no,' said Daniel. 'It was a chance remark; Pat got your name wrong and called you Vera. And I knew from the registrar that your own mother's name was . . .'

'Deveral,' nodded Veronica. 'After the way my father behaved, I just wanted to get away from him . . . it was such a long time ago.'

'Thirty-eight years,' said Daniel. 'So, I twigged, but then thought, it can't be, it just can't be, but then when the chance of the job came up, I took it, and then I saw you . . . and being in the same profession. I mean, it was just too weird.'

'So you've been working with me all this time thinking I

might be your mother?' mused Veronica, shaking her head. 'It seems so very strange.'

'It was,' said Daniel. 'Especially when you were so kind to me. I wanted to tell you before, but it didn't seem fair till I knew for sure.'

There was a long silence.

Veronica knew she badly needed to go somewhere and cry; howl at the universe and screech at the injustice: that she should have created this person; a lovely person, but had missed it all. Every fall she could have kissed better; every sticky first day of term, with new pencil cases and trousers grown out of; making the football team; unwrapping Christmas presents; sending him off to college. It was as if a speeded-up version of the life they'd never had together flashed in front of her eyes, but she couldn't look at it; it was too painful.

And her own life hadn't been wasted, surely? Nonetheless, right now she had a fierce need to be alone.

'So what now?' said Veronica.

'I'll have to tell Mum and Dad,' said Daniel. 'They know I was looking for you . . . Penny will have to know too.'

'Of course,' said Veronica, although she had no idea what was proper protocol under the circumstances. 'Please . . .' She mustn't cry. She mustn't. But why could she feel him, the sense memory so strong, feel him as a baby in her arms as if it were yesterday, before they took him away?

'Please thank them from me, for the wonderful job they have done,' she managed to get out eventually.

'I will,' said Daniel stiffly, holding the emotion from his voice. 'And, once we've delivered the assessment, will I be able to come back and see you?'

'I would like that very much,' said Veronica.

*

Veronica sat still at her desk for a long time. She was in no fit state to see anyone. Her head was buzzing, absolutely full of conflicting thoughts. At the fore were two: one, how wonderful, how amazing; how very much Daniel was exactly what she would have wanted for a son. Happily settled, handsome, polite, with a good job. And she wondered to herself if she could have provided him with the stable home life and good example that had obviously worked so well for him. Very possibly not.

She also felt a cold hand at her neck. This ... well, it wouldn't be ideal. For the school. For prospective parents. Who would want to send their child to the care of a woman who had abandoned her own child, however compelling the reasons? She thought of those awful stories she'd seen in the magazines Evelyn liked to read: 'I found my Long Lost Son on the Internet' and such like.

The idea of something so private becoming common knowledge, to be gossiped about and discussed by the girls at home ... that was an insupportable thought too. But would Daniel wish for secrecy? He could already be out, spreading the news. She clutched her teacup so hard her knuckles went white. Surely not. No, of course not.

They would discuss it sensibly. Yes. She could gradually feel her breathing ease, get back under control. She must control herself, that was it. And perhaps she could meet his adoptive parents, thank them. And ... she hardly dared to think it, hardly dared to breathe or admit to herself how great her longing was. But if she could meet his children ... be involved with his two little boys and the little baby girl, Eliza her name was. Being their other grandmother ... it was a desire so strong, it frightened her. Breathing out hard, she rose to stand at the window, the view of the cliffs and the sea normally one she found infinitely calming. Today, though, the choppy April waves and grey sky, filled with fast-moving clouds, reflected her own tempestuous mind, which couldn't settle.

To look at her, though, you wouldn't suspect a thing.

Chapter Fifteen

Post-Easter, the school seemed to divide in two. For half of them there were looming exams, barriers to be surmounted; for the eldest, university interviews and coming to terms with the next phase of their lives, whether that was travelling on a gap year, or moving straight into higher education. Hanging over this for the teachers was the huge pressure on results, which meant that their desire to help the girls and not make this time too difficult for them was compounded by the need to make this year the best ever; to beat other schools in their league and show Dr Deveral that everything was running as smoothly as ever (she had been uncharacteristically reserved lately). Clarissa Rhodes, expected to get an unprecedented six starred As, was frequently to be found mopping her eyes in the loos, even as she was being wooed by several top universities in the UK and the United States.

'I just can't help it,' she wailed to Maggie, who still felt slightly nervous teaching someone whose work was rather better than hers and whose legs certainly were. 'What if I don't go to Harvard and someone else comes along and discovers a successful alternative to OPEC?'

'There there,' said Maggie encouragingly. 'You are going to be just fine.'

Maggie felt a little sunnier too – she and Stan had managed

to get away at Easter. It was just a week in Spain, but she felt better for having a bit of colour, lazy days sleeping in without bells and fun nights drinking horrible local spirits and cutting it up a bit on the dance-floor, just like they used to when they were at school. It had been fun, good straightforward fun, and all the stresses of daily life and heavy conversations had been put behind them. Maggie knew many of the other girls had spent Easter in Mustique, or Gstaad or on safari, but sipping a ridiculous cocktail out of a coconut shell whilst inexplicably wearing a balloon crown, she and Stan laughing their heads off, she hadn't felt envious in the slightest.

It made such a change, at this time of year, when she had normally been in a frenzy trying to help the few children who were going to even turn up for their exams, versus those who started chafing at the bit to get outside as the days got longer and the sky clearer. It was a tricky balancing act.

Here, all the girls in her upper classes looked likely to pass, even Galina Primm, whose dyslexia was so bad it was often hard to tell what she was writing at all. But special arrangements had been put in place so that she could take longer and dictate her exam papers, which meant she shouldn't have any problem with the GCSE papers at all; it wasn't her brain that was at fault, just the wiring between her brain and her fingers.

And her lower class was, finally, falling into place. It was such a luxury to enter the classroom without worrying about Simone being in tears, again, or Alice and Fliss giggling and gossiping behind their hands. Knowing girls as she did, Maggie knew these acts of class solidarity rarely lasted for long but, in the aftermath of the stealing incident, and Simone's subsequent new-found and hard-won popularity, it was nice to see them all working well as a group.

So it was with a sunny heart she walked into class on a warm Wednesday morning in mid-May, wondering if it was time to give the girls some time off from the Ben Jonson they'd been looking at, and wondering if they'd all read Laurie Lee. If not, they'd like him.

This, and thinking about Claire, who'd become very quiet and clammed up about her love life lately, was what was going through her head, as she walked into the classroom, only to find all the girls with their noses jammed in horror against the glass windows on the eastern side of the building.

Alice had been planning her trick for months. She needed to gain back the respect of her classmates, many of whom thought she had been unjustly hard on Simone, but were too frightened of her sharp tongue to say so to her face. She couldn't bear all this lovey-dovey atmosphere in class. The fashion was for girls to walk arm in arm. Next they'd be giving each other bead bracelets. Alice sniffed. Well, this would wake them up, and give that common Glaswegian witch something to think about too.

It wasn't normal for Alice to feel the one sidelined, particularly for someone she didn't think much of. Normally girls looked to her for guidance, but now it was all sweetness and light and everyone spending most of the day speculating romantically about that stupid English teacher from the boys' school. Well, she'd show them.

It took a while to arrive – her grandfather, and frequent partner in crime, had had some trouble digging it up from his attic, but had managed it eventually. Miss Starling had asked her what was in the large parcel, but she'd looked wide-eyed and explained her grandfather had sent her a small stool, and that had seemed to satisfy her.

Fortunately there'd been heavy rain the night before. She'd risen silently at one a.m., when the whole house was asleep, creeping over to wake Fliss, who finally had the plaster off her ankle and was back to active service.

Fliss awoke to see Alice leaning over her with a torch, and nearly screamed out loud.

'What!' she finally managed to whisper.

'Larks afoot,' said Alice. 'Come on. Remember I mentioned our prank?'

Fliss searched her memory. Hadn't Alice forgotten all about that ages ago?

'Uh huh,' she said, slowly.

'Well, it's time,' said Alice.

Fliss sat upright. 'What do you mean?'

'It finally arrived. The thing I need. And it needs to be done now. So are you in or not?'

'I don't know!' said Fliss. 'I'm behaving myself now, you know. Any trouble and I'm going to get into absolutely serious s-h-i-t.'

'Does that include, you know, swearing to yourself,' said Alice sarcastically.

'No,' said Fliss. 'But I just don't want to . . . you know. Show myself up again.'

'OK,' said Alice. 'I promise I'll take all the blame if we get caught.'

'Blame for what?' came another voice. Alice rolled her eyes.

'Go back to sleep, Simone.'

'But I want to know.'

'Me too,' said Fliss, folding her arms and looking slightly mutinous. Alice sighed. Roll on next year when she'd be able to boss around the younger pupils.

'OK,' she said. 'I'm going to explain. But Simone, you can't come. You just have to keep mum. Or, better still, you could be our "Credulous Stooge".

'All right,' said Simone. She was delighted not to have to go, but to be included at the same time. Then Alice explained the prank and it was simply beyond Fliss's powers not to go along with it.

'We'll need waterproofs,' she whispered.

'I've got it all sorted,' said Alice. 'Here, grab this mallet.' Fliss's eyes widened. But she did as she was told. And with Alice clutching the heavy box, they crept silently downstairs to the unmanned fire escape.

The night was mild, and lit brightly by the moon and the stars, but evidence of the recent heavy rainfall was everywhere; the mud was thick and glutinous and it was hard going in the socks Alice had insisted on, to minimise footprints.

'I've got it all mapped out,' she said. Fliss shivered; half of her wanted to collapse in hysterical laughter, half was just plain terrified.

'We'll never get away with it,' she whispered.

'It is our duty to try,' said Alice solemnly. 'Now, be quiet, get down in the mud, and start rolling.'

Two hours later they had made it back to the dorm unnoticed – Simone was lying awake, fearfully, and had thoughtfully stuffed pillows down their beds.

'In case Miss Adair came past,' she said.

'Smart thinking,' said Alice, surprised. They cleaned the dirt off as well as they could in the little sink in their bathroom; the macintoshes she'd borrowed from the gardeners' shed had gone back in there – a new coating of mud hadn't made much difference. The really important thing was that their footprints didn't show – only the huge, unmistakeable footprint of her grandfather's wastepaper basket, trophy of a century-old hunting trip in Africa . . .

'What's that?' timid Sylvie was saying, staring out into the mud, now lit up brightly by the spring sunshine. The light made the tops of the great marks sparkle.

Maggie could now hear an excited uproar from the other classes up and down the halls, as well as windows opening. The refectory had high windows, too high to see out of, but this side of the building the view went all the way to sea. She could see Harold and two of the groundsmen, just starting work, following something and looking puzzled. As she watched, one of them peeled off and ran up in the direction of Dr Deveral's office.

'What is it, for goodness' sake? Girls, get down.'

As she came up she could see them, right across the lawn, straight past the windows and heading out to the pond: a huge set of hoofprints, with three large stubby toes, set in a galloping motion.

'I thought I heard something last night,' said a voice behind her. She turned, and it was sensible Simone. 'Kind of like a rumbling. But I didn't think much of it. But now I think of it – it could have been galloping!'

'I did too!' said Felicity Prosser, her face looking full of colour suddenly. 'Kind of like a rumbling, bashing noise.'

Suddenly the rest of the class nodded and started loudly agreeing that they'd heard it too, until even Maggie was wondering if she'd woken in the night – surely not.

Now Miss Starling and Claire Crozier were both outside, being given details by the groundsmen, and Maggie turned to her class.

'Calm down all of you.'

'Calm down?' said Sylvie. 'There's a wild animal escaped from the zoo!'

'All the better reason for you to stay indoors then,' said Maggie. 'Let me find out what's going on.'

She stalked outside.

'This is ridiculous,' Miss Starling was saying.

'I know,' the gardener was saying. 'But there are no foot-prints or anything near it, and it's definitely rhinoceros.'

'That's absurd.'

'I went on a safari,' said the younger gardener. 'We were tracking them. They were exactly like that.'

'And where do the tracks go?' said Miss Starling.

'You know, there ees the safari park just at Looe,' said Claire.

'That's monkeys,' said Miss Starling.

'Perhaps they have expanded,' said Claire.

'Ring them,' said Miss Starling. She bent down to examine the marks. 'I can't imagine how they got here . . . did you hear anything, Miss Adair?'

Maggie shook her head. 'Though some of the girls are saying they heard rumblings in the night.'

Miss Starling stalked ahead following the markings. They were set, two by two on the diagonal, and deep in the mud, as if an extremely heavy animal had indeed been running. It was entirely mysterious. The undergardener took his hat off and stared at them.

'I tell you, I've seen rhinoceros tracks, and they look just like that.'

Behind them, some of the older girls had strayed into the grounds and were also following the tracks. Seeing their lead, more classes had come out to see what was going on. There was much squealing.

Miss Starling's mouth was pursed. The tracks went all the

way down to the pond, where there was a broken-down wooden bridge. This area was out of bounds to pupils, and anyway dank, unpleasant and hardly an attraction.

This morning, however, a huge part of the bridge was knocked through. It looked exactly as if a huge creature had barged through it, only to tumble into the watery depths below. The group stood there for a moment, staring into the pond.

'What a terrible thing to happen,' said the under-gardener. 'He must have been scared out of his wits.'

Maggie was busy wondering how she was going to explain to Stan that there were wild animals on the property as well as everything else. And would they have to evacuate the grounds now they'd found its final resting place? And would they have to dredge the pond?

She glanced at Miss Starling and was surprised to see her shoulders shaking. Surely she couldn't be that upset? Maybe she was a real animal lover.

Then she looked closer. Miss Starling's shoulders were shaking ... surely it couldn't be ... it couldn't be with *laughter*.

'Miss Starling?' she said, moving forwards. But it was true. The lady was rocking back and forth, her eyes moist, clutching her fist to her mouth.

'Are you all right?'

'I'm fine,' said Miss Starling. 'Tee hee hee! I mean, I'm fine.'

Claire and Maggie swapped incredulous looks. Then they started laughing too.

'That,' said Miss Starling, 'is a new one on me. And it's not often anyone gets the chance to say that.' She managed to compose herself in record time and looked around to see that they were being watched by a crowd of wide-eyed girls.

She marched up to them. 'There has been some damage here,' she said, sternly. 'If anyone believes they can assist to repair it in any way, please come and see me. In the mean-time' – and her face was so straight, Maggie could fully believe she had imagined the last five minutes – 'I recommend nobody drink from the pond until we get it fully drained. Now, everyone back to class *immediately*.'

Alice, Fliss and Simone lay breathless on the floor of their dorm. Every time they felt they couldn't possibly laugh any more, it was too painful, someone would recall the look on Maggie's face when everyone mentioned hearing the noise, or the under-gardener's scientific insights into hoofprints, and they'd all set off once more.

'I said I'd get that Miss Adair,' Alice would howl again, and the hysterics would rise again.

When their sides actually hurt, there wasn't a breath left in them, and Fliss thought she was going to throw up, Alice finally rose.

'OK,' she said. 'Off to face the music.'

'Are you going to own up?' said Fliss, impressed.

'God, yes,' scoffed Alice. 'Of course, who do you think I am, Imogen? My granddad said if I could pull it off he'd pay for the fence.'

'I'd like to meet your granddad,' said Simone, wonder-ingly.

'Oh, maybe you will,' said Alice carelessly, and Fliss's heart leapt, recognising in it a simple acceptance of her new friend.

'They won't send you down, though, will they?' said Fliss, suddenly worried.

'Unlikely,' said Alice. 'I didn't actually do anything too bad, and that bridge needed demolishing anyway. Few detentions,

I think. Which will be well worth it. And I won't mention you guys, don't worry.'

'Thanks,' said Fliss.

As it turned out, Alice was exactly right. Miss Starling was less strict than her usual self, and Alice merely received lines and a sharp telling off. The rhinoceros-foot wastepaper bin was ordered home to its rightful owner, and although everyone in Middle School 1 knew that Alice was behind it – and treated her with reverence and incredulity because of it – it also somehow made its way into Downey House folklore that, one night, an escaped rhinoceros had run through the grounds and drowned in the pond. It was to keep generations of Downey juniors well out of reach of the water.

The other positive outcome was that Simone's willingness to support the prank cemented the girls' friendship in the dorm. Three was never an easy number, and Simone would always have a residual distrust of, and admiration for, Alice's quick wit and sharp tongue – but the three girls were now inseparable.

Chapter Sixteen

If it hadn't been for Alice and Fliss, Simone would never have gone up for the hockey team. But they encouraged her, and it wasn't as if she was going to need too much time to study for end of term exams – she'd done so much work throughout the year, it would really just be a case of going in and writing down the answers.

All year Miss James had been putting them through their paces in various sports. Unlike most games mistresses, she wasn't keen on forcing girls into teams too early. It took some girls a while to find their feet and confidence; telling a girl she couldn't do sport too early was likely to put her off for life, and she would probably finish her career on the games field hanging around the goal chewing nonchalantly and gossiping with chums.

So she tried different sports; shook up teams, encouraged everyone to play every position. Obviously some were stronger than others, but rotating often showed unexpected skills, and some girls found, for example, some talent in trampolining where they'd failed elsewhere.

In summer term, however, there were special netball and hockey play-offs between all the houses and that's where it got really serious. Not everyone had to try out, but there was kudos, time off other classes, and the chance to travel to other schools in later years if you made the team, so competition was fierce.

Try-outs were late in May on a Saturday morning. It was shaping up to be another lovely day. Seniors, bored with their A-level revision, glanced fondly out of their study windows, remembering past try-outs from their first year as if it were a lifetime ago.

'Right everyone,' said Miss James. She had her usual brisk manner, but no one could prevent the nerves from getting through. Fliss was sitting out this year, despite loving netball; it wasn't worth risking the ankle just yet, but she firmly hoped she'd be allowed to play next year. Alice wasn't auditioning at all, she thought sport was stupid. But Simone was there, making a feeble attempt at warming up, and her friends had gone to cheer her on.

'This is going to be super embarrassing,' she said at the sidelines. 'Andrea runs like the wind, and Sylvie is totally brilliant. They're all going to laugh at me.'

'They're not,' said Fliss. 'You're great at hockey.'

'I suppose I could stop the ball with my thighs,' said Simone. 'They're bigger than the net.'

'Is that legal in hockey?' said Alice.

'Maybe I could sue them for not letting a person of unrestricted growth play,' muttered Simone. Alice laughed, but Fliss didn't like Simone's habit of always putting herself down. Maybe if she got in the team she could drop a bit of weight anyway, and it wouldn't be such a problem.

'Go Simone!' she said. 'Go for it!'

Simone raised her eyes to heaven. 'Will you look after my glasses? I'm much more aggressive if I can't see what I'm doing.'

Miss James ran them around for a warm-up which didn't do Simone's cause much good – she was puffed out almost before they had to zigzag in amongst the mini traffic cones. And when it came to shooting at the goal, star shots Ursula and lanky sporty Andrea were streets ahead. But at Simone's turn in goal she stolidly and carefully blocked every shot, and Miss James made a mark on her paper anyway.

Maggie was delighted to see Simone's name up on the team list the following morning. Simone hardly ever came to see her now, only infrequently to change a book.

'I'm not reading so much now,' she'd said last time. 'I'm so busy.' Then she'd blushed. She'd be rather pretty if she could drop a little of that weight, thought Maggie. Then she had to get on. There were final assessment sheets to be dropped off – the assessors were counter-marking the mock examinations, which had made everyone terribly nervous – end of term exams to be set for the juniors, and exam supervision to be arranged for the seniors. The end of term concert she wasn't involved in. Probably just as well. The less time she spent with David McDonald the better. And anyway, she'd managed to persuade Stan to come down for sports day, tempting him with sunny weather and the promise of walks on the beach with frequent ice cream stops. She was sure if he just spent some time in Cornwall he'd learn to love it too.

Maggie sometimes surprised herself by thinking how much she'd forgotten now her once fierce ideals about returning to the poorer areas of her homeland, though she knew somewhere in her heart that she would have to – one day. Anna kept reminding her about it, telling her how Dylan and Cody's local park had been closed down due to council cuts and how they were driving her crazy kicking about the house all day. Maggie felt guilty and vowed to get them down here too, maybe when the Scottish schools broke up, earlier than the English ones, to let them, too, run about in the fresh air; play on the crags and the beach, jump in the enormous swimming pool. It wasn't, she knew, the solution.

Veronica waited for the final assessment meeting with some trepidation. Even the idea of being in the same room as Daniel again made her feel nervous. She was desperate just to stare at his face, even though she realised how peculiar this would be.

Pat and Liz had not been best pleased to have their previous meeting cancelled and were huffy and self-important when they turned up, fussing about with unnecessary flip charts and bar charts. Present, in the small lecture auditorium, were Veronica, Miss Starling, and three representatives of the board of governors, who were normally very hands-off: Dame Lydia Johnson, a local JP, Digory Gill, a local council officer, and Majabeen Gupta, a paediatrician from London who had a holiday cottage there and had sent all three of his girls through the school. The report, once it was bound, would go to every governor, every teacher, and from then on to every parent who requested it. It had been such an eventful year, Veronica reflected ruefully. She hoped it wouldn't have a negative impact on their score.

'Now,' said Liz, looking officious in a white polyester shirt which strained over her large bosoms. It was lucky she'd never attempted to button her suit jacket; it was very unlikely she'd succeed. 'When we approached this task, we used the 1989 matrix inversion schedule, as popularised by McIntosh and Luther, in the Northern Schools Initiative of 1991.'

Veronica glanced briefly at Digory. He was not one for jargon and tended to either complain through it or fall asleep. From the looks of him this morning, it might well be the latter.

'First we looked at how effective, efficient and inclusive is the provision of education, integrated care and any extended services in meeting the needs of learners,' droned Liz. 'We found that in many circumstances there were some problems with developmental acquisition of the proper non-discriminatory religion, disability, difference and gender instruments.'

Even Veronica was finding it hard to understand what she was talking about, and she had a PhD in economics. Perhaps a PhD in horrible waffle would have been more appropriate.

Over the space of the next forty minutes, however, it transpired that Pat and Liz had decided the school was not socially-minded enough, did not include enough work on environmental issues and wasn't inclusive. Veronica mentally struck this from her head. Inclusive wasn't, sadly, their business. They had girls here from every part of the world, from every race and religion, although she was well aware that the one thing they all had in common was that their parents were wealthy, and believed in educating girls. But her job was only to teach them to be tolerant and kind, not slavishly trying to right wrongs.

It didn't really matter, though, as she was hardly concentrating. She was watching Daniel. Her son, Daniel. She couldn't even believe the words as she thought them. 'My son Daniel.' She'd hardly slept since he'd been to see her.

Daniel was sitting, looking grave and making notes on a piece of paper. Veronica hoped he would stay behind so they could have lunch together, and she could ask him about his parents. Daniel felt nervous too. What was expected of him now? he wondered. Maybe it would be all right if they just tried to get to know each other. What on earth were the others going to say when they found out he was Dr Deveral's . . . he couldn't keep thinking of her like that, it was ridiculous, but so was 'mother' so he'd have to keep thinking of an alternative. Anyway. What were people going to think when they found out? It was going to be strange for everyone.

'There are also some extreme safety and security issues at the school,' Liz was now saying, touching as if sensitively on 'breakouts' and 'injuries' as if they were much more serious than she could bring herself to mention. 'We have enumerated these at some length in our final report.' Digory did look like he was nodding off. Just as Veronica was thinking this, she noticed June Starling give him a sharp dig in the ribs.

'However,' said Pat, taking back the baton. 'There are some other matters to consider.'

Another sheet came up on the overhead projector. This Veronica understood immediately.

Attitude of learners
Attendance of learners
Enjoyment of learners
Involvement of learners
Attainments of learners

And lined up under those headings were the exam marks of girls from the last five years, and the projections for this year, which were higher than ever.

Everyone gazed at this slide for some time.

'So,' said Pat, somewhat reluctantly. 'We'll have some recommendations to make about truancy, safety procedures and some suggestions as to how to promote inclusivity . . .'

'Yes,' said Veronica, her heart beating slightly faster.

'But these aren't problems, however pressing, that are believed to be significant enough to affect the school's standing in the long run,' said Liz, sounding grudging. 'The girls, it seems, have spoken for you. And they like the school as it is.'

There was a pause.

'Well done,' said Daniel, who'd known the results in advance. He rose to his feet. 'It's a top score all round.'

And he came forward to shake Veronica by the hand. It was only when he did so that she realised how nervous she had been. As usual, she didn't betray herself by even a tremor. She's amazing, thought Daniel. You would never think they were more than just colleagues.

'Thank you,' said Veronica. 'Thank you so much everyone. And thanks for your hard work.'

Pat and Liz gave thin-lipped smiles.

'You'll get the full report in the post in eight weeks,' said Liz.

Eight weeks? thought Veronica, but she didn't say anything, except, 'Lunch?'

Daniel caught up with her as they walked round the outside of the building – it was such a beautiful day. He approached her nervously; Veronica turned, equally nervous, having walked on ahead alone in the hopes that he would come and walk with her.

'Hello,' she said, checking to see no one was near them.

'Hello. How are you? Are you well?'

'I'm well. Yes. I'm well. You know. It's strange and everything. What about you?'

Veronica looked at the nervous young man beside her. What must he be thinking? she thought. After all, he'd been through all the work of finding her. Was he pleased? Disappointed?

'Oh, you know,' she said, trying to carry off a little laugh. 'Starting to come to terms with the world being a little different to how I thought of it before.'

246

'Quite,' said Daniel. He wasn't sure if it was the right thing to do, but he touched her lightly on the arm. Veronica tensed up, realising this was the first personal contact they'd had in nearly forty years.

'Sorry,' said Daniel.

'Not at all,' said Veronica. He didn't remember when she'd held him; buried her face in his head and smelled his brand new, bloodied fresh-bread smell. She'd never forgotten it.

'I, er . . . spoke to Mum and Dad.'

'Oh yes?'

'They think I should go slow. You know. Take it a step at a time.'

Both his parents in fact had been a little worried that he'd tracked Veronica down and confronted her, but loved him too much to tell him. Daniel swallowed.

'But I'm happy to tell the world. I don't mind.'

Something in his tone made her think that suddenly he didn't sound like a thirty-eight-year-old at all, but like the little boy he must have been. She must remember that; he was not an adult when he was talking to her, not really.

Veronica smiled at him. 'Well, I understand completely your parents' reticence. Of course it's too early, we don't want to go broadcasting anything until we've got to know each other a little.'

She realised immediately by the way his face twisted that this wasn't what he'd been expecting.

'What do you mean?' said Daniel, suddenly feeling as if he'd just been snubbed. Why not? Why couldn't they be a family? Wasn't that the whole point of him telling her? His parents would be so welcoming too.

Veronica felt conflicted. For a moment she thought he was

going to turn round and announce it to the others behind them, which made her shiver with horror. And she'd been looking forward so much to getting to know him slowly, on their terms, without being a topic of gossip and intrusion for the rest of the world . . . surely that was best.

'I just meant, I understand that a more cautious approach . . .'

Daniel didn't understand this at all. He'd thought she was so pleased. 'You mean, you're ashamed of having an illegitimate son? In this day and age?'

'Don't be ridiculous,' said Veronica, stopping short and looking straight at him. 'Meeting you again has been one of the best things that has ever happened to me.' She took a deep breath. 'After having you.'

Daniel took this in. Wow. That was . . . that was so amazing, so what he'd hoped she'd feel and say. But then why on earth would they have to keep it a secret?

'But in my position . . .' went on Veronica.

Daniel stopped short. His face looked red.

'I see,' he said and started to head back to the others.

'No, no!' said Veronica, reaching out as if to hold on to him, but dropped her arms immediately. 'It's not like that at all. I want to get to know you so much, Daniel. I was hoping to meet your family one day . . . even, I was thinking, you know Mrs Sutherland retires next year from the history department, and I even thought you might be interested in coming to work here . . .'

But how could she say this and mean something else?

'But in secret?' said Daniel, rubbing the back of his head.

'Please, Daniel. I just . . . I just don't want to rush things.'

'Well, you've already offered me a job, but apart from that you don't want to rush things.'

Veronica looked down at her elegant hands, noticing

unavoidably, as she always did, the way the veins grew uglier and more prominent every year.

'I . . . I . . . I seem to be making rather a mess of this, don't I?' she said. What could she say to him to make him realise how important he was; how important this was to her?

Daniel couldn't believe this. She really would offer him a job but not tell anyone he was her son. After everything he'd done to find her. She said she wanted him but when it came down to it, it was just like before – she didn't really want to acknowledge him at all. He felt his ears going pink, felt once more like a little boy .

'I don't . . .' he said, then decided to leave before he said something he couldn't take back. 'Uh. I don't think I'll stay for lunch.' And he strode off towards his car.

As Veronica watched him go, she felt a piece of herself break off; plummet into blackness. Her boy . . . her boy . . .

'Are you all right?'

It was Majabeen, come up beside her.

'It's wonderful news, isn't it?'

'What?' said Veronica, trying to wrest her brain back from where it had gone, down the road with her only son. 'Oh, yes. The report. Yes, I suppose it is.'

'Come on, then. I think everyone wants to celebrate. Is that young chap gone?'

'Yes,' said Veronica, slowly. 'Yes he has. Let me just go and freshen up.'

Chapter Seventeen

End of term! There was a heady atmosphere in the dorms as the girls were getting ready to go home, or abroad on exciting trips. Astrid was spending the summer on the special programme at the Royal College of Music in London. Alice was joining her parents in Cairo. Fliss couldn't believe how much she was going to miss her friends.

'I'll only be in London,' said Simone. 'You can come and see me.'

'No, no, come to Guildford – you can ride my pony,' said Fliss. 'It'll be great.'

All exams were over, and all that was left was to slack off, lie tanning on the grass at lunchtime, and make plans for the summer.

'I am going to sleep till eleven o'clock every day,' said Sylvie, dreamily.

'Is that the most wonderful thing you can think of to do?' said Alice, but not in as sneering a tone as she'd have used before.

'Yes, actually,' said Sylvie, uncowed. 'I'm very sensitive to bells.'

Clarissa Rhodes was off to the Sorbonne, where she would take a vast number of high level courses, all in

French. Maggie had felt entirely embarrassed when Clarissa came by especially to thank her.

'Well done with that Rhodes girl,' she now said, banging loudly on Claire's door. Hearing no answer she popped her head round – Claire ought to be here by now.

She was lying full length on her bed, howling her eyes out.

'What's the matter?'

'Eet does not matter. *Tant pis! Je déteste les hommes.*'

'What, all of them?'

Sitting down, Maggie got from her that the affair with the married man had ended catastrophically, and that he had gone back to his wife, tragically just in time for the summer holidays.

'There there,' said Maggie, patting Claire on the back. 'At least you won't have to see him any more.'

'Ah have to see him ALL THE TIME!' said Claire furiously.

'Why? What do you mean?'

Maggie had always imagined Claire's paramour to be some rich glamorous Frenchman, like Nicolas Sarkozy, only taller, who bought her jewels and had a beautiful apartment in an *arrondissement*.

'Mais non, it's Mr Graystock.'

Maggie shook her head. 'Mr Graystock at Downey Boys? The classics teacher?'

She dimly remembered the lanky posh chap, but had hardly given him a second glance as it was, she remembered with some embarrassment, at the height of her David mooning phase.

'Isn't he a bit of a chinless wonder?'

''e ees BASTARD!'

Maggie stayed with her for some time, amazed at what

was going on under her nose at the school that she'd managed to completely miss.

It was still a lovely morning though. Many of the Downey Boys would be coming over to see their sports day, and vice versa. She'd make excuses for Claire.

And all her girls had done well in their exams. She was so proud of them, this term they'd really got their heads down. And now all that was left was the sports day, then back to Glasgow for eight glorious weeks. Her parents were incredibly excited already and had made all sorts of plans; Stan was still here and threatening to drive the Fiat Panda all the way back to Scotland, which was fine by her. Nothing else had been said, but she knew, she just knew deep down that she wanted to come back next year. She'd had a short interview with Veronica that had confirmed what she'd hoped very much – that it was working out for her at Downey House, and they'd like to keep her. She had accepted, telling herself she'd sort it out later. But she just didn't know how long Stan would take 'no' for an answer.

Frowning slightly, she wandered past the sports pitch to walk down and pick him up from the village. Lessons were cancelled today as the girls all dressed up in house colours, in preparation to fight it out on the hockey pitch and athletics field. The gardeners had done an amazing job; flower beds were blazing with June flowers, reflecting the colours of the houses – rose-pink for Tudor, white for York, surrounded by green wreaths for Wessex, and fresh blue and yellow broom for the Plantagenets. Fluttering bunting had been hung up along the running track and around the stall that would be providing much-needed barley water later. It was an amazingly hot day, butterflies thronging up from the long grass beneath her feet.

She hailed the familiar figure at the foot of the driveway.

'Well met!' she shouted.

David grinned back at her, but she thought he looked a little nervous, and there was no sign of Stephen Daedalus.

'What's up? Where's Stephen Daedalus? Are you here on school business?'

David looked uncomfortable and glanced around. He was wearing long baggy khaki trousers, and a grey collarless shirt; if he hadn't seemed so awkward he would have appeared cool and fresh in the summer heat.

They couldn't be seen from the school where they were, far away from the high towers, close to the copse. She moved closer towards him.

'Uh,' he said. It wasn't like David to be speechless. He couldn't be blushing, could he?

'Here's the thing.' he said. 'And I'm just going to say it, all right?'

Maggie found that she was holding her breath.

'I . . . I've broken up with Miranda.'

Maggie squinted at him. She felt her heart start to beat faster. Why was he telling her?

'Oh, I'm so sorry.'

'It doesn't matter. She didn't like having a lowly school-master for a beau, and didn't really bother to hide it too much. Always pestering me to go to Portsmouth and get a job there. Like it wasn't all right to be happy in your job if you didn't make that much money . . . anyway, forget that,' he said, taking a deep breath. 'I . . . I. Well. I think you're . . . Anyway. Huh. This is difficult. Anyway. Listen. I'm going on holiday. I'm going to walk the Cinque Terre. In Italy. It's gorgeous, apparently, and some friends have a villa down there and I'll be staying with them, and, well, of course you can't, it's totally stupid to ask. But if you wanted to come. You could. That's all. Right. Sorry.'

His dark eyes had been fixed on the ground throughout this speech, and Maggie could barely think straight. But did this mean . . . what? What did it mean?

She stood there, staring at him.

'I know. I'm sorry. I shouldn't have said anything. I'll go. Sorry. Sorry. I'm really sorry.'

And he turned round. Maggie couldn't take her eyes off him. David. Her David. He was walking on now, not looking back, towards the gates of the school, his shoulders bent. She couldn't bear to watch him so . . .

'DAVID!!!' she shouted, just as he reached the entrance, even though she didn't have the faintest idea of what she was going to say to him after that. But she so wanted to say his name.

His long body stiffened, and, very slowly, he turned around. She found herself staring straight into his eyes. Very slowly, and with a faintly incredulous look on his face, he started to walk back towards her up the hill. Maggie caught her breath. Oh my. Oh . . .

'HEY!'

They both froze, still several metres apart.

'Can I come through this door, or do I get arrested as a sex pest immediately? Useful to know, like,' said Stan, hovering just at the very edge of the gates. 'Thought I'd come and get you, but I forgot about the paedie bit where I can't come in.'

Stan was wearing odd-length shorts that seemed to stop halfway down his calves, like they'd been bought for a toddler, and his beloved Celtic top. Maggie stared at him. David was looking at her still, so intently.

'I've brought sausage sandwiches,' said Stan. 'Miss a meal here, you're stuffed.'

David dropped his gaze, shaking his head. Then he pasted on a smile.

'Stanley,' he said. 'Hi there.'

'Hello,' said Stan, not friendly or unfriendly. 'Come on love.' This to Maggie.

Maggie felt her head spin. Had she taken leave of her senses? What, was she just going to suddenly dump this man, her Stan, when she'd agreed to marry him only six months before? Had she gone crazy?

She tried out her voice experimentally. It sounded weird, like she was listening to it on tape. 'Eh, hello, Stan.'

Stan didn't seem to notice.

'Are they really going to let me watch all these foxy girls in sporty skirts?' he grumbled. 'I'm not sure this is such a good idea.'

Unable to stop herself, Maggie found herself going towards him. You do not, she told herself very firmly, confuse what is real with what is a fantasy. That is madness. Madness.

'Must go,' said David. 'Get the dog, you know.'

'I reckon he's married to that dog,' said Stan, watching him head down the lane. Then he took Maggie in his arms and kissed her. 'School's nearly out, eh? Nearly finished! Yay!'

'Yay,' said Maggie, slightly more quietly, then she buried her head in his shirt, taking in his familiar scent.

'Steady on,' said Stan. 'I don't want your terrifying Miss Starling having my guts for garters. And she would too. She'd claw them out with her bare fingernails, and smile while she did it.'

'She's not that bad,' said Maggie.

'Not that bad? After everything you've told me . . .'

And Stan followed a very thoughtful Maggie up the hill.

Simone was nervous as she got ready in the blue and yellow polo shirt they'd had specially made up. All she had to do, she knew, was stand in the goal and do as well as she could. But it was one thing being surrounded by her own form, who supported her and had grown to like her. Girls from other classes, older girls were watching now. She bit her lip. Well, it was too late now. Fliss was plaiting her hair to keep it out of the way.

'And don't let them go for your glasses,' she was saying.

'No,' said Simone.

Miss James got her teams together. Two ten-minute halves for six-a-side teams per game; York versus Tudor first, then Plantagenets v Wessex, followed by a play-off.

The whole school was out on the benching, in a festive mood; the senior sports coming up later. The little ones' hockey tournament was always fun, the older girls shaking their heads in disbelief that they were ever so small and immature, and laughing if things got aggressive, as they could do.

Miss James blew her whistle as the whites and pinks faced off. The game was fast and furious played with this number of players in such a short time frame, and it took a while to get a goal on the table. But at the eighth minute, Eve McGinty, a tough-faced girl from Tudor, whacked one across the goal line, followed in the second half by two more. She was clearly a formidable opponent, and York retired sulkily.

'Go, Simone,' shouted Fliss, as she stood up to get on the pitch. Everyone, it seemed to Simone, was yelling.

Maggie was watching, trying to clear her bewildered head. Had David really . . . suddenly she had a vision of them both, walking through Italy, eating in simple trattorias, getting brown with the sun and healthy with the exercise; spending balmy nights with sweet pink wine in little towns where whitewashed churches rang out their bells as the stars above swelled and the velvety soft nights washed over them with the scent of heavy lilies . . .

'You all right?' said Stan, nudging her. 'This fat girl's one of yours, isn't she?'

With effort, Maggie pulled herself back. And indeed, it was wonderful to see Simone out there, blocking, passing the ball back and forward, hearing the shouts from the crowd.

No one, though, it seemed, could get in to score. It looked like being sudden death in the second half when, suddenly, Andrea broke through at the last moment and hit the little ball straight into the corner of their opponents' net.

The Plantagenet girls erupted into a bouncing mass of blue and yellow from their place on the benches, jumping up and down and hugging each other.

'Well done,' said Miss James, as they took five minutes before the final. 'Now, watch out for Eve McGinty. She's the best in the year. Simone, do you think you can stop her?'

Simone was getting her breath back and polishing her glasses, but she nodded nervously nonetheless. She'd felt very strange out there and was thankful that the ball hadn't really come too close to her goal.

That all changed when the next match began. There was no doubt that Eve was the star, and she went for the ball with all the aggression of a national rugby player. Simone saw the ball come straight for her, and, in a temporary loss of nerve, closed her eyes. The ball went straight between her legs and landed in the goal, glinting up at her.

There were roars from the Tudor side, and groans from the Plantagenets; even a couple of solitary boos. Maggie winced in disappointment for her, and again as Eve slammed the ball in two more times in that half alone. It was going to be a massacre.

Simone knew she was purple at half-time, partly with exhaustion, and partly with embarrassment.

'Would you like me to take you off?' said Miss James.

'She'll be all right, won't you Simone?' said Andrea.

And at that, Simone felt her confidence rise a little. If tall, capable Andrea thought she could do it, there was no reason not to.

'I'll do my best,' she said.

'Well, do better than that,' said Andrea, spitting out her orange peel. 'Do your job. Block these bloody goals.'

And my goodness, she did! Simone was everywhere over the back of the pitch; feinting, blocking, and whacking the ball back with gusto. Even the most indifferent of pupils, who thought sport was a complete waste of everyone's time, were riveted by the chubby commando of the hockey pitch. As Eve's frustration started to show, Andrea went for her, allowing little Sylvie to slip in at the last moment and pocket one. Goal! In the ensuing kerfuffle, Andrea went headlong in again and scored almost immediately. Goal!

Almost roaring with frustration, Eve ploughed down the field with the ball, heading straight, it seemed, for Simone's glasses. Everyone waited for Simone to move. But she didn't. She held her ground, and as Eve whacked the ball with full force straight at Simone's left side, Simone merely leaned over and planted her stick on the goal line. And WHACK, the ball was off and back in the game; picked up by Ursula, passed to Sylvie, who as usual was dancing unnoticed right up at the front line, and one more was in. GOAL!

The Plantagenet girls were on their feet now, shouting and roaring like little savages. There were two minutes of the game left as Miss James threw the ball back into play. Tussling at the front was absolutely vicious, and ankles were whacked willy-nilly as both sides fought for their lives. But the ball wasn't getting anywhere up or down the field – the girls were all over it, any concept of tactical play gone completely. Finally, desperately, Eve McGinty made a huge swing at it.

The hit connected, and the ball flew through the air, as the girls all stopped to follow its parabola. Once again Simone saw it. And she did not close her eyes this time, but said to herself, 'DO YOUR JOB.'

Whereupon, with tremendous skill, she trapped the ball and hit it full flight across the pitch, straight to Andrea, who putted it gently into the back of the net just as the whistle blew.

The noise levels were absolutely extraordinary. Miss James was grinning like a Cheshire cat; nobody could say sport was unimportant now! Maggie, to her surprise, found herself not thinking about David for the moment, but standing up in her seat, unapologetically cheering the Plantagenet girls' victory. The team were now surrounded by the rest of their classmates, jumping up and down and screeching with excitement, a mass of colour in the blazing sunshine. Miss Starling was shaking her head at the noise. Maggie rushed down to congratulate them – she couldn't help it – and was touched and heartened by the warm welcome the girls gave her.

'All right,' said Stan, when she returned to her seat in the stands – the middle school second year were about to start on their javelin throwing.

'All right what?' said Maggie, still pink with happiness.

'All right. You were right,' said Stan.

'What?'

'You were right. It is good for you here. You do belong.'

This was so unexpected, Maggie just stared at him.

'Lots of people have long distance relationships for a bit – ours has been going all right, hasn't it?'

Maggie felt a surge of guilt that she squashed down as far as she could.

'Yes.'

'OK. I'll stop bugging you. You stay here and . . . well, we'll see in a year or two, yeah?'

Maggie would have liked to hug him, but it was rarely advisable when surrounded by pupils. Instead she squeezed his leg, hard. Inside she was a mass of contradictions – but women were like that, weren't they? she told herself. Weren't they?

'Thank you,' she said. 'Thank you.'

'So, anyway,' said Fliss's mum, as they drove back up the motorway. They were heading straight for Gatwick for a couple of weeks in France, even though Fliss would rather have gone back to Surrey to catch up with her old friends. Oh well, it wouldn't be for long.

'And then we never thought Simone was going to be one of us, but then it turned out she's OK really, then she helped me out a lot with my English, so I think my marks are going to be really good now, I mean, the exam was totally easy and everything, but she's all right that teacher, and I'm going to definitely try out for the team next year, my ankle's completely fine, and next year you get to travel and play other schools, and . . .'

'So,' said her mother when she could get a word in edgeways. 'We did say we were going to look again at whether you wanted to stay on at Downey House.'

'Oh,' said Fliss. She'd forgotten about that. Then she saw her dad at the wheel, smiling.

'I suppose it's OK,' she said.

'I knew it!' crowed Hattie triumphantly. 'I knew she'd think it was the best school in the world.'

'Shut up, swotto,' said Fliss.

'Shut up yourself.'

'No, *you* shut up.'

Veronica took a final turn around the empty classrooms before leaving the buildings in the capable hands of Harold Carruthers for the next few weeks. It was amazing how still the place felt; all the eternal noise and bustle and colour of four hundred girls, bursting with life, vanished overnight.

Dust was already settling on the desks and the radiators and work peeling from the walls, and the school had a characteristic, slightly deadening smell of old ink and gym shoes, as if it knew its rightful inhabitants were missing.

She wondered, as usual these days, about Daniel. She'd written to him once or twice, hoping to hear from him, but she hadn't. She'd poured her heart out into those letters; telling him exactly what he'd always meant to her and what she hoped he could mean in the future. She could only hope it was enough. Losing a child once had been bad enough . . . losing him again would be such a heavy burden to bear.

She went through classroom after classroom, running her hands across the desks, checking that there were no left-behind apple cores or milk bottles or anything that could cause them problems at the start of the new year. It had been an eventful time. With some good new people, and sad losses. But sometimes she felt she loved the school most of all when it was empty, with only its faint scent and her own quiet footsteps to remind you that its halls were once full of laughter and chatter and young minds being formed. And if she half-closed her eyes, she could almost hear an echo of singing, from far away and down the hall . . .

We are the girls
The Girls of Downey Hall
We stand up proud
And we hold our heads up tall
We serve the Queen
Our country God and home
We dare to dream
Of wider plains to roam
We are the girls
The Girls of Downey Hall.

Maggie's Poems

The Choosing

We were first equal Mary and I
with the same coloured ribbons in mouse-coloured hair,
and with equal shyness
we curtseyed to the lady councillor
for copies of Collins' *Children's Classics*.
First equal, equally proud.

Best friends too Mary and I
a common bond in being cleverest (equal)
in our small school's small class.
I remember
the competition for top desk
or to read aloud the lesson
at school service.
And my terrible fear of her superiority at sums.
I remember the housing scheme
Where we both stayed.
The same house, different homes,
where the choices were made.
I don't know exactly why they moved
but anyway they went.
Something about a three-apartment
and a cheaper rent.

But from the top deck of the high school bus
I'd glimpse among the others on the corner
Mary's father, mufflered, contrasting strangely
with the elegant greyhounds by his side.
He didn't believe in high school education,
especially for girls,
or in forking out for uniforms.

Ten years later on a Saturday –
I am coming home from the library –
sitting near me on the bus,
Mary with a husband who is tall,
curly haired, has eyes for no one else but Mary.
Her arms are round the full-shaped vase that is her body.
Oh, you can see where the attraction lies
in Mary's life – not that I envy her, really.

And I am coming from the library
with my arms full of books.
I think of the prizes that were ours for the taking
and wonder when the choices got made
we don't remember making.

Liz Lochhead, 1970

266

Daffodils

I wandered lonely as a cloud
That floats on high o'er vales and hills
When all at once I saw a crowd,
A host, of golden daffodils;
Beside the lake, beneath the trees,
Fluttering and dancing in the breeze.

Continuous as the stars that shine
And twinkle on the Milky Way,
They stretched in never-ending line
Along the margin of the bay:
Ten thousand saw I at a glance,
Tossing their heads in sprightly dance.

The waves beside them danced; but they
Out-did the sparkling waves in glee:
A poet could not but be gay,
In such a jocund company:
I gazed – and gazed – but little thought
What wealth the show to me had brought:

For oft, when on my couch I lie
In vacant or in pensive mood,
They flash upon that inward eye
Which is the bliss of solitude;
And then my heart with pleasure fills
And dances with the daffodils.

William Wordsworth, 1804

The Silver Tassie

Go fetch to me a pint o' wine,
An' fill it in a silver tassie,
That I may drink, before I go,
A service to my bonnie lassie.
The boat rocks at the pier o' Leith,
Fu' loud the wind blaws frae the ferry,
The ship rides by the Berwick-law,
And I maun leave my bonnie Mary.

The trumpets sound, the banners fly,
The glittering spears are rankèd ready;
The shouts o' war are heard afar,
The battle closes deep and bloody;
But it's no the roar o' sea or shore
Wad mak me langer wish to tarry;
Nor shout o' war that's heard afar:
It's leaving thee, my bonnie Mary!

Robert Burns, 1788

The Journey of the Magi

'A cold coming we had of it,
Just the worst time of the year
For a journey, and such a long journey:
The ways deep and the weather sharp,
The very dead of winter.'
And the camels galled, sore-footed, refractory,
Lying down in the melting snow.
There were times we regretted
The summer palaces on slopes, the terraces,
And the silken girls bringing sherbet.
Then the camel men cursing and grumbling
And running away, and wanting their liquor and women,
And the night-fires going out, and the lack of shelters,
And the cities hostile and the towns unfriendly
And the villages dirty and charging high prices:
A hard time we had of it.
At the end we preferred to travel all night,
Sleeping in snatches,
With the voices singing in our ears, saying
That this was all folly.

Then at dawn we came down to a temperate valley,
Wet, below the snow line, smelling of vegetation;
With a running stream and a water-mill beating the
    darkness,
And three trees on the low sky,
And an old white horse galloped away in the meadow.
Then we came to a tavern with vine-leaves over the lintel,
Six hands at an open door dicing for pieces of silver,
And feet kicking the empty wine-skins,
But there was no information, and so we continued

And arrived at evening, not a moment too soon
Finding the place; it was (you may say) satisfactory.

All this was a long time ago, I remember,
And I would do it again, but set down
This set down
This: were we led all that way for
Birth or Death? There was a Birth, certainly,
We had evidence and no doubt. I had seen birth and death,
But had thought they were different; this Birth was
Hard and bitter agony for us, like Death, our death.
We returned to our places, these Kingdoms,
But no longer at ease here, in the old dispensation,
With an alien people clutching their gods.
I should be glad of another death.

T. S. Eliot, 1927

Christmas

The bells of waiting Advent ring,
    The Tortoise stove is lit again
And lamp-oil light across the night
    Has caught the streaks of winter rain.
In many a stained-glass window sheen
From Crimson Lake to Hooker's Green.

The holly in the windy hedge
    And round the Manor House the yew
Will soon be stripped to deck the ledge,
    The altar, font and arch and pew,
So that villagers can say
'The Church looks nice' on Christmas Day.

Provincial public houses blaze
    And Corporation tramcars clang,
On lighted tenements I gaze
    Where paper decorations hang,
And bunting in the red Town Hall
Says 'Merry Christmas to you all.'

And London shops on Christmas Eve
    Are strung with silver bells and flowers
As hurrying clerks the City leave
    To pigeon-haunted classic towers,
And marbled clouds go scudding by
The many-steepled London sky.

And girls in slacks remember Dad,
    And oafish louts remember Mum,
And sleepless children's hearts are glad,

      And Christmas morning bells say 'Come!'
Even to shining ones who dwell
Safe in the Dorchester Hotel.

And is it true? and is it true?
    The most tremendous tale of all,
Seen in a stained-glass window's hue,
    A Baby in an ox's stall?
The Maker of the stars and sea
Become a Child on earth for me?

And is it true? For if it is,
    No loving fingers tying strings
Around those tissued fripperies,
    The sweet and silly Christmas things,
Bath salts and inexpensive scent
And hideous tie so kindly meant.

No love that in a family dwells,
    No carolling in frosty air,
Nor all the steeple-shaking bells
    Can with this single Truth compare –
That God was Man in Palestine
And lives to-day in Bread and Wine.

John Betjeman, 1951

The Crystal Set

Just as the stars appear, Father
carries from his garden shed
a crystal set, built
as per instructions
in the *Amateur Mechanic*
Mother dries her hands. Their boy
and ginger cat lie beside the fire
He's reading – what – *Treasure Island*
but jumps to clear the dresser. Hush
They tell each other. *Hush!*

The silly baby bangs her spoon
as they lean in to radio-waves
which lap, the boy imagines,
just like Scarborough. Indeed,
it is the sea they hear as though
the brown box were a shell. Dad
sorts through fizz, until, like diamonds
lost in dust: 'listen, ships' Morse!'
and the boy grips his chair. As though
he'd risen sudden as an angel to gaze down, he
     understands
that not his house, not
Scarborough Beach, but the whole
island of Britain
is washed by dark waves. *Hush*
they tell each other. Hush.

There is nothing to tune to
but Greenwich pips
and the anxious signalling

of ships that nudge our shores.
Dumb silent waves. But that
was then. Now, gentle listener,
it's time to take our leave
of Mum and Dad's proud glow, the boy's
uncertain smile. Besides,
the baby's asleep.
So let's tune out here
and slip along the dial. *Hush*.

Kathleen Jamie, 1995

Stopping by Woods on a Snowy Evening

Whose woods these are I think I know.
His house is in the village, though;
He will not see me stopping here
To watch his woods fill up with snow.

My little horse must think it queer
To stop without a farmhouse near
Between the woods and frozen lake
The darkest evening of the year.

He gives his harness bells a shake
To ask if there is some mistake.
The only other sounds the sweep
Of easy wind and downy flake.

The woods are lovely, dark, and deep,
But I have promises to keep,
And miles to go before I sleep,
And miles to go before I sleep.

Robert Frost, 1922

If you loved *Class*, read on for the first chapter of *Rules*,
which details the second year at Downey House.

Rules

Jenny Colgan
Writing as Jane Beaton

For the second year at Downey House, it's getting harder
and harder to stick to the rules...

It's about making them...
Now she's engaged to sweet and steady Stan, Maggie's just
got to stop thinking about David McDonald, her opposite
number at Downey Boys... hasn't she?

It's about breaking them...
Headmistress Veronica Deveral has more to lose than anyone.
When Daniel Stapleton joins the faculty, she's forced to
confront her scandalous secret. How long will she be able to
keep it under wraps?

'Funny, page-turning and addictive'
Sophie Kinsella

Chapter One

Maggie was dancing on a table. This was distinctly out of character, but they *had* served her cocktails earlier, in a glass so large she was surprised it didn't have a fish in it.

Plus it was a beautifully soft, warm evening, and her fiancé Stan had insisted on watching the football on a large Sky Sports screen, annoyingly situated over her head in the Spanish bar, so there wasn't much else to do – and all the other girls were dancing on table tops.

I'm still young, Maggie had thought to herself. *I'm only twenty-six years old! I can still dance all night!*

And with the help of a friendly hen party from Stockport on the next table, she'd found herself up there, shrugging off any self-consciousness with the help of a large margarita and grooving away to Alphabeat.

'Hey, I can't see the game,' Stan complained.

'I don't care,' said Maggie, suddenly feeling rather more free, happy and determined to enjoy her holiday. She raised her arms above her head. This was definitely a good way to forget about school; to forget about David McDonald, the English teacher she'd developed a crush on last year – until she'd found out he was engaged. To just feel like herself again.

*

'Isn't that Miss Adair?' said Hattie.

They'd been allowed down into the town for the evening from the discreet and beautifully appointed villa they'd been staying in high on the other side of the mountain. Fliss turned round from where she'd been eyeing up fake designer handbags, and glanced at the tacky-looking sports pub Hattie was pointing out. Inside was a group of drunk-looking women waving their hands in the air.

'No way!' exclaimed Fliss, heading towards the door for a closer look. 'I'm going in to check.'

'You're not allowed in any bars!' said Hattie. 'I promised Mum and Dad.'

'*I promised Mum and Dad*,' mimicked Fliss. 'I am fourteen, you know. That's pretty much the legal drinking age over here.'

'Well, whilst you're with me you'll obey family rules.'

Fliss stuck out her tongue and headed straight for the bar. 'You're not a prefect now.'

'No, but we're in a position of trust, and . . .'

Fliss stopped short in the doorway.

'Hello, senorita,' said the doorman. Fliss had grown two inches over the summer, although to her huge annoyance she was still barely filling an A cup.

Maggie and the girls from Stockport were shimmying up and down to the Pussycat Dolls when she saw the girl. At first she thought it was a trick of the flashing lights. It couldn't be. After all, they'd come all this way to leave her work behind. So she could feel like a girl, not a teacher. So surely it couldn't be one of her—

'MISS ADAIR!' shrieked Fliss. 'Is that you, miss?'

Maggie stopped dancing.

'Felicity Prosser,' she said, feeling a resigned tone creep into her voice. She looked around, wondering what would be the most dignified way to get down from the table, under the circumstances.

Normally, Veronica Deveral found the Swiss Alps in summertime a cleansing balm to her soul. The clean, sharp air you could draw all the way down into your lungs; the sparkle of the grass and the glacier lakes; the cyclists and rosy-cheeked all-year skiiers heading for higher ground; the freshly washed sky. She always took the same *pension*, and liked to take several novels – she favoured the lengthy intrigues of Anthony Trollope, and was partial to a little Joanna for light relief – and luxuriate in the time to devour them, returning to Downey House rested, refreshed and ready for the new academic year.

This time, however, had been different. After her shock at meeting her adoptive son after nearly forty years, Veronica had handled it badly and they had lost contact. And although there were budgets to be approved, a new intake to set up and staffing to be organised, she couldn't concentrate. All she seemed to do was worry about Daniel, and wonder what he was doing.

Now back from her unsatisfying trip, she was staring out of the window of her beautiful office two days before term was due to start, when Dr Robert Fitzroy, head of Downey Boys' School over the hill, arrived for their annual chat. The two schools did many things together, and it was useful to have some knowledge of the forthcoming agenda.

'You seem a little distracted, Veronica,' Robert said, comfortably ensconced on the Chesterfield sofa, enjoying the fine view over the school grounds and to the cliffs and the sea beyond, today a perfect summer holiday blue. They weren't really getting anywhere with debating the new computer lab.

Veronica sighed and briefly considered confiding in her opposite number. He was a kind man, if a little set in his ways. She dismissed this thought immediately. She had spent years building up this school, the last thing she needed was anyone thinking she was a weak woman, prone to tears and over-emotional sentimentality.

Robert droned on about new staff.

'Oh, and yes,' he said, 'we have a new History and Classics teacher at last. Good ones are so hard to find these days.'

Veronica was barely listening. She was watching the waves outside and wondering if Daniel had ever taken his children to the seaside for a holiday. So when Robert said his name it chimed with her thoughts, and at first she didn't at all understand what she'd just heard.

'Excuse me?'

'Daniel Stapleton. Our new Classics teacher.'

'Mom!'

Zelda was throwing ugly things in her bag. Ugly tops, ugly skirts, ugly hats. What the hell? School uniform was the stupidest idea in a country full of stupid ideas.

'Did you know I have to share, like, a bathroom? Did they tell you that?'

Zelda's mother shook her head. As if she didn't have enough to deal with, what with DuBose being so excited about the move and all. Why they all had to go and up sticks and live in England, where she'd heard it rained all the time and everyone lived in itty-bitty houses with bathrooms the size of cupboards . . . well, it didn't bear thinking about. She doubted it would be much like Texas.

'Don' worry, darlin',' DuBose had said, in that calm drawl of his. He might get a lot of respect as a major seconded to the British Army, but it didn't cut much ice with her, nuh-huh.

'An' we'll get Zelda out of that crowd she's been runnin' with at high school. Turn her into quite the English lady.'

A boarding school education was free for the daughters of senior military staff on overseas postings, and Downey House, they'd been assured, was amongst the very best.

As Mary-Jo looked at her daughter's heavily bitten black-painted fingernails, so strange against the stark white of her new uniform blouses, and so different from her own perfect manicure, she wondered, yet again, how they would all fit in.

Simone glanced at Fliss's Facebook update – *Felicity is having a BLASTING time in Porto Caldo!* – and tried her best to be happy for her. The Pribetichs weren't having a holiday this year. It just wasn't practical. Which was fine by Simone: she hated struggling into her tankini and pulling a big sarong around herself, then sitting under an umbrella, hiding in case anyone saw her. So, OK, Fliss might be having great fun without her, and Alice was posting about being utterly, miserably bored learning to dive with her au pair in Hurghada, and she was jealous and she did miss them – but she was doing her best to be happy for them.

It had been a long seven weeks, with not much to do but read and try to avoid Joel, her brother, who had spent the entire time indoors hunched over his games console.

She'd spent the summer dreaming of school and reading books, whilst eating fish finger sandwiches. Her mother had tried her best to get her involved in some local social events, but it wasn't really her thing. She winced remembering an unbelievably awkward afternoon tea with Rudi, the ugly, gangly teenage son of one of her mother's best friends. His face was covered in spots and his hair was oily and lank. They were shuffled awkwardly together on to a sofa.

Simone's misery on realising that this was the kind of boy her mum thought she might like was compounded by the very obvious way Rudi looked her up and down and made it clear that he thought he was out of her league. She sighed again at the memory.

'You go to that posh school then,' he'd muttered, when pushed by his mum.

Simone had felt a blush spread over her face, and kept her eyes tightly fixed on her hands.

'Yeah.'

'Oh. Right.'

And that had been that. It was pretty obvious that Rudi, over-stretched as he was, would much rather be upstairs playing Grand Theft Auto with Joel.

Simone sighed. It would have been nice to go back to school with at least some adventures to tell Alice and Fliss. Still, they would share theirs with her.

'Tell me about her thighs again,' said Alice, leaning lazily on shady manicured grass, watching tiny jewel-coloured lizards scrabble past and running up an enormous bill on the hotel phone.

'Jiggly,' said Fliss, under an apple tree two thousand miles away in Surrey, tickling her dog Ranald on the tummy. 'Honestly, you could see right up her skirt and everything.'

'I never really think of teachers having legs,' mused Alice. 'I mean, I suppose they must and everything, but . . .'

'But what, you think they run along on wheels?' Fliss giggled.

'No, but . . . oh, it's so hot.'

'FLISS!' The voice came from the next room.

'Oh god, is that the heffalump Hattie?' drawled Alice.

'I'm not going to answer,' said Fliss.

'FELICITY!' Hattie huffed into the orchard garden, her tread heavy on the paving stones. '*Felicity.*'

'I'm on the *phone*,' said Fliss crossly.

'Well, I have news.'

'Is she pregnant?' said wicked Alice.

'Ssh,' Fliss told her.

'Fine,' said Hattie, turning to go. 'So I guess you DON'T want to hear who's starting Downey Boys this year?'

Fliss turned and looked at her.

'What are you talking about?'

'Just that I was down in the village . . . and was talking to Will's mum . . .'

And just like that, Alice was talking to an empty telephone.

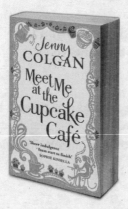

Meet Issy Randall, proud owner of *The Cupcake Café*

After a childhood spent in her beloved Grampa Joe's bakery, Issy Randall has undoubtedly inherited his talent so when she's made redundant from her job, Issy decides to seize the moment. Armed with recipes from Grampa, The Cupcake Café opens its doors. But Issy has absolutely no idea what she's let herself in for …

One way or another, Issy is determined to have a merry Christmas!

Issy Randall is in love and couldn't be happier. Her new business is thriving and she is surrounded by close friends. But when her boyfriend is scouted for a possible move to New York, Issy is forced to face up to the prospect of a long-distance romance, and she must decide what she holds most dear.

'Gorgeous, glorious, uplifting'
MARIAN KEYES

Life is sweet!

As the cobbled alleyways of Paris come to life, Anna Trent is already at work, mixing and stirring the finest chocolate. It's a huge shift from the chocolate factory she used to work in back home until an accident changed everything. With old wounds about to be uncovered and healed, Anna is set to discover more about real chocolate – and herself – than she ever dreamed.

Can baking mend a broken heart?

Polly Waterford is recovering from a toxic relationship. Unable to afford their flat, she has to move to a quiet seaside resort in Cornwall, where she lives alone. And so Polly takes out her frustrations on her favourite hobby: making bread. With nuts and seeds, olives and chorizo, and with reserves of determination Polly never knew she had, she bakes and bakes and bakes. And people start to hear about it ...

Remember the rustle of the pink and green striped paper bag?

Rosie Hopkins thinks leaving her busy London life, and her boyfriend Gerard, to sort out her elderly Aunt Lilian's sweetshop in a small country village is going to be dull. Boy, is she wrong. Lilian Hopkins has spent her life running Lipton's sweetshop, through wartime and family feuds. As she struggles with the idea that it might finally be time to settle up, she also wrestles with the secret history hidden behind the jars of beautifully coloured sweets.

Curl up with Rosie, her friends and her family as they prepare for a very special Christmas...

Rosie is looking forward to Christmas. Her sweetshop is festooned with striped candy canes, large tempting piles of Turkish Delight, crinkling selection boxes and happy, sticky children. She's going to be spending it with her boyfriend, Stephen, and her family, flying in from Australia. She can't wait.
But when a tragedy strikes at the heart of their little community, all of Rosie's plans are blown apart. Is what's best for the sweetshop also what's best for Rosie?

'A naturally funny, warm-hearted writer'
LISA JEWELL

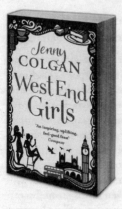

The streets of London are the perfect place to discover your dreams...

When, out of the blue, twin sisters Lizzie and Penny learn they have a grandmother living in Chelsea, they are even more surprised when she asks them to flat-sit her King's Road pad while she is in hospital. They jump at the chance to move to London but, as they soon discover, it's not easy to become an It Girl, and west end boys aren't at all like Hugh Grant ...

Sun, sea and laughter abound in this warm, bubbly tale

Evie is desperate for a good holiday with peaceful beaches, glorious sunshine and (fingers crossed) some much-needed sex. So when her employers invite her to attend a conference in the beautiful South of France, she can't believe her luck. At last, the chance to party under the stars with the rich and glamorous, to live life as she'd always dreamt of it. But things don't happen in quite the way Evie imagines ...

'Colgan at her warm, down-to-earth best'
COSMOPOLITAN

How does an It Girl survive when she loses everything?

Sophie Chesterton is a girl about town, but deep down she suspects that her superficial lifestyle doesn't amount to very much. Her father is desperate for her to make her own way in the world, and when after one shocking evening her life is turned upside down, she suddenly has no choice. Barely scraping by, living in a hovel with four smelly boys, eating baked beans from the can, Sophie is desperate to get her life back. But does a girl really need diamonds to be happy?

A feisty, flirty tale of one woman's quest to cure her disastrous love life

Posy is delighted when Matt proposes, but a few days later disaster strikes: he backs out of the engagement. Crushed and humiliated, Posy wonders why her love life has always ended in disaster. Determined to discover how she got to this point, Posy resolves to get online and track down her exes. Can she learn from past mistakes? And what if she has let Mr Right slip through her fingers on the way?